also by Tim Sandlin

Sex and Sunsets
Western Swing
Skipped Parts
Sorrow Floats
Social Blunders
Honey Don't
Jimi Hendrix Turns Eighty
Rowdy in Paris
Lydia
The Pyms: Unauthorized Tales of Jackson Hole

THE FABLE OF BING

The Fable of Bing

Tim Sandlin

Oothoon Press

GroVont Wyoming
New York
Los Angeles

OOTHOON PRESS

ISBN: 978-0989395755

Cover by Cynthia Huyffer

For Carol

ACKNOWLEDGEMENTS

Thanks to the kind folks at the San Diego Wildlife Safari for their patience and help.

And to Army Feth who went into Tijuana so I didn't have to.

And Julia Kardon for handling the technical end.

And, forever and always, for Carol who makes it matter.

September 1991

*H*istory of the name: Bing Crosby sang "Blue Hawaii" in Waikiki Wedding *in 1937 and fifty-four years later Dale Konigsberg danced with his wife in Zaire. They found the album of mixed movie tracks in their predecessor's leavings, along with an aged RCA Victor stereophonic record player and a packet of three new needles. The abandoned treasures were stuffed in urine-stained crates in a closet off the boxing room where meerkats, zebras, and various primates lay caged and crated before their long journeys around the world.*

Dale pressed Mary's flushed torso against his own, the palm of his left hand in that divot in her lower back that he knew so well. He stared into her bottomless blue eyes. "What shall we name the tyke?"

Mary floated in Dale's arms across the concrete slab floor. His dancing prowess had been the hook that snared Mary's love, way back at the Tri Delt Spring Fling at UT. Before dancing, Dale had been nothing but a tall frat boy with a thick mustache and a receding hairline faking sophistication beyond his years in order to impress Mary and her cousins from Chattanooga. But, as the strains of a fairly decent Lionel Richie cover oozed over the student union ballroom, Dale strode across the hardwood floor and asked if he might have this dance, and that was all she wrote for Mary's discretionary dating period.

Together, Mary and Dale danced through grad school, marriage, internships at the Cincinnati Zoo, dream jobs in Zaire with the Wildlife Nature Conservancy, followed by pregnancy and the birth of Franklin, who at the moment was staring at a rusted crack in the corrugated tin ceiling above his hammock crib hung between two hoist stakes.

Franklin's name had been the closest the couple ever came to a bone of contention. Dale's grandfather — Franklin — offered a Vanderbilt

1

education to any family offspring named after himself. This blatant bribe rankled Mary's sense of fair play.

"You should name a child after a relative from respect, not cash flow."

"We can respect Grandpa Franklin and take his money," Dale said. "It's the American way."

They argued for three days until Dale led Mary into the lobby of the Kinsangani University Hospital and slow danced her to the sound of air conditioner hum while nurses snickered at the back gap in Mary's gown and she forgot her anger.

Now, five months further into the happily ever after part of the story, they were still dancing, and it was time to name another baby.

Dale swayed his hips to the steel guitar waves, gliding and guiding Mary between the prep table and the storage cabinets, over to the crate that an overweight black man wearing a striped railroad engineer cap was nailing around a cage.

"Our lady is within moments of being ready, Boss," Oudry said. "The truck should arrive at this spot in fifteen minutes." Oudry had a cauliflower ear and had been educated at Cambridge, England. The Yes, Bwana, No Bwana attitude was an affectation meant to needle Dale who considered himself racially advanced.

"You call me Boss one more time and I'll drop you in the soldier ant pit," Dale said.

"Yes, Boss."

Dale spun Mary out to the tips of his fingers where she froze, one arm poised over the orchid decorating her right ear, to peer down into the cage of a female bonobo — long black hair, pink lips, deep, dark eyes — nursing a hairless wisp of a baby. The female was named Betty, some sort of a stretched take-off on Betty Boop.

Betty blinked thick eyelids and stretched a tongue elastic as a Gumby doll.

"Betty knows she and I are sisters under the skin," Mary said. "We should be sipping oolong tea and swapping delivery stories."

Bing Crosby finished his last Buh Buh Buh Blue and after a short, scratchy silence, Martha Raye broke into a ditty complaining about men in general and Hawaiian men in specific.

Dale leaned into Mary for a look down at the bonobos. "She does resemble you a touch, except her lips are larger, proportionately."

Mary popped a right fist punch to his chest.

Dale backtracked. "Hers flop in space where your little plums point directly at me."

Mary said, "I choose Bing."

"He'll be back in a few minutes. They let Martha Raye sing the comic relief between love songs."

"The name for the baby." As if he knew Mary was speaking about him, the baby bonobo's eyes came up, looking over his bald forehead and directly into Mary's eyes. His head looked like a Bocce ball painted by a Tijuana velvet artist. He wreaked vulnerability.

"We'll call him Bing," Mary said.

"Not Bing Bing?"

"One Bing is plenty. You wouldn't like being called Dale Dale by drooly tots throwing peanuts at you. Let's leave the poor child a semblance of dignity."

Dale stood beside Mary with his arm around her waist. He lived for the stance. It made him feel a part of her, more partners than any of the interesting positions they'd learned from the lovemaking book. "He doesn't look a bit like Bing Crosby. Observe the ear holes."

The baby bonobo — Bing — clutched his mother with both tiny fists. He made a kitten-like mewl sound. As if in commiseration, Franklin began to fuss.

"I don't give a snap about ears. I love our little Bing. He'll grow up to be a crooner." Mary broke free of Dale's arm and crossed over to baby Franklin. Franklin was a chubby, hairless version of his mother. Same pistachio shaped eyes. Same dimple. Even his nostrils flared in a Mary-esque button kind of way.

He gurgled when Mary scooped him from the crib.

Dale examined the bonobos while Oudry hammered on the front panel. All he had left was the lid and the paperwork and they'd be ready to ship.

"Load her with bananas," Dale said. "Those bureaucratic bumble brains in Kinshasa Airport are supposed to check her, but they never do."

"You always say that and I always do," Oudry said. "Always have, always will, from the beginning of time. Perhaps you should give me credit for having a memory."

"I don't recall saying the same thing — always."

"Thus you prove my point, Boss."

Baby Bing shifted under the warmth of his mother. Even without hair, he had the distinctive facial bones of the male bonobo. High forehead, regal nose, wide eyes. He could have passed for a senator from Wisconsin.

Dale said, "His nose is more Bob Hope."

Mary dropped the strap of her sleeveless blouse and guided Franklin to a breast. Dale left off the bonobos to admire his wife nursing their child. If possible, Mary was even more wondrous than she'd been before giving birth. Her skin glowed. Her demeanor was that of the original Mother Mary had she been a ballerina. No matter how long he lived, Dale would never tire of the sight of his wife.

Oudry, on the other hand, stared hard at the crate slats. He wasn't used to this behavior in a white woman.

"Come, come," Mary said. "We can't send out an animal named Bob. It would destroy our reputation."

"We have a reputation?" Dale cocked his head toward the double garage loading doors. "What's with the racket in the compound? Sounds like a tiger attack."

"The natives must be celebrating a successful circumcision," Oudry said.

"Natives? As opposed to fat devil invaders like you and me?"

Mary's eyes came off her feeding baby. "That doesn't have the ring of a celebration to me."

High-pitched wails bled through the walls, more in the lines of terror than ecstasy, although it was hard to pin down. Had this been west Tennessee, Dale would have recognized the tone. These Bantu had a way of mixing their extremes.

"Oudry." Dale took two steps toward the door. "I want you to go out there and discover the scoop, as it were. Find out who is winding up the compound and if it's an uprising, throw them some red meat. I'll finish Betty and Bing."

Oudry spoke through roofing nails between his teeth. "You do not follow procedure."

"I've been shipping wildlife since you were white, Oudry. Get out there."

Oudry mumbled complaints, setting his hammer and nails on the prep table. He squared the engineer's cap on his head, pulling it low in hopes of *hiding the cauliflower ear. His deportment as he glided through the double loading doors was nothing less than majestic.*

Mary said, "That smacked of racism."

Dale dug into a stack of files and folders strewn across the table as if by a stiff wind. "Oudry hates it when I treat him as ginger."

Mary translated. "Gingerly."

"He craves to be one of the good old boys. Like you and me."

She faked offense. "Since when did I turn into a good old boy?"

"Since we're the only true Americans within a hundred miles, except for the Peace Corps do-goodniks and they don't count." Dale slipped the bonobos' invoice from its plastic sheath. "Always with the drums. If God wanted white girls on African drums she'd have given them big feet."

Mary said, "What?"

"Those faux-black chicks all keep journals. Natives don't keep journals."

"I don't know which mortifies me most, you saying faux or chicks."

Dale popped the top off a Sharpie and wrote: WE NAMED THE BABY BING on the descriptive page, in the margin next to birth date and weight.

Mary placed Franklin back in the crib hammock and tucked a rice sack under his little chin. The fluorescent lighting that Mary hated with so much passion gave Franklin a shimmering pink look. Or maybe it was the suffocating heat laced with diesel fumes. Most five month olds don't sweat like cowboys, but Franklin seemed to be giving himself a bath.

"You're turning into a character out of Joseph Conrad. By next winter you'll crown yourself King Dale of the Congo. What was that?"

From outside, a noise popped, distinctly like small caliber gunfire followed by more shouts. Betty Bonobo stirred from her crouch and stood with the baby hanging off her neck. Franklin opened his eyes to stare out at his mother.

Mary said, "Why, Dale. This feels just the way I always imagined a movie moment would feel."

"It's the modern version of déjà vu," Dale said. "In a crisis we react as if we've been transported into a movie because that's the only level we can relate to. We've seen life and death many times, but never experienced it first hand."

"But, this isn't a movie moment, is it?" Mary said, a little sadly.

Dale pulled himself up to his best posture, the one he saved for facing situations. "No, my dear, it isn't."

The doors banged open and Oudry strode in, fighting to maintain a standard of dignity he no longer felt. Only his breathing, or lack thereof, gave away a heightened sense of involvement.

"What is the problem?" Dale said. "Speak up."

"Let him catch his breath," Mary said.

"He can breathe on his own time."

Oudry shut and locked the doors, then he turned back to the room. He was now collected. "Bad news, sir. Mobuto's goons have lost self-control."

Another large object hit the wall. Mary said, "Be specific."

Oudry glanced from her to Dale. "Armed with government issue machetes, they are hacking up the staff. Cook, the gardener. Both interns. Not a living soul is being spared."

Dale stared at his precious Mary. "I hate it when they do that."

He hoped she might rush into his arms, but instead Mary stayed by Franklin. "I've rehearsed this a thousand times since we left the States. I always thought I would fall apart from fear."

Dale smiled. "Look at you now,"

"Yes, look at me. It's the oddest thing, how calm I've suddenly become."

"That's because we are together."

Mary's eyes slicked over and her voice quavered. "I only regret what we are doing to Franklin. He is innocent. He deserves a life." She reached down to touch her son on his little chin. He laughed and grabbed her finger. Mary raised her eyes to her husband. "I would take it kindly if you could save him."

Dale walked a circle around the bonobo crate. He touched his mustache, which was as close to nerves as he felt comfortable displaying. "The truck will arrive in ten minutes. Those UPS guards carry firepower enough to stop an army of machete wielding maniacs."

Oudry sniffed, as if smelling an offensive odor. "I estimate we do not have ten minutes to spare."

Dale strode to his charcoal gray file cabinet. He opened the bottom drawer and pulled out a huge mother of a pistol. One of the originals, perhaps carried by an Earp brother.

"Where did you find that thing?" Mary asked.

"It was stuffed in the crate, under the record player."

"Why didn't you tell me about it?" Mary wasn't certain she liked the idea of Dale hiding the gun's existence from her. He'd never kept secrets, in the past.

Dale shrugged. "I'm not certain how the mechanism works."

"Pardon me." Oudry lifted the pistol from Dale's hand and broke open the breech. "Did your firearm come with bullets, Boss?"

Dale flinched at the Boss crack, but there didn't seem time to go there. "Bullets?"

"Firearm don't fire with no bullets," Oudry said, his Cambridge accent replaced by Swahili roots. The words came fast and mumbled, as if by a man with gravel between his teeth and gums.

Mary stared at him, wondering if, while he was outside, Oudry had been replaced by his jungle twin. "Oudry, where is this accent coming from? You never talked native before."

"I was never on the edge of being chopped before."

Dale shut the file drawer with a bang. "My love, I fear we are screwed."

Mary didn't approve of the word screwed used in that context. It beat the F-thing, barely. The F-thing would show a total breakdown of moral fiber. Still, she would have preferred We are in dire straits, or Our number is up — terms that fit her self-image as the civilized woman in an uncivilized land.

"Dale, you save Franklin or I will go to my grave cursing your name. Your family's name, starting with Grandfather Franklin and working down to those neckless cousins from Ohio who believe in intelligent design."

Dale's attention traveled from the bonobo crate to the pistol in Oudry's hands to his baby. He ended the scan of options by staring into Mary's blue eyes. Her eyes were the oxygen in his lungs. The blood that beat through his heart. He could not bear the possibility of disappointing Mary.

"Oudry," he said. "Do you very much mind stepping outside and buying us some time. Wave the weapon about. You may frighten the boys into breaking off their massacre."

"I'll step," Oudry said. He had regained his Britishness — a positive sign when Mary needed one most. "However, the goon gentlemen are drunk on Motubo whiskey. They are not likely to break off."

"Do what you can."

Oudry removed his cap and, with ceremony and whispered words to the baby, placed it in the crib beside Franklin. As he turned to go, Mary had the irresistible urge to kiss him on both cheeks and the forehead. Due to his girth, the forehead kiss required a stretch.

"Goodbye," she said.

Oudry smiled. "You are a blessing to your race and gender."

"You too."

Then, with a nod to Dale, he was gone.

Mary locked the double doors behind him. She braced herself, then turned to face Dale. "We had so much more we wanted to do."

"At least, it was perfect while it lasted."

"That is true. We shall never grow tired of one another."

"Darling, if I'd lived to a hundred and four, I would never have grown tired of you."

A scream came from the other side of the doors. Oudry.

Mary winced. "Dale, my husband, I can't for the life of me decide if you are hopelessly romantic or just full of shit."

Dale did his utmost to appear enigmatic.

Three minutes passed before the front and back doors crashed open and machete-wielding madmen flooded the room. Crazy-eyed, froth lipped, spattered in blood and entrails — your basic nightmare of lust in the rain forest. Howling and cursing, the men moved with the random purpose of a force of nature. A tidal wave of hatred.

But then, the murdering mass froze. From the record player rose the tinny sound of Bing Crosby singing "Sweet Leilani."

Sweet Leilani, Heavenly Flower

I dreamed of paradise for two

You are my paradise completed

You are my dream come true

In that space between the empty hammock and the shuttered crate Dale and Mary danced. Her hands locked behind his neck, her thumbs in his curly black hair. His arms around her waist with the fingers alongside her spine. Their eyes held each other in a gaze both infinite and final. Beyond love. Beyond death.

Neither Mary nor Dale blinked when the doors crashed in. Not so much as a glance did they bestow on their killers. No one, no time, existed beyond the love that held them to one another.

The machete goons stood, slack mouthed and speechless, frozen in the moment as the song drifted to a close.

You are my paradise completed

You are my dream come true.

Mary and Dale danced.

Then, silence — a needle scratching in the groove at the end of the record. The littlest goon who had never been loved howled his fury. The wave surged.

February 2010

Chapter One

We — you and I — are observers. On a blue morning in late winter, we observe a young man lounging among the upper leaves of an acacia tree overhanging the savannah habitat in the San Diego Zoo Safari Park. He sits wedged in a fork of the acacia, astride a dappled limb, legs dangling, back braced against one of the forks, hands lazily crossed at the wrists several inches above the shock of blond straw that is his hair. The young man would appear representative of his age and time — Padres t-shirt, Dockers cargo shorts, — except for these facts: he is barefoot with his toes splayed against the bark, the arms that drape over his head hang in an awkward position, and as he keeps track of the comings and goings below, the young man emits a soft, panting, mechanical sound in his throat punctuated by the *wisp* of sucking air through his teeth.

Along with his physical oddities, his hovering in a tree on the habitat side of the zebra moat would make the young man worth a second look, had any of the visitors on a slow February weekday peered up through the screen of flat leaves on the acacia. But, of course, no one sees him. Not the visitors nor the zoo employees nor the zebras and the bearded lizards in the savannah environment know of the young man in the tree. We are the only ones to see him there.

He is a young man different from other young men in that he is not intrigued by what he cannot see. He sees his bed in his mother's nest. He sees the endlessly circling shuttles filled with pointing Outies. He sees the mammals and the birds and the amphibians that mostly come from Africa but so far as the young man knows, are commonplace. Men and women in khaki uniforms feed the animals and shovel their scat. Men in dark green uniforms pick up trash and clean the restrooms. Light green shirts save lost children. Red shirts pass out maps. Sky blue shirts lecture on lore. Outies flow in through the huge gate with its turnstiles and kiosks and, so far as the young man knows or cares, they have no being outside the gate. He has never considered the likelihood of life beyond the Park. He assumes the entire world exists within his view.

Perhaps this isn't different from others his age after all. Who knows? The young man knows the odors of animals in captivity, and the sounds of wild creatures in anger, lust, and boredom. The permanent aspects of his world are well known, and, therefore, not as interesting as the beings who come in and go away.

The young man in his tree shows a keen interest in the types and shapes of people who haunt zoos. Mothers with toddlers in umbrella strollers and nowhere else to go. Foreign tourists with cameras and checklists. February is a month of disproportionate numbers of Asians, lured to San Diego by the promise of warmth and group rates, off-season prices. Children on school trips group and regroup with a swarm intelligence the young man sees in flocks of birds.

The young man is quite good at spotting loneliness by the posture of those who have it as they stand before the animals. Their hands are rarely visible, either kept in pockets or clutched to one another in supplication. Lonely people don't see what they are looking at. Their eyes have the inertness of an animal beaned with a club.

Most of all, the young man is interested in lovers. From adolescents through to those much too old to reproduce, he watches lovers wander aimlessly from exhibit to exhibit, as if partially blinded to external stimuli. They strike the young man as moving in a bubble — no contact from outside passing into the bubble, but neither can the lovers recognize anything outside of each other. They often touch — not rubbing scrotums like the bonobo — but hands and shoulders, sometimes wrapping arms across one another's upper body in an exchange of bacteria.

Not that the young man knows these dazed people he observes are lovers. He has never heard the word *love*. Dr. Lori calls the smitten pairs *couplers*.

"Couplers are the most pitiful of Outer Ones," she says. "They've forfeited self-realization for a vapor lock."

"They do not appear pitiful. They seem pleased."

Dr. Lori snorts, a sound not unlike a duiker defecating on dust. "Hypnosis. Outer Ones are forced to feel in direct contrast to their condition."

"Does not thinking they are happy define them as happy?"

Dr. Lori takes off her spectacles and leaves them dangling by the thin, gold chain around her neck. She stares at the young man. "Bing," she says, for that is his name — Bing. "Bing. Thinking you are above water when you are underneath won't save you from drowning." She pauses to watch his reaction, which consists of pursing his lips and baring his incisors. "Am I correct?"

He inhales quickly, twice, with a whistle noise. "Yes, Dr. Lori, you are my elder and you know truth from lies."

Dr. Lori replaces her glasses to the bridge of her nose. "Keep that in mind."

CHAPTER TWO

On this specific February day we find Bing lolling in his crook of the acacia, studying Outies as they scuttle from exhibit to exhibit, seeing their world through a view finder. Bing is toying with a blue and brick red spotted caterpillar that hunches, slowly, methodically, its way up and down Bing's knuckles, from thumb, down the dip and over onto the pointer finger, down the dip and up over onto the middle finger. Bing sniffs the caterpillar. He likes the feel of tiny legs on the soft web between his fingers. It makes him happy. The caterpillar has black eye liners, like a panda. Ear tuffs. A spray of prickly fuzz halos its body. The fuzz feels like tiny slivers against Bing's skin.

When the caterpillar accordions itself onto Bing's little finger, he turns his hand, palm side up, then watches as the caterpillar works its way back thumbward. Bing knows that so long as he turns his hand, the caterpillar will go on forever, round and round in a never ending loop. This means something important, although Bing isn't sure what.

Bing's nostrils flare. He snorts, for he has spotted a young woman who doesn't fit categories. She sits, weight forward, on a prefabricated concrete bench with curlicues stamped in the arm-rests. The bench is positioned on the far side of the sidewalk, so passersby obscure her view of the savannah, but she doesn't seem to care. She isn't looking at the savannah. She isn't looking at anything or away from anything. She isn't aware of vision, and this makes Bing observe her more closely. In his narrow experience, the girl-woman below him appears unique.

The female strikes Bing as long — long wavy to curly hair, long tapered fingers like a sloth, long legs that keep going from the long feet up and up until they disappear beneath her lemon yellow sundress that isn't long. She looks like a girl who belongs in a magazine, only she isn't. Bing can see the girl is real and Dr. Lori has promised him that magazine girls are not real. She says photographers have a trick to erase flaws on the magazine girls. This girl is without flaws.

The main thing that draws Bing to her is the clean hair. Or it starts with the clean hair. Later it moves to her hands, particularly her index fingers that are longer than her middle fingers. Then his interest goes to her long neck with its delicate tendons and soft planes, but this is much later and we're getting ahead of ourselves.

That first morning when Bing sees the girl from on high, looking down at her as she reads what must be a letter, Bing hangs mesmerized by the wavy, almost curly iced-tea brown waterfall of hair. It is hair to go into and become lost. It glitters. It flows over her shoulder when she flicks it away from the letter.

Besides the yellow sundress with its plunging V neckline molded to her white, white cleavage and held to her shoulders by the thinnest of straps, the girl wears brown sandals. Her toenails are painted light purple.

She holds the pale blue sheet of stationery in her left hand and twirls a lock of hair with her right index finger, next to the ear that holds two silver posts in the upper cartilage and a golden ellipse hanging from the lobe. Bing, who has never touched a person from outside the park, in all his twenty years, feels an ache to run his fingertips along the female's ear, lobe first, then working his way up to the studs and on into her hairline.

As Bing edges forward in his tree to watch, the girl closes her eyes. She holds them closed for a long time, several of Bing's breaths. He thinks perhaps she sleeps, although her chest doesn't rise and fall like a person sleeping, and her head doesn't loll. If she is asleep, she has amazing control of her body.

Her eyes open. She stares into the acacia, and, for a moment, Bing thinks she is looking at him, which alarms the young man. No one ever sees Bing. Invisibility is his task and gift, literal invisibility when he is on the exhibit side of fences and a salamander-like invisibility when he walks the asphalt walks. No one notices Bing. He reflects no light.

The girl stares into the acacia, then she reaches into her leather bag and withdraws a turquoise blue cigarette lighter. Bing knows what it is. Even though smoking is against park policy a group of reptile keepers and an elephant vet often meet in a small enclosure behind the snake staging area where they smoke cigarettes and disparage women. The elephant vet uses a cigarette lighter much like the girl's, only his is silver.

The girl flicks at the top of the lighter twice before a blue to red flame shoots an inch over the turquoise tube. She stares into the flame, her breath causing it to flicker both forward and back, then she places it under the upper right hand corner of the stationery page and sets the paper on fire. She watches it burn. A couple of little boys who had been throwing sticks at the zebras turn to marvel at the audacity of this grownup firebug. They tell her she is breaking a rule. She ignores them. As the page burns down she turns it over so the flames are flowing up the page instead of down, toward her fingers. Just as it appears she will be scorched, she drops the paper on the asphalt where it burns a few more seconds until she steps on it. Then the girl with the wavy to curly hair makes her right hand into a fist and punches air. After that, she walks away.

By now our young man Bing is utterly smitten. The girl has done something he's never seen. She has acted with directness and purpose, without question. That is a rare and wondrous quality to behold and Bing either knows this and is properly flabbergasted, or he has no idea what he has seen but he doesn't want to go forward in his life without seeing more of it. Whatever his reasons, any male or female in the position of spying from a tree on this particular girl burning a sheet of paper would be equally smitten. That's how life is.

CHAPTER THREE

B ing eats the caterpillar. Imagine a worm with prickles. Then he shimmies down from the tree and knuckle walks alongside the steep hill dividing the savannah from the fence and public. By sticking close under the ridge he is out of sight from almost but not all the Outies. A person on the far side of the field with a spotting scope might have seen him, but Bing has developed confidence in his invisibility.

"You don't emit any sign of being," Dr. Lori said once when he was younger and she found him keeping watch over a dead shoebill, in plain sight of gawkers. "They see you as a stone."

"Is that positive?" Bing asked.

"It means you'll be safe. But you still must stay on guard every instant. Some people see stones better than others."

Bing comes to a wire gate covering a drainage pipe under the berm. He lifts the gate out, slides in backwards, then replaces the gate. It was made for animals with hooves. Any chimp could have broken through.

The pipe comes out in the storage closet of the employee bathrooms next to the flight landing. Bing hears someone coming and ducks into a stall for a drink of water. While there, a man he knows to be an electrician on the zip line goes pee at the urinal. From the stall, Bing listens to the man mutter to himself, something about stinking tourists and then he goes to the sink to wash his hands. Bing cannot understand what that is for — the washing of hands — but he does not worry over his lack of understanding. There are things he knows the cause of and purpose for and things he doesn't. The things he doesn't are not a concern.

Bing emerges onto the sidewalk as an Asian tour group passes. Mostly female, they cluster around a skinny gentleman carrying a paper flag of South Korea on a narrow pole. Dr. Lori has taught Bing his tour group flags, so he knows South Korea from Denmark. What he doesn't know is what a country is. The Asian Outies take no notice of Bing. They fuss with camera equipment. A child drops his ice cream on the dirt. A Twittering man ignores the zoo completely.

Bing walks upright — no more knuckle dragging — back down the sidewalk to the stone bench with the curlicue armrests where the unique woman read and burned the letter. Bing drops to all fours and sniffs the bench where her bottom had been only minutes before. He smells sweetness, like a tangerine. And salt. He licks the bench seat, tasting her. She tastes like leaves soon after they fall off a tree. She tastes like the yellow butterflies he finds from time to time outside the bee-eater aviary. Bing has enough experience spying on them to know human females do not as a rule smell or taste like yellow butterflies. They mostly smell damp and their residue is mushroomy. Only this one is not like others.

The ashes from the light blue paper are still on the sidewalk, at least some are. He can make out where her sandal crushed them into the asphalt. They are grey to white. The larger flakes have crinkled edges. Bing wets the tip of his finger to picks up the ashes because Dr. Lori told him not to lick the ground in front of Outies. He tastes the ash on his finger.

It isn't enough of the girl. Bing wants more.

Chapter Four

R ain doesn't fall so much as permeates. Warm mist, like precipitation sprayed on vegetable bins at Trader Joe's complete with artificial thunder to make shoppers believe the vegetables are outside even when the lighting resembles nothing found in nature. Rosemary Faith thinks it is late afternoon, near closing, but she isn't certain because low clouds block the sun. No others loiter on the observation platform at the tiger overlook. This isn't unusual during rain. The out-of-towners who are at the zoo because today is their scheduled day and they can't wait for a better afternoon cluster together under the safari barn or in the butterfly habitat. Not many have the energy to climb to the tigers.

Rosemary of the shiny hair and long fingers is one of those people who find respite in a zoo, even more so than a city park. Much more so than a city park. She likes the quiet and the timelessness of the animals. They calm her nerves, as opposed to parks full of loud kids and competitive grownups.

This specific afternoon — the first week of March, ten days after the burning letter incident — Rosemary is distracted by her personal problems. She is so distracted she forgets to open the black umbrella she rented at Jambo Outfitters before starting her climb. She has no hat. The rain flattens her wavy hair so it sticks to the sides of her neck. Water trickles into her eyes.

Surreptitiously, Rosemary smokes a Kent 100 cigarette. Not all 100 millimeters. She takes five or six puffs, carefully making sure no one is near, then drops the cigarette to the deck where she grinds it under the toe of her trainer, then she bends to pick the butt up and she tucks it into a plastic pouch inside her bag. Rosemary tries to be thoughtful smoker.

Had Rosemary been asked to describe herself she would have used the term *heavy laden.* Spiritual oppressiveness shows in the droop of her shoulders. Her lips are not animated. Her eyes do not sparkle. As happens quite often at the tiger overlook, she sees no tigers. She thinks they are asleep across the ravine, behind a barkless fallen log. Or maybe the tigers have a cave to retreat to when it rains. Rosemary supposes the zoo provides an artificial den tucked into the hillside back in the grass.

Rosemary draws her phone from her jacket pocket and checks for messages. She does this roughly twelve times an hour, which puts her close to the national average for people in her age and economic demographic. She keeps the ring tone off always. When a call comes in the phone vibrates. With a text message or e-mail, it doesn't vibrate but a red light blinks on and off. Because Rosemary turns off the ring tone for calls and the buzzer for messages, she thinks the phone does not control her.

This time, there is a message from her boss, Turk Palisades, wanting to know where his call sheet is. Turk runs a radio station and he gets so many phone calls he has to delegate keeping up with them to an employee. Rosemary texts Turk back, telling him the call list is where it is supposed to be and where it always is, although those aren't the words she uses. What she says is *Look on my desk.*

After texting Turk, Rosemary checks her sister's location on the GPS. This is something else she does twelve times an hour. Rosemary's sister Sarah tends to wander and Rosemary is driving herself sick for fear Sarah will wander away forever. Rosemary feels this is a possibility and only her constant vigilance can keep Sarah safe.

As Rosemary walks down the boardwalk toward the exit two teenage boys come crashing down along behind her. Thundering over the boards, racing to no end point, the one in back shouts a slang term for homosexual to the one in front, who doesn't seem to mind. Rosemary freezes in place as the boys veer right to clatter past. Black hooded sweatshirts, bizarrely oversized shorts, ankle high black tennis shoes; the boys wear the uniform of their time and place.

Like so many women Rosemary's age — 26 — she observes the boys closely and asks herself if she has a child, would he or she grow up to look and behave like those two. The answer, of course, is *God, I hope not.*

The boardwalk slopes down a fairly steep incline through overgrown greenery — not quite Rosemary's idea of a jungle, but lush as a forest in a warm, wet climate. At the base of the hill the path passes a murk-filled pond shaded by overhanging cypress and acacia before crossing a hanging bridge and starting back up the other side. At the pond, Rosemary comes upon a groundskeeper — late 40s, mustache favored by Latinos of his generation, sea green uniform, hip boots such as worn by irrigators as opposed to fly fishermen.

The man wades the shoreline, using a net to scoop trash from the water. With each scoop, he flips the trash over his left shoulder into an orange plastic bag held open by a thin hoop. He's very good at what he does.

Rosemary feels the usual upwelling of resentment against people who throw garbage at beauty. Trashing a place as nice as this goes beyond thoughtlessness to mean-spirited aggression. She wonders if Turk would care to do a show on the yang elements of litter.

The man looks up the rise at her and smiles. He tips his hat, causing a rivulet of rain water to spill into the pond.

He says, "Pleasant day."

Rosemary takes in the drops striking the pond surface, like tiny bombs. "If you're a goose."

The man laughs. Then he scoops an M&M wrapper from the water and flips it over his shoulder.

A thin, gold-to-brown banded snake falls from an overhanging acacia and lands on the groundskeeper's shoulder where the snake sinks its fangs into the man's neck. The groundskeeper grabs the snake in a two-handed chokehold and throws it into the pond.

It happens so quickly at first Rosemary isn't certain it has happened at all. Like blinking your eyes and seeing a dream, then flashing back to present tense. But the man's face has gone bruise purple and the snake is slalom skimming across the water. What happened is real.

Rosemary steps off the path toward the pond, her hand out as if to hold the groundskeeper aloft. His chest heaves for breath with an asthmatic wheeze, then his right hand gropes for his neck. He staggers two steps toward the shore, one step back. His eyes go to Rosemary's, pleading a question she can't form. He seems to hold the eye lock for a long time, before falling backward, slowly, buckling from the knees. As Rosemary watches — fascinated, repulsed, terrified — the groundskeeper's body rotates over, face down in the water.

She looks up the path and sees the two teenage hoodie boys watching from atop the ridgeline, toward the main entrance.

Rosemary shouts, "Get help!"

The boys stare, mutely, not moving.

Rosemary stumbles down to the pond's edge. She kneels on one knee and reaches out for the groundskeeper's foot, but he is in too deep to grasp from shore and the snake slithering through the rank water off the man's elbow frightens her. She knows she should go in. It is the right thing to do, only she is afraid.

She looks back to the boys, who have vanished, then she claws her phone from her jacket pocket and punches nine-one-one.

The snake's head V comes closer. Rosemary backs, away and upright.

"Nine-one-one. What is your name and location?"

A boy drops into the pond.

Rosemary goes rigid. Physically and mentally, she seizes up at the sight of the boy who seemingly fell from the sky, although he'd come out of the same acacia as the snake. Nothing makes sense to Rosemary. Her suspension of disbelief backfires.

The boy — more young man now that she can focus on him — slogs though waist deep water to the groundskeeper's side where he slides both arms under the body and turns it around. As water courses off the face that is more black now that purple, Rosemary can see twin tracks of blood from the nostrils and another track off the lip crease. She knows he is dead, probably from a heart attack that led to a drowning. Surely a snake bite can't kill that quickly. This is America, for God's sake. Not some Amazonian jungle.

"What is the nature of your emergency, please?"

The boy lifts the groundskeeper in his arms, baby-style. Water pours from the top of the rubber boots, leaving a stream in their wake as the boy wades to shore. He passes right by the snake without a glance. As the boy kneels to gently detach the hoop and trash bag device before sliding the groundskeeper to the dirt, Rosemary gets her first good look at him — the boy. She's already seen the groundskeeper.

Worn out t-shirt, canvas shorts, bare feet, dark blond hair in need of a haircut sticking out from a train engineer's cap, water streaming from cheeks, chin, and chest — the expression on his face is nearly unique in Rosemary's experience. She recognizes it though. It is the alive look of a person — generally a woman — who's fallen madly in romantic love sometime in the last twenty-four hours. Rosemary had an irritating college roommate who took on the new-love gawky look once every couple of weeks. It's definitely not an expression Rosemary has ever seen in a mirror.

Bing — for that's who the boy is although, of course, Rosemary has no idea of that — straightens the groundskeeper's legs and traces an arc in dirt around his head.

"Nine-one-one. Do you need assistance?"

Rosemary hangs up the phone. She drops to her knees on the opposite side of the groundskeeper's body, away from Bing. "Is he dead?"

Bing runs his hand from the groundskeeper's breastbone over his throat and holds it, palm down, over the nostrils that give no sign of breath. Bing's other hand hovers over the man's navel.

A low, guttural hum strums from Bing's throat. Like a garbage disposal full of coffee grounds, Rosemary thinks, or Turk when he's winding up for a final run at climax. Bing's hum grows quieter, smoother, now more of a ceiling fan sound. Rosemary almost speaks, but she bites off the words. They don't matter. Something is going on here and her questions or asides hold no relevance. She is one rare person who knows when the appropriate time has come to shut up.

The rain falls. The wind whispers. Far away, a lion roars. Bing hums. Rosemary sees a V slide through the pond, off into a cypress root. She thinks about the mystery of death. What happens in that special moment when a person leaves their body behind? The spirit and body separate. The body goes from alive to being a thing, an inert object. Where does the spirit land? Turk would want her to note her impressions.

The groundskeeper opens his eyes.

Rosemary flinches. *"Holy moly!"*

Bing's humming tapers to silence. He and the groundskeeper stare at one another, as if not certain what comes next. The groundskeeper is flabbergasted at being alive. Bing is more fascinated than surprised. Now, it is Rosemary's turn to stop breathing.

The groundskeeper smiles. Bing nods. The groundskeeper nods back.

Rosemary says, "I don't understand this one iota. What just happened?

She needs answers, right now, and both men are ignoring her. Rosemary reaches across the now-live groundskeeper and touches Bing on the upper arm.

The boy explodes. Imagine sticking a cattle prod to an innocent child. He jerks away, an expression of livid horror in his eyes. Rosemary would later think about that instant change — from beatific love to terror in the space of heartbeat.

Bing stares at his arm, the spot where her fingers brushed his skin. He looks back at Rosemary.

"It's okay," she says. "You're cool. I don't bite."

Bing leaps to his feet and runs into the forest.

CHAPTER FIVE

Rosemary watches Bing bound away, like a deer vaulting through ground cover. He goes straight up the hill opposite the pond, making long leaps on the steep slope. She watches until he vanishes into the gloom, then she turns to see the groundskeeper has sat up next to her. He also watches Bing run. The only evidence of his ordeal is the blood track from his nostrils and lips. She can't locate fang marks on his neck.

He says, "Water."

She twists the top off her blue cylindrical water bottle with the Centered Soul logo in white and hands it to the groundskeeper, feeling a certain smugness for not minding that a person of a different ethnic group is going to drink after her and she will soon be drinking after him. Then she calls crap on herself. Her pride at a lack of squeamishness is just as bogus as if she'd been squeamish because the enlightened person would be so enlightened she wouldn't notice that the man is a different ethnic group, much less feel smug for behaving like a human should. Finally, the moral nuances snarl so badly Rosemary gives it up.

When the groundskeeper tips his head back and pours water down his throat she notices a nametag sewn into his uniform — CARL FLORES. Now, she can at least think of him as Carl instead of a nameless member of the service industry.

Rosemary says, "I'm lost here. Why aren't you stretched out there dead?"

Carl drinks till water runs off his chin. Drops glisten against his mustache.

He says, "I have never felt such thirst."

"Were you thirsty before —" She hesitates, wondering how to word it "— whatever happened to you happened?"

"I do not recall. I think not."

"So what did happen, I mean, after the snake? I'm pretty clear on events through the bite and falling into the water."

He drains the entire bottle. "I was dead. Maybe. I think I was dead for a period of time."

"Did you see a light or a tunnel? Maybe your passed-on mom?"

"My mother is alive. At least, she was this morning." Carl isn't taking anything for granted.

"Did you see any passed-on loved ones?"

He shakes his head. "I was gone away to someplace else." Carl studies Rosemary, as if memorizing her features. "You must know more of what went on than I do. While I was gone."

Rosemary leans back on her heels. She looks at the pond. The rain has stopped. The acacia drips along the edge, but the center of the pond lies flat. There is no movement from within the cypress root where the snake was last seen. She looks up into the acacia, as if searching for something else to fall from the sky.

"Let's start with — who was that kid?"

Carl the groundskeeper makes it to his knees and, with a grunt, upright. Rosemary stands with him.

"I wish I had a cigarette," he says.

Rosemary pulls her pack from her purse and offers Carl a Kent 100. She says, "Keep it hidden. The zoo doesn't allow smoking."

"They bend the rules for dead men."

It takes Rosemary more than a moment to realize Carl has made a joke. She wonders if she would be able to joke if she had been dead and come back. It would be such a life-changer. How can you emerge out of that the same way you went in, and, therefore, isn't it pathetic not to take into account the possibility? Shouldn't we all pretend we've died and been given a second chance, whether we have or not, for the sake of prioritization.

Rosemary loans Carl her lighter. He lights up, draws deeply and says, "I've never seen him and I don't know his name, but I believe he is the Park wild boy. He lives here. Hides out. No one has ever had a good look at him. Before today."

Rosemary says, "Jesus. The Tarzan of Escondido."

Carl walks to the pond and, looking carefully for snakes, he wades back in to fish out his hat. Rosemary thinks he is braver than she would ever be. She would have kissed that hat goodbye.

Carl talks through the cigarette between his lips. "I have heard stories since I began work at this place. There was a trainer in Condor Gardens claimed he lives in the hills up there." Carl made a vague motion toward the hill backing up the zoo. It is mostly bare rocks and juniper scrub.

"Vivian down at the gift shop says he stays in the closed off part of the Park, with the primates. She says he has mated an orangutan."

Rosemary peers into the undergrowth where Bing disappeared. She wonders if he is still watching her.

He is.

"Thousands of people pass through, on most days, anyway. How can a person live in the park without anyone knowing?" Rosemary asks.

Carl grabs his hat and turns to slosh back. He comes ashore healthy and strong as he'd been before the snake.

He says, "Same way he made me breathe again, I think."

"This is the other thing I can't wrap my mind around," Rosemary says. "How did he do that?"

CHAPTER SIX

Bing stands at the short side of a rectangular table with a cutting board top, catching fruit Dr. Lori hacks with a cleaver the size of a machete.

WHACK! A mango cleaves into two equal chunks. *WHACK.* A cantaloupe. *WHACK! WHACK!* Grapefruit. Melon. After each chop Dr. Lori sweeps the halved fruit toward Bing. Her left arm swings forward horizontally in counterpoint to the right wielding the cleaver vertically. *WHACK!* Sweep. *WHACK!* Sweep.

The fruit flies to Bing who grabs each juice-laden section and tosses it into a plastic laundry basket on the floor. As each basket fills, he uses his bare feet to maneuver a full basket out of the way and an empty basket into position.

Bing says, "I want an iPhone."

Dr. Lori pauses in her chop motion. Dr. Lori is a tall woman, 58, although she looks older due to severity and skin brown from years outdoors and a disdain for sunscreen. She has cropped grey hair and fingers with practically no fingernails. Bing often thinks of her as a tree.

"You can't have an iPhone."

"You have one."

Dr. Lori splits a watermelon, like firewood on a stump. She falls into her wise woman voice. *"Why of the sheep do you not love peace."*

Bing considers the sheep that climb boulders up next to the condor habitat. They eat and crap. Is that peace? He isn't good with abstractions along the lines of *peace.* Dr. Lori never explains words.

"Can I play a game on your iPhone?

"How do you know about games?"

"The Outie adolescents. They hardly look at exhibits. They play on their toys."

Dr. Lori sweeps watermelons halves to Bing. Pink juice glistens on the hairs of her left arm. "You touch my phone and I will neuter you."

Bing dunks the halves into a fresh basket. "Is that an example of exaggeration?"

"Don't try me."

He thinks sadly of the thousands of post-puberty children his own age, their concentration fixed on the box machines between their opposable thumbs. Sometimes they focus so hard on the boxes that they walk into light poles. He's never been close enough to see the games they play, but their vocalizations indicate great joy and frustration.

"Where do Outies go when they leave the zoo?"

Dr. Lori has known the day would arrive when Bing asks that question. Since his toddler time, she's come up with hundreds of answers. Now, with forethought, she says, "They cease to exist, outside our walls, until it is time to return."

"You go out. Do you cease to exist?"

"I am an administrator."

Bing has never doubted Dr. Lori's word. How could he since she is his sole source of information? He has no one to compare with her.

"I saw an interesting Outie today," Bing says. "She burned paper."

Dr. Lori stops at the top of her backswing. She turns her glare on Bing. She means to be menacing, but he misses it. He is looking into the basket at watermelon seeds. Several appear to move.

Bing says, "She had shiny hair."

Dr. Lori lets loose a vicious chop. "You stay away from Outies."

"They can't all be foul, disease-ridden vermin."

"Bing." Dr. Lori reaches across the table and pokes his sweatshirt with the back side of her cleaver. "If you touch an Outie your flesh will rot off your carcass, you will bleed from boils. You recall the boils on the hippopotamus?"

Bing nods, mutely. The hippo smelled like week-dead worms.

"You will bleed from open sores and die in agonizing pain."

Bing puffs out his lower lip — bonobo fashion. He pouts. "Outies touch each other."

"And they die in agonizing pain."

Bing has seen agonizing pain. A giraffe blew his ankle — which most people think of as his knee — when Outie children threw firecrackers over the moat. Agonizing pain is to be avoided.

"Terror in the house does roar, but pity stands before the door."

Bing has heard that sentence often, so he nods, knowingly. He's learned it is better to falsify understanding than to pursue questions.

He arches his back, moves up on his toes, and commences to scratch his neck — not gently. This is a vicious, hard scratch that draws blood.

Dr. Lori crosses the gap between them and catches him by the wrist, freezing him in mid-scratch.

"Who found and saved you?" she asks.

Bing stares at the floor drain.

She tightens her grip on his wrist. "Who raised you from a baby?"

"You did, Dr. Lori."

"Who protects you from Outies? Who knows what is best for you at all times?"

"Dr. Lori."

Dr. Lori releases Bing's wrist. Her look is one of purest motherly love. Bing is the center of her existence.

"That is correct," she says. "Go feed your family."

CHAPTER SEVEN

At the time of our story, when the San Diego Wildlife Park is on the cusp of becoming the San Diego Zoo Safari Park — still in Escondido and not San Diego — five bonobos live in a private habitat in the closed part of the zoo. Zoo officials say they are kept off display in order to acclimate the bonobos to Southern California, but the truth is showing bonobos to the public can be awkward. They go through spells of having sex several times an hour — oral, homosexual, missionary, inappropriate incestuous touching. The female orgasm can be long and loud. Bonobos tend to be educational at a level that makes human parents uncomfortable.

Three females and two males live in the zoo, besides Bing who is in the unique situation as a non-species member of the family. His mother Betty is there. Remember Betty from Zaire? And his brother Kano who should have been Bing had not a human baby been added to the crate leading to misinterpretation of the paper work. There's also a very young female named Lola and a very old female named Taeyondo. Taeyondo is the oldest bonobo in captivity. She may well be the oldest bonobo on the planet. She is considered wise by the press, although it is hard to pin down what they are basing this on, other than age. Old age doesn't suppress vanity in bonobos anymore than it does in humans.

The fifth bonobo is a male named Ubu. You might think that by being the prime candidate for procreation Ubu would rule the enclosure, but, if so, you're confusing bonobos with chimps. Nature doesn't work that way for bonobos. For example, two years ago when Ubu tried to steal a watermelon from Taeyondo, she tore his thumb off. The myth that bonobos are a bunch of make-love-not-war hippies was started by hippies.

When Bing brings the basket of fruit through the back gate into the compound, Ubu paces to and fro along the front fence. He holds out his thumbless hand, palm up, begging. Bing ignores him. Kano charges over and steals a bunch of grapes. The old and young females watch, knowing Betty will kick the crap out of anyone gives her son grief. Only Bing bares his incisors and growls Kano away.

Bing then tosses bananas, cantaloupe, mango, melons, apples, and grapefruit toward each female who sits like a queen in waiting. As Bing feeds the extended family, he undergoes an interesting transformation. His posture droops — shoulders down, knees bent. His jaw thrusts forward. His lips poof. When he crosses the compound he knuckle walks. His breathing turns to pants and grunts. When Kano charges in for another theft, Bing emits a high-pitched shriek.

With the basket nearly empty, Bing overhand throws a couple of bruised mangos to Ubu, then he settles into peeling bananas for himself. Maybe it's the matriarchal thing, opposed to male rule, but bonobos take their time with dinner. They enjoy meals. Bing peels his bananas. Most primates eat the peels.

Bing squats on his heels and tilts his face to the setting sun as he chews. He thinks about the girl with the wavy hair. The girl burned a sheet of blue paper. Bing wonders why. As a generalization, Bing doesn't wonder the why of things he sees. The girl has him thinking new thoughts. Bing pictures the cup between her collarbone and throat. In his mind, the cup pulses with the fragileness of a hummingbird's throat. In reality, he'd been too far away to see any pulse in her collarbone cup. That doesn't matter. Bing's vision has replaced reality. It doesn't take long.

A lump soon forms in Bing's canvas shorts. Betty comes across the yard to look at it. Lola tries to touch him there, but Betty backhands Lola in the ear. Bing wouldn't have minded Lola touching him. Sometimes, he thinks having two mothers — bonobo and human — is not that great a deal.

Betty reaches over and rubs Bing's scalp with the palm of her hand. Bing reaches out and pinches a tick from Betty's neck. Betty grunts, appreciatively.

Bing eats his banana.

Chapter Eight

Rosemary Faith lives in a little yellow house built by an architect who takes pride in building tasteful, small homes. His theory — and therefore Rosemary's theory — is if you have less you'll need less. People like him call themselves the Small House Movement.

The house has three rooms plus a bathroom. The floors are blond oak. The furniture is the best you can buy at IKEA. The kitchen is neatly organized and feng shui correct.

Every night before sleep, Rosemary steeps a pot of tea using clay utensils she bought at an art fair in Solano. The tea is white leaves from a Japanese herbal shop on Venice Beach. While the tea steeps she sits at her kitchen table and deals out, from bottom to top, ten whole grain Wheat Thins in the pattern of a baobab crowned by a single star, although without size perspective it looks as much like a mushroom as a tree. Rosemary thinks of it as baobab, anyway. Then in a certain order that hasn't varied since she was eleven years old and first read *The Little Prince*, Rosemary dips the crackers in hot tea and contemplates her day. This night, she has much to consider. The long-awaited other shoe has dropped, so to speak. She has seen a miracle.

It's no accident that Rosemary produces shows for a spiritual-ist radio network. She is drawn to individuals who know what they believe. Rosemary herself is informed when it comes to chi, tao, Durga Puja, and the Arapaho Medicine Wheel. She can speak fluently on Kabbalah. If anyone understands Revelations, it is Rosemary, but, bottom line, she doesn't believe in Santa Claus and that fact sweeps everything else away with it.

Rosemary desperately wants to believe Impossible Shit happens. Miracles, synchronicity, transmigration of souls — she would give her life for proof that a person's stuff goes on before birth or after death.

The folks she works with at Centered Soul seem to believe. Turk makes too much money off God not to believe in him, and the colorful eccentrics she books on their shows certainly believe, but Rosemary has never been able to push herself though that final window. She's never witnessed an example of undeniable Impossible Shit, until today.

She sips her tea — no sugar, one slice of lime — and nibbles her Wheat Thins in the correct order, and tries to reconstruct what she'd seen. Was the groundskeeper, whose name she's already forgotten, dead? Could he have been almost but not quite dead and when the boy laid him out in the air he came around? He hadn't coughed up water the way near drowning victims do in the movies. The man had simply gone from not breathing to breathing. Surely that is the sign of a miracle.

Rosemary stands up and walks around her combination kitchen table/chopping block, clockwise, then she knocks on it twice, as a focusing ritual. Turk is big on focusing rituals. He believes in physical mantras. Rosemary is willing to try whatever works for anyone else. Turk claims to have inner peace, but what he has is confidence that manifests itself as a curtain of serenity.

Rosemary covers all bases by reciting a prayer taught to her by her Grandma Ellie when she'd been losing her mind in a nursing home. It was the one with the *If I should die before I wake* line. Rosemary's grandma tended to shriek that part.

Rosemary walks into her cozy bathroom, loads her water flosser toothbrush with fluoride-free paste, and flips over her two-minute sand timer.

That gives her two minutes to consider the wild boy. His shirt had writing on it, the logo of a university sports team, but she doesn't know which one. If he never leaves the park, how does he get clothes? Who buys him deodorant? He'd been wearing a train engineer's cap that didn't fall off when he came from above into the pond. As her mind slowly puts him together, like dressing a paper doll, the more she thinks about it the more she thinks his shorts had been inside out. What was that all about? Rejection of consumerism? The kid had not looked like a being given to symbolism. His face had been alight with joy.

And the sounds he made over the groundskeeper's either dead or nearly dead body were not from a tradition she knows of, and she can differentiate repetitive chants from Dervish to Zulu to Navajo and most in between, including Catholicism. It had been an animal code, of some sort.

After brushing her teeth, Rosemary washes her face carefully and rubs moisturizer into her legs, the backs of her hands, and her throat. A woman's bedtime ritual is at least as stylized as any voodoo priest.

She wanders into the bedroom and checks on her sister's whereabouts on the Droid GPS. A digital photo frame on Rosemary's nightstand shows Sarah as she'd been, pre-sickness. They had climbed Mount Whitney one summer. The photo up now is of Sarah at the top, with her arms raised like a champion. Her mouth is open in a shout of triumph. Her blond hair blows in the wind and her smile is proud and glorious. Her bare skin glows with life. At that moment, Rosemary had known Sarah would never die.

Rosemary punches 1 on her speed dial.

"Good morning."

Rosemary doesn't say, "It's not morning." There is no point.

"Sarah, it's Rosie. How are you feeling?'

"I am alive, thank you."

"Listen, Sarah, I may have found a way to save you. I'm not completely sure, but we might be able to make you whole again."

"That would be pleasant."

"I've found someone who can help. You need to hang on for a few more days and everything will be okay. I promise, I'm going to find a way. We'll get out of this."

Rosemary waits for Sarah to process the information. She expects questions and she can't decide how far to push Sarah's hopes. Her sister needs hope. Without hope there is no call to go on. But false hope would build her up only to smash her down again.

After thirty seconds of quiet breathing, Sarah's voice comes back across the phone.

"Who is this?"

"Rosie. Rosemary. Your sister."

"I don't know a Rosie or a Rosemary. You must have reached a wrong number."

Rosemary's phone goes dead.

CHAPTER NINE

D r. Lori removes her glasses and lets them drop to the end of the gold chain hanging around her neck. She thumb-and-index-finger rubs the bridge of her nose, giving herself a shiatsu treatment along the frontal plate. She feels for the edge of the skull, where it meets the nasal cavity. It doesn't help her headache much. What she needs is a drink followed by bed.

She rises from the desk and walks down the hall to the bonobo compound. In the daytime, a bevy of vets, cleaning crews, and marketing minions swarm the area, but at night the enclosure is left to Dr. Lori. She guards this privacy with fierce determination, quick to light into anyone who invades her sanctuary.

As on most — but not all — nights for the last twenty years, Dr. Lori enters the bonobo enclosure and crosses to the sleeping nests. This is against policy. She's not supposed to approach any primate alone, but Dr. Lori looks at policy as a guideline and a guideline as a suggestion. No one tells her what to do.

The bonobos are stretched out on their nests — tree limbs and leaves woven across tire bases. Taeyondo sleeps sitting up, like Buddha in repose. Ubu, away from the others, whimpers in his sleep. Bing sleeps on his stomach with his head on Betty's thigh. Kono's hand is wrapped around Bing's ankle.

As Dr. Lori watches Bing she runs through the same thoughts parents around the globe think while watching their children sleep. First, overpowering love — kids are easy to love when they're asleep. Then, in roughly this order: anxiety for the future; amazement that this being could exist and be yours; fear of messing the child up; and finally softness.

Dr. Lori feels a wave of loss for something that isn't yet lost. The feeling vexes her. Why nostalgia for the present? There must be a term for missing something you have. Bing is right there in front of her. She can see him breathing. His eyes twitch in a dream. He mumbles to someone or something. Dr. Lori feels excluded from his dreams. She feels a penetrating sense of sadness caused by the knowledge that this incredible joy is doomed.

Dr. Lori touches Bing's face. He snuggles deeper into Betty. A twinge of jealousy flashes through Dr. Lori, that Bing is more attached to his animal mother than her. Maybe she can do something about that. She'll think on it later.

Chapter Ten

osemary Faith haunts the wildlife park. For eight weeks,
throughout March and into April, whenever she isn't producing at Centered Soul, Rosemary drives to Escondido, buys a one-day
pass, and walks the paths. She climbs the hill to the tiger overlook
almost daily. She circles the Heart of Africa. She weaves her way
through the throngs at Thorntree Bazaar, always looking.

While more or less two million people pass through the park
in a year, only a handful haunt the place. The regulars — the every
day visitors — stand out to each other, like an urban coffee clique.
At least, they stand out to Rosemary who is paying attention. Some
of the regulars seem to move in a fog.

Such as: A dapper gentleman — no other words fit him —
maybe seventy. He uses an umbrella as a cane and parks himself
on the same bench in front of the lowland gorillas. He chews gum
and stares at the huge beasts who themselves rarely move either.
It is as if the gentleman and the gorillas are playing a game of
whoever-blinks-loses.

A woman in Dacron with twin toddlers. These three barely
make it through the entrance gate before plopping onto the rocks
at the flamingos. The woman and both kids drink 64-ounce Big
Gulps. They eat snacks all day. The kids run wild while the woman
ignores them, although Rosemary can't decide where her attention
lies instead. She wears earphones and carries an MP3 player in a
holster on her belt.

Two women in Sundance shorts and ironed Cabela safari
shirts power walk the lower circle every afternoon at six. Neither

so much as glances at the animals. They both have devices on their upper arms for measuring bodily functions. Once early in her quest, Rosemary found herself caught in their path. She braced for a collision or at least a scathing remark, but instead the women shot around her on either side, like a raging river bypassing a rock.

A mixture of haunters meander the park aimlessly, like Rosemary. She imagines they too are searching, although she can't imagine what they are searching for. Inner peace, maybe. Or lost love. Some appear to be schizophrenics, but that may just be head set cell phone use. She hopes they aren't searching for the same thing she is. That would be depressing. Rosemary is realistic enough to see herself as grasping at a straw, and if everyone else walking aimlessly day by day is as pitiful as Rosemary feels she is, then she might as well give up and scream.

One afternoon in April, a young man breaks the unspoken barrier between regulars. He tries to pick Rosemary up.

It happens at the shoebill lagoon where she is scanning the treetops on the other side. The trees are filled with large birds. There may be something else among the leaves, but it's hard to say.

The boy steps up next to Rosemary and says, "I've seen you before."

Rosemary glances at him. Young, nervous, bad skin. Squashable as a bug. "Is that so?"

He takes this as encouragement. "You come every day. I didn't see you Friday. I looked but if you was here, I missed it."

She is a bit impressed he's kept track. Had the kid said *were* instead of *was*, she might have been tempted to take him seriously. "I had to work overtime Friday."

The kid gathers all the courage he has in him. "Would you care to accompany me for an ice cream. I'll buy."

"I am sorry, but I'm kind of in a hurry."

"In a hurry for what? You don't look in a hurry."

"Don't force me to be rude to you."

Now the kid is hurt. He pouts. "I'm not forcing you to do anything. I just asked if you'd care to go for ice cream. I even offered to pay. I don't see how that makes you be rude against your will."

The kid has a point. Rosemary turns from her search to bring the full brunt of her attention to the boy. "You are skipping school."

He doesn't speak, but his face blushes.

"I'll bet twenty dollars your mother thinks you are in high school but you sneak off here every day instead. You hide your books somewhere and walk around all day and at three o'clock you pick them up and go home and tell Mama what a good day you had in algebra."

The boy flushes the color of sliced beets on a salad bar. "I was only trying to be nice."

"Yeah, well, you failed miserably. Now go off and let me do what I need to do here."

CHAPTER ELEVEN

Rosemary Faith sits perched on a bench in Chandler's Garden when Bing appears at her elbow. Chandler's is a quiet, out of the way garden surrounded by yet apart from the exhibits. Because there are no wild animals, few visitors loiter along its paths. The garden is filled with herbs, mostly, and a few flowers. The herbs grow behind stake-mounted cards explaining what each plant is and what part of the world is its home.

Rosemary sits on the bench, her palms aligned, one on each thigh. She is pretending her mind is a deep well and, one by one, she is dropping coins into the well. Fifty-cent pieces. She waits for each coin to *plink* into the water, causing first a nipple splash and then concentric circles of waves. The coin turns slowly over as it sinks to the bottom of the well. When one half dollar settles to the bottom, she drops another.

This is a technique Turk taught her. Its purpose is to empty her mind, and, that day, Rosemary dreams of an empty mind. The search isn't going anywhere. She is out of ideas.

"Do you have an iPhone?"

Rosemary opens her eyes and there he stands — the object of her search. His hair drips under the engineer's cap, as if he just stepped out of a shower. He is wearing cargo pants instead of shorts.

"Do you have an iPhone?"

Rosemary's hand moves to her bag. She'd recently taken to carrying her phone in a drawstring pouch because Sister Starshine says a cell phone in your pocket causes cancer.

"It's a Droid."

"Is that the same?"

"More or less."

Bing says, "Give it to me."

Like almost everyone will when given a direct order, Rosemary obeys. She hands her phone to Bing. Their fingers do not touch.

He glances at the phone, then sticks it into the back right pocket of his pants.

Rosemary says, "What are you doing?"

Bing tries to think of an answer. It seems obvious what he is doing. He is standing next to a girl, speaking with her, and even though it is something he's never done before, anyone can see that's what it is.

"Thank you for the possession."

"Give back my phone."

Bing's eyebrows draw up in a muscle flex. "You gifted it to me."

"Not to keep. I thought you wanted to borrow it."

"Borrow?"

"To telephone someone."

Bang pulls the phone from his pocket. He looks at it with a combination of desire and envy. "Who would I telephone?"

Rosemary takes the phone back. Once more, their fingers do not touch. "How should I know who you would call? Who do you usually call on the phone?"

"Dr. Lori is the person I know with a phone of her own. She won't allow me playing on it. And I couldn't borrow her phone and call her at the same moment. They don't operate like that." He enjoys the way *borrow* comes out of his mouth, as if it is a word he's known for always. Bing likes new words. He's learned all the words Dr. Lori is liable to say.

"I know two persons with phones now."

"Counting me?" Rosemary says.

Bing nods.

"How many people do you know in the world, all put together?"

Bing thinks. "Human people?"

"That's correct. How many human people do you know?"

Bing counts on his fingers. "Two. First there was Dr. Lori and now you."

CHAPTER TWELVE

Two young people — him, twenty, her, a few years older — study one another, as if in a zoo, looking into cages, or more like watching television unaware that the object of scrutiny is scrutinizing back. Bing admires a soft vein pulse against Rosemary's throat. It is a fine throat, strong and evenly planed. A throat to be proud of. He would like to place his ear over that vein, to listen.

She watches his eyes, searching for mystery.

Bing says, "You have been looking for me."

Rosemary says, "Yes."

Bing scratches his bottom. Not a subtle, nuanced scratch to relieve a tickle. Bing digs deep, he tears at his anus with all his attention.

For Rosemary, it is spellbinding. "When did you figure it out?"

Bing twists to look back at his rear end. His hole itches like he has ants. "I can't keep in mind how time passes," he says. "You come and go and you look."

He suddenly leaps onto the back of Rosemary's bench. The seat is concrete, but the backrest is made of green wrought iron in a scroll pattern. As Bing jumps, Rosemary stands and turns. She watches him walk barefoot three steps along the back edge of the bench before he turns in a semi-circle and comes toward her.

"I need to know how you made the groundskeeper start breathing," Rosemary says. "After he was gone."

Big spins back the other way. He speaks without looking at her. "The man wasn't gone anywhere."

45

"He was dead. Or close to dead. You healed him by that – " She holds her hands out flat, the way Bing had held his over the groundskeeper. "Gobbledygook."

Bing stops. He looks down at Rosemary. "I do not fathom *gobbledygook.*"

"The chant. It wasn't works, more like magic sounds. Could you do it again? Make a person well when they are sick?"

Bing hops up and comes down at Rosemary's level, directly facing her. His eyes are sly. "Maybe. For an iPhone."

They both drop back into stare mode. Rosemary is good at the unblinking eye challenge that comes with sexual politics. The dare. The question. The submission.

Bing is lost.

Rosemary says, "The groundskeeper guy told me you live in the Wildlife Park. You don't go outside the gates."

It isn't a question, so Bing doesn't answer. He is basking in the flavor of Rosemary's breath. He's never inhaled an air similar before. It smells like sweet life mixed with timothy hay.

"How long have you lived here?" Rosemary asks.

Bing can no longer stand the pressure. Again, he leaps onto the bench back, only now he walks on his hands. His face swivels to keep an eye on Rosemary.

"Since Dr. Lori saved me."

"What did Dr. Lori save you from?"

Bing hand walks to the end of the bench. He performs a move dancers call spotting, where he looks at Rosemary, then spins his head lightning fast as he turns to look at her again. It's hard to pull off, upside down.

"Outies. They would have touched me and given me diarrhea and I would have died in misery. She protects me from those outside. People like you."

"You need no protection from me."

Bing's look is dubious.

"I touched you the day you healed the man and you didn't die. You didn't even get diarrhea, did you?"

Bing lowers his head until it aligns on the iron bench back. "That is true."

"This Dr. Lori has been feeding you horse manure."

Bing loses his purchase and falls. He bounces off the bench seat and lands in a pile of elbows, knees, and wounded dignity. He jumps to his feet. "I did that on purpose."

Rosemary takes no note of the fall. She is on a mission. "So you've never been outside the park?"

From the top of Elephant Lookout, Bing catches a flash of light. He tilts his head sharply right and the light goes out. He brings his head back straight and the light glints again. Sunlight on glass. A tourist must have propped a pop bottle on the rail.

"Do you ever go out there?" Rosemary gestures toward the big world beyond the zoo.

"I don't want to catch the plague. People outside are shreds of broken humanity."

"Do I look like a shred?"

What she looks like to Bing is everything Dr. Lori isn't — youth, beauty, possibility. Sex. She brings a trickle of sweat to his ribcage.

"Perhaps you are a shred in places I cannot see."

Rosemary moves closer, bathing Bing in female scent. She says, "I need you to come with me. Outside."

Bing shows fright. "That is not possible."

"It is possible." She glides even closer. He feels cool breath on his eyelids. "What's your name?"

"Bing."

"I'm Rosemary Faith." She extends out her hand to shake. Bing looks at Rosemary's hand. He sees the length of her fingers — longer index than middle — and the gloss on her nails. He has no clue as to what he is supposed to do.

CHAPTER THIRTEEN

Two nuns from Waterloo, Iowa, make their slow way up the steps to the Elephant Overlook. They are dressed in nurse shoes and the modern wool habits that make nuns look like Mary Poppins wannabes. The older one who considers herself the ept member of the team has her face turned down toward a guidebook called *1,000 Must Sees in Southern California*.

"What is this place?" she asks.

The other nun actually believes in Jesus as opposed the older one who chose her career based on job security. This younger devout nun searches the railing area until she finds a sign.

"Elephant Overlook."

The older nun who doesn't believe pulls a number 2 pencil from behind her ear where it is held in place by a white cotton scarf and checks a box next to ELEPHANT OVERLOOK in the guidebook.

"What next?" the younger one says.

"Lion Camp."

Neither of the nuns glances across the rail at the elephants. These are checklist tourists. The attraction is irrelevant.

As they turn to make their exhausted way back down the board steps, they pass Dr. Lori who isn't watching elephants either. Dr. Lori has her elbows propped on the viewing rail to stabilize the binoculars through which she is watching Bing and Rosemary. When Rosemary grasps Bing's wrist and teaches him how to shake hands, Dr. Lori lowers the binoculars and says, "God damn little bastard. I'll cut off his nuts."

The nuns from Waterloo ignore her. They are too tired to take offense.

CHAPTER FOURTEEN

Our young man Bing stands, legs spread, on the lip on a tractor tire that hangs horizontally by a three-rope rig from a beam across the top of the bonobo enclosure while Kano stands on the opposite side. Their purpose: to jump up and down until the other brother, on the far side, falls off. The game requires much energy. Doesn't give Bing time to think about any girl with shiny hair and sage breath. Bouncing, laughing, chirping. Two brothers at play.

"Bing." A harsh voice sounds behind him. "Come to me."

Bing ignores her. He has Kano off balance and is moving in for the kill, game-wise. Bing goes from jumping to a slide and shake twist motion. Kano's feet fly off the tire but he hangs onto the rope by one hand.

"This minute."

The threat in her voice pierces Bing's glee. He thinks *uh-oh* and stops to look back at Dr. Lori standing in the dark doorway to the support hall. She's wearing a black turtleneck, black pants, black cloud. Posture of a lion trainer. Bing starts to say, *"I didn't-"* just as Kano makes a savage jump that jerks Bing into the apex of the ropes.

Bing screams. *"Aieee!"*

Dr. Lori says, "One."

His voice is a slur. "Ah bit mah thung."

"Two."

Bing drops off the tire. Holding his mouth open in an off-kilter slant fashion, he approaches Dr. Lori. Bing lowers his body, drags his hands along the ground, keeps his eyes downcast — classic submission posture.

Bing lisps. *"Hurts."*

"You deserve pain."

Behind his inferior body language, Bing is hyper-alert. He doesn't know how Dr. Lori knows about his talk — and touch — with Rosemary Faith, but he has no doubt that she knows. Dr. Lori has convinced Bing that she sees all things at all times. Bing assumes there is an ever-present security camera with Dr. Lori on the monitor.

Dr. Lori stares down at Bing. "You have had contact with an Outer One."

Bing hangs his head. Busted.

She doesn't wait for denial. "Bing, you must go directly to the decontamination chamber. I only hope we have caught the infection in time."

Bing's lower lip protrudes much farther than you normally see in even the most recalcitrant of human children. "I don't feel infected. I feel pleased."

She expected tears and begging for forgiveness. She hasn't planned for a lack of remorse. "Do not contradict me. You will spend today in the chamber. No food. No toys. You may use your time in dwelling on the horror of your actions."

Dr. Lori pauses to check the power of her words. Bing stares ahead like a stubborn four year old who thinks he's being unfairly attacked.

"You must be made to understand the seriousness of your transgression."

Bing sulks. Kano moves to the front of the enclosure. All the bonobos move as far from Dr. Lori as they can get.

"You do understand the seriousness, don't you, Bing?"

Bing is petulant. Not petulant enough to meet Dr. Lori's glare, but he isn't going to roll over and accept the punishment this time.

"She said you are feeding me a line of horse manure."

Dr. Lore goes apoplectic, which in this case means her nostrils flare and her hands form fists. An electric current passes up her spine. In the shadow of the late afternoon light she appears as an angry tall predator. A leopard walking upright.

"You told the female about me?"

"Just what you said — that touching her would give me diarrhea." Bing glances up at Dr. Lori, then away to Betty, who is watching nervously. "She touched me and I didn't get diarrhea."

Dr. Lori also glances over at Betty. She wonders if she slaps Bing in the face would Betty charge. The bonobo is properly submissive now, but Dr. Lori has seen the maternal instinct kick in in violent forms in the past. It can be a mess.

"How long ago did this touch from an Outie take place?"

Bing shrugs. What does he know about time? "Before."

"Before what?"

"Before now."

Dr. Lori crosses her arms over her chest. She leans back on her heels. "I assume you have been meeting this licentious woman on a regular basis."

Bing holds up two fingers off to his side, like pointing a direction. "Two. I've talked with her two times."

"Do not lie to me."

Bing's forehead wrinkles, washboard fashion. He stares hard at the ground. It has never occurred to Bing to lie to Dr. Lori. He thought it impossible. He may omit information if she doesn't ask, but he's never thought it possible to lie directly to her. The fact that she thinks he might be telling an untruth but she isn't certain means she doesn't know all. He senses a crack in her omnipotence.

Dr. Lori lifts his chin, forcing his eyes to meet hers. He doesn't like this. "Bing, you know I am your only link to the world."

Bing motions toward the bonobos. "Except for the family."

"The only link to the human world. Your real world. Just like the bonobos raised in captivity, you would never be able to survive in the wild." She skewers him with her eyes. . "Alone. Without me."

Bing nods. He's heard this in the past and he knows it is true. Outside Dr. Lori's protection, he is lost.

"You must promise me, Bing. Promise. Never to go out the front gate. Never risk your life in the outside world. If something happened to you it would kill me, and you don't want to kill me, do you?"

Bing sulks.

Dr. Lori tightens her grip on his chin. "You hear me?"

Bing nods.

"You *hear* me."

Bing snaps. "I hear you."

With her free hand, Dr. Lori grabs the front of Bing's sweatshirt and yanks him toward her face.

"Promise me, Bing."

"Okay."

Promise!"

"I promise I will never leave the animal park. Not ever."

Dr. Lori releases both Bing's sweatshirt and his chin. She pats her hair at the nape of her neck. Her voice dials way down. She whispers. "*Great things are done when Men and Mountains meet. It is not done by jostling in the street.*"

She studies Bing's face to see if he is properly moved. He nods, as if he knows what she has in mind and he agrees.

Dr. Lori rests her hand lightly on Bing's right shoulder. "Now, report to decontamination."

CHAPTER FIFTEEN

Bing squats on an overturned bucket with his knees up at his shoulders. He is crammed between cases of toilet paper, Pine Sol, floor wax, mini-pads, glass cleaner, and three types of mop. When he was younger the decontamination chamber was even more packed by paper towel wheels and refills, but now that the park has gone to paperless drying machines the room isn't quite so crowded as it used to be.

The first time Bing was sent to decontamination — for eating a urinal cake back when urinals sported cakes — it had been pitch black and Bing cried. He wouldn't stop. Dr. Lori was afraid someone would hear him, so now she allows Bing the use of a six-volt flashlight. A big bugger.

Bing sets the flashlight upright on the floor with the beam aimed at the ceiling. He crouches over it and creates shadow puppets with his fingers. No one ever showed him how. This is spontaneous art Bing taught himself during the long hours of decontamination. He makes a dik-dik, then a wattled crane. No dogs or kitties for this boy. The cape buffalo is a snap. Giraffes are funny because he sticks his middle finger out to make the neck, but birds are the hardest. Bing has spent hours on the laughing kookaburro. Tonight, he has it. The moment of triumph and no one to share it with.

As he creates a two-dimensional zoo on the ceiling, he hums a song he learned from riding the Conservation Carousel. It's a simple organ tune originally meant to convey the light-heartedness of a circus midway. Bing is quite good at imitating the organ. He can imitate almost any sound in the park. He hasn't had much contact with music in his life — Dr. Lori doesn't listen to the radio while she works, only tabla.com later in the security of her trailer — and he enjoys it when he can. Music does bubbly things to his insides.

The truth is this: Decontamination terrifies Bing. He plays games with himself and hums to turn his mind to a blank. Thinking is bad. No matter how much he hums or how many shadow animals he makes, the walls and ceiling, even the floor, press against him. There is not enough air. Bing needs air. Dr. Lori tried to frighten him with spider and rat stories, but spiders and rats don't frighten Bing. No air frightens Bing. Not being able to move his arms and legs frightens him. Fat toilet paper rolls frighten him. He can't stand to look at the mop for fear it will jump up and hit him in the face. Decontamination is the nightmare of Bing's life.

CHAPTER SIXTEEN

That night as Bing creates wattled cranes on the ceiling of his chamber, Rosemary Faith cleans her house naked. She vacuums the bathroom, the only room with a carpet. She sweeps the hardwood floors, then wet mops, then waxes. She empties her kitchen cabinets, takes out the natural fiber paper liners, and replaces them. She scrubs the microwave oven plate.

At first, she listens to Persephone's past lives regression show on Centered Soul — *Know who you are by knowing who you were.* Persephone is guiding a housewife from West Covina back through the sixteenth century. That's how the woman describes herself — *housewife.* An old-fashioned term to Rosemary. *Homemaker* is more politically proper. Or *self-employed.* The woman died in childbirth in India, Persia, and what is now South Dakota something like thirty incarnations in a row before being born into French royalty. Most of Persephone's guests have been royalty in some era or another. Rosemary used to laugh with Sarah about that back when Sarah laughed.

Sarah's laugh sparkled like a club soda waterfall. "We can't all have been Empress Josephine."

Rosemary said, "Just you and me and sometimes I wonder about you." That had been a saying their mother used when she was being sarcastic, before she discovered love of mankind and lost love of immediate family.

The thought of Sarah and their mother causes Rosemary anxiety and she changes the radio station to lite jazz, the sort of music you hear in the dressing room at Bon Marché. The purpose

55

of all-night naked cleaning is to clear the mind — meditation for Americans who can't sit still — not to dwell on troubles. Rosemary spends enough time obsessing on troubles. Tonight, she wants to lose herself in grout.

Which is what she does. Rosemary digs out an old toothbrush from before she went electric and a tin of Ajax and attacks her shower. She pictures the germs as little animated blobs exploding into tiny fragments of chaos as her toothbrush scrubs them into eternity. Rosemary the Scourge.

She Simple Green cleans the back and sides of the toilet. She shines the pipes under the sink. She organizes her hair products by expiration date, throwing out a hundred dollars of deep conditioner. She unscrews her energy efficient fluorescent light bulbs and carefully dusts between the spirals. She Brassos each charm on the charm bracelet she hasn't worn in fifteen years. She dusts the books, not just the spines but the top and fore edges.

The music plays. Her digital timepieces change numbers. The stars rotate clockwise across the sky. As Rosemary cleans a sheen of perspiration glistens on her bare skin. The folds where her breasts meet her rib cage are damp. A lock of hair clings to her temple. And she cleans on.

At dawn, Rosemary checks the GPS to make certain Sarah is asleep, or at least not on the move. Sunrise is often a restless time when the pain crests and breaks. Finally, Rosemary steeps a pot of white tea. She sits at her kitchen table — still nude — cradling the teacup, and she weeps. Cleaning has not given her control. She is still overwhelmed.

When the tea is no longer hot, Rosemary wipes the tears away with back of her hand, gets up, and showers in her shower stall that smells like bleach.

CHAPTER SEVENTEEN

The Kupandi Falls Botanical Pavilion may well be the most restful spot in California, although for a spot to be restful it probably shouldn't compete for the title. Long-needled trees, bubbling, babbling brook, rocks that appear soft to the eye. The very air is comforting. The pavilion itself has the romanticized Buddhist temple look. The only thing missing from Kupandi Falls is a waterfall. Kupandi Riffle might me a more apt name.

When Bing approaches he finds Rosemary standing next to a concrete column, working the keyboard on her Droid. Her hair is limp, in the humidity. She has a blemish on her forehead. It looks as if she hasn't slept properly.

Rosemary stares at Bing and Bing stares at Rosemary's feet. She's wearing cloth flats.

She says, "I waited for you all day yesterday."

He says, "I got stuck in decontamination, because of you."

"Do you have any concept how creepy that is?"

Bing is dressed in white. Canvas pants. White shirt that, from the buttons on the left, is obviously to anyone other than Bing made for a woman. He's barefoot. The only non-white article of clothing is his engineer's cap.

He nods toward her phone. "Are you calling someone else, or are you playing a game?"

She glances down at the phone. The downward glance causes a curl to fall across her face. "I was checking my schedule. My time frame got scrambled when I shuffled appointments to wait for you to show up."

Bing removes his hat and brushes hair off his own forehead. Her locks hanging down make him aware of his own. "I don't fathom *schedule.*"

"It's what I do when I do it."

"What do you do when you do it?"

"I'm a producer for a talk radio network called Centered Soul. You know what radio is?"

She lost Bing on *producer* and *soul,* but he doesn't go there. He sticks with what he does know. "The box young people listen at, like a phone but not a phone. It makes a hideous sound."

"Our network makes beautiful sounds." Rosemary is instinctively loyal. "We help searchers discover the essence of being from pre-birth to post-death. Our spirit guides connect to the inner soul that vibrates the cosmic web."

Bing has no clue. Post-death? Cosmic? "Are you searcher or spirit guide?"

Rosemary's neck is hot. She spreads a cloth-covered rubber loop between her fingers and works her hair into a ponytail. "I facilitate. I book the seers on the spirit guide shows, then they initiate the searchers into truth."

The words wash by Bing like so much foam. He's more interested in Rosemary's skin tone than he is in hearing her speak gobbledygook, which is a word he now knows. He wants to sniff the air under her nostrils.

Rosemary says, "A wise and gifted teacher created our network. He has raised the universal awareness through syndication to twelve million listeners. If he puts you on the radio, those millions plus more will know your story of isolation and imprisonment. Your recognition factor will skyrocket. It has to. At this second, you may have the lowest profile of anyone in America."

A family of two adults and five juveniles are working their way up the paths, downstream a hundred yards. The children squeal and push each other into the water. The mother lectures on the importance of sharing. The father is wearing ear buds.

Bing wants to move on. "Do you mind if we walk? Up there." He nods toward the nativescapes where almost no one goes even on busy days.

They walk, at first side-by-side, then as they leave the creek and the trail narrows, Bing in the lead. The lushness of Kupandi gives way to desert. They come to a sign: BEWARE OF SNAKES. STAY ON TRAIL.

Rosemary laughs. "You think the snakes can read and they know hikers on the trail are off limits?"

Bing enjoys her laugh. It's even better than the sound made by running water. "I do not understand."

"The sign. It says the trail is safe and off the trail is dangerous. How can the snakes know the difference?"

Bing studies the sign. It's all symbols to him. "I can't read. I don't know what the snakes know."

Rosemary looks from the sign to Bing. His face is perplexed, as if he's up against an insoluble mystery. She says, "I never met anyone who can't read. You hear about it all the time, usually from the First Lady, but it just doesn't come up in my circle."

"There never was need. Dr. Lori takes care of me. Is a recognition factor something to be desired?"

"My mentor says fame is the only worthwhile temporal attainment in modern civilization. He says wealth is no longer relevant."

"I am not familiar with modern civilization."

He turns to walk up the trail. Rosemary speaks to his back. "That's what I'm talking about here. You *must* see the amazing world outside this zoo. Zoos are artificial environments. Cages inside a cage. San Diego is real, but you're trapped by terrible limits."

She reaches out to grasp his upper arm. He doesn't flinch. "I do not enjoy limits," he says.

"Outside you can discover the amazing things civilization has accomplished. Ten-lane freeways. Malls. Starbucks coffee shops. Surfboards. Machines that spit out money. Have you ever seen a machine spit money?"

"I've seen money."

"You can meet human beings who will teach you and learn from you. You will achieve enlightenment."

She turns Bing around and zeros in on eye contact. "There is no enlightenment in staying here."

Bing doesn't enjoy eye contact. He refuses to go there. "Will I get a phone with pictures?"

Okay. He won't buy enlightenment. Maybe a phone will pry him loose. "Of course, we'll buy you a phone. And clothes. Where do you get these clothes?"

Bing looked down at his ladies blouse and white pants. He'd worn them on purpose today, knowing he might see Rosemary. "Lost and found, mostly. When the cloth is soiled, I swap. Dr. Lori brings my under pants. I was found with this." He takes off the engineer's cap to show her. It's worn gray in the sweatband "What is wrong with my clothing?"

Where to start? He looks like a kid dressed by his grandmother. "You'll never know until you see the possibilities, Bing, and this Dr. Lori woman has stolen your possibilities. She is selfish. You understand selfish?"

Bing scrunches the bridge of his nose. Rosemary thinks it gives him a hint of cuteness.

"Dr. Lori says that's what I am when I cry for Cheetos."

"Wanting Cheetos isn't selfish. Wanting to keep others from having Cheetos is. She wants to smother your potential. You must leave this place, with me. We must set your potential free."

Bing sneaks a peek into Rosemary's eyes. Green. Flecked by bits of darker green. Very white whites. Lack of sleep hasn't lessened her eye allure. Rosemary's eyes have the depth of moss-covered diamonds under clean water populated by tropical fish. Anyone looking in them would think so.

He looks down at his hands clutching each other. "I promised Dr. Lori I would never leave the park."

Gently, Rosemary takes both Bing's hands in hers. She rubs his palms with her thumbs. "Dr. Lori doesn't want what is best for you. You don't owe her a life spent behind a wall."

Bing's confusion is complete.

Chapter Eighteen

"The boy was raised in the wildlife park, by animals and an insane woman. He's spent his whole life inside the fence."

"Never trust a Nature Boy. I've gone far with that policy and I'm not backing off now."

Rosemary can never tell for certain when Turk is joking, or when he's being sarcastic which means he's pretending to joke but isn't, or when he really is serious. He always looks serious, behind his ebony desk the size of a Hummer, in his Jay Kos suit, open necked silk shirt, intense blue eyes made even more blue and intense by contacts. Turk has an elk ivory stud in his left ear that she knows he pierced with a cactus thorn. Big honker of a diamond on his right hand pinkie. Turk reminds Rosemary of an Easter Island statue.

He twirls a Mont Blanc pen between his fingers. Rosemary knows the pen can hypnotize if the person on the far side of the desk isn't careful. "I've seen hundreds of these John the Baptists. Ten years in the wilderness and they come out thinking they're prophets."

"Bing doesn't claim to be a prophet. And the zoo isn't the wilderness. He's around thousands of people every day. They can't see him. He's invisible, or something strange. I can't understand it."

Rosemary isn't at ease talking to Turk in his office. She's more comfortable texting, or even in his bed. The office is as big as her Small Home house. It was professionally decorated by a designer who stressed intimidation. One entire wall is lined by photos of Turk standing beside or shaking hands with gurus, spiritualists, religious fanatics, and politicians. A second wall holds racks of CDs of every radio show Turk has ever hosted. The coffee machine in the corner is appropriate for commercial use. Rosemary knows which door leads to a full bathroom and a marble shower. The wall behind the desk is made of smoked glass. It looks out over the San Diego skyline.

"There's no artifice with this boy." She sits forward on the edge of her chair, knees together and hands in lap. "He wouldn't know what a lie is."

"We at Centered Soul thrive on artifice," Turk says. "Artifice is the oil that keeps society's engine from blowing a gasket."

"Society needs one innocent, so that it can tell the difference between what it is and what it could be." Rosemary is making this up on the fly. She is desperate. Turk can smell desperation like a wolf on a hamstrung moose, so she's desperate to hide her desperation. "We need to expose our listeners to extreme innocence. Prove it still exists."

Turk twirls his pen, staring at Rosemary, feeling for the hidden agenda. He knows that every person who wants something from him comes with a hidden agenda. "Can the monkey prove this staggering level of naiveté?"

"He's not interested in proving anything. Bing doesn't want publicity."

"Everyone wants publicity. Shunning publicity is nothing but a dishonest way to get it."

"What makes Bing ideal for C.S. is that he can heal the afflicted. I saw him bring a man back from death."

Turk's eyes flicker, then close down on himself. His is an evolved consciousness beyond emotional arousal. "Do you know how many bozos come in here claiming they can heal the sick? Even I can do it, if I choose to. Any fakir can use hypnosis and hysteria."

"But I saw him. The man was bitten by a coral snake. He was face down in the lake. He couldn't have been saved by hypnosis. The guy was either in a coma or dead. I'm fairly certain he was dead."

Turk twirls the expensive pen between his fingers, in and out, walking it through the knuckles like Bing and the caterpillar. Then he eases it up and spins it around the manicured fingertips.

"Making the lame walk and the blind see are revival circuit stunts. They don't translate to radio. Nobody buys faith healing they can't see these days."

"What if we had him perform a miracle? Live. We could line up witnesses."

Turk clicks his pen in and out. In and out. The tip appearing and disappearing like a phallic symbol. He stares. Rosemary knows they've come to the point where she can go flustered and blow it, or she can prove herself worthy. Proving herself worthy to Turk is important to her. The most important professional goal she aspires to. She meets his stare, head-on.

Turk stops clicking. "This is about your sister. What's her name?"

"Sarah."

"You think monkey boy can save your sister Sarah."

Rosemary's hand rises to her hair. She blinks quickly, three times. "No. No. It's about the show. The network."

"Rosemary, we both know you took this job to put yourself in the position of finding a miracle cure."

"I took the job to learn from you."

Turk doesn't speak. He doesn't have to. There's no call to hammer her with words when waiting will do. He can wait all day.

"Okay." Rosemary breaks. "I admit I'm interested to see what he can do for Sarah, but most primarily, I mean, primarily, my first thought is for you, Turk. You and the enlightenment of our listeners. I think this boy can raise the self-awareness of our audience. That's the point."

Turk tosses the pen onto his desk. The meeting is over. "He can have six minutes with Sister Starshine."

"That's not enough time for a miracle."

"Six minutes, Rosemary. Don't push your luck."

CHAPTER NINETEEN

D r. Lori washes Bing's hair. Bing perches on a stool and leans forward over a square, galvanized tub originally meant for delousing. Dr. Lori holds a green hose with a nozzle that adjusts for spraying, spritzing, or hard streaming cold water, which, coming from an Escondido spigot, isn't really cold. More luke cold. Bing enjoys the water, but he doesn't like Dr. Lori's fingers digging into his scalp, working up a lather that runs down his forehead and gets into his eyes.

He cries out. *"Owww!"*

"Be still."

"You're stinging me."

"It wouldn't sting if you'd close your eyes."

"You're getting gobbledygook in my ears."

"What?"

Bing shuts up. When he was a small boy he used to like Dr. Lori washing his head. It was almost the only time he touched a human person. Dr. Lori wasn't much of a toucher. She cut his finger and toenails, and hair. That was it. For Bing, touch meant losing a part of himself. Over the years, he developed a deep aversion to touch, especially his head. Even with Dr. Lori, the overwhelming urge when she touches his head is to bite her hand off.

"Here." Dr. Lori hands him the hose. "Rinse." She goes to the canvas bag that she carries everywhere so she won't have to choose between paper and plastic. "They had an underwear sale at Costco. I bought you a three-pack."

Bing speaks through running water so his voice sounds gurgly. "Do they have colors and stripes?"

"Of course not. You wear white undergarments. You've always worn white. What makes you think it comes in colors?"

Bing turns his head so the water is running over his right ear. He likes the sound. "I've seen it sticking up above boys' trousers on field trips. I thought it was a belt, but it's visible-colored undershorts."

She tosses the plastic wrapped three-pack at Bing. He misses the catch and it drops into the sink.

Dr. Lori says, "I better not ever see you flaunting your underwear."

Bing fishes out the pack. Tight, white boxers. Crack riders. "I want colors."

"You'll wear what I tell you to wear."

Bing doesn't like this. "You're stealing my possibilities."

Dr. Lori goes on high alert. She knows every phrase Bing is likely to use because she taught him all he knows.

"Did that reprobate tramp tell you to say that?"

The moment has come to lie to Dr. Lori. "No."

"You are lying to me."

He knew he wouldn't get away with it. "She said it that first day, before decontamination," which is also a lie, but not quite so direct as No when the answer should be Yes.

"You know what will happen if I catch you with her again."

Bing knows enough not to go there. This is the time to change the subject. "I just want to wear what I want to wear."

"You'll wear whatever is on sale. And white."

He plumps his lower lip. "You're not my mother."

Dr. Lori stalks to the tub and hovers too close to Bing. "I am better than your mother. I am your owner. You're mother is a bonobo. When she goes to Costco, she can pick out whatever color you want."

The owner crack causes something deep in Bing to break. The unthinkable decision is suddenly thinkable. "I do not want to be around you."

"You're stuck, Bing. Get used to it."

"I am not stuck."

Dr. Lori says, "You will never be able to live without me." What she means, of course, is, *I'll never be able to live without you.*

Chapter Twenty

Night. Bing the boy crouches on his haunches in the far back corner of the enclosure. His arms wrap around his legs. His butt almost but not quite brushes the packed dirt. His nose quivers slightly, smelling the hot wind blowing off the desert side of the mountains, northeast to southwest, opposite the way the wind generally blows. It brings a hint of smoke from fires in the canyons above Escondido.

Bing's lower lip protrudes. A soft hum emanates from his chest and the lower end of his throat. A deer fly lands on his cheek and walks across his face. Bing doesn't notice. He is in a trance of waiting. His brain has been put on hold until the event he is waiting for comes to pass.

We hear a soft murmur and Betty crosses over from the sleeping nests to sit in front of her ward. The two don't stare directly at each other. They both look a bit to the right, slightly off center. A distant security light casts a glow to the yard, little more than you would get under a full moon.

Betty's hands waggle back and forth, patting air. Bing emerges from his trance, although you'd have to have spent most of his life with him to tell his awareness has moved from inside to out. His eyes are the same, as are his shoulders. He touches Betty on the ankle. She ruffles his hair.

Her other hand moves to his chest. The fingers are spread, the index finger providing a slight pressure to Bing's sternum. He blinks, gradually, more like a closing of the eyes and then a reopening. He places his palm on her face.

A door slams and Dr. Lori enters the compound, come to say goodnight. She is carrying a bucket of water and a sponge. She plans to clean the feeding station where Ubu vomited earlier in the afternoon.

"Look at you two droopy mouths," Dr. Lori says. "Why are you still awake?"

Betty ignores Dr. Lori, but Bing turns to the voice. "The night is too pleasant to sleep."

Dr. Lori sniffs the air. It's hot and dry, no more pleasant than any other night.

"Phooey with that. Go to bed now. Both of you."

Bing shuffles over to his nest, leaving Betty facing the empty corner of the fence line.

CHAPTER TWENTY-ONE

Rosemary Faith buys a hat. A floppy straw affair suitable for gardening by the aged who are melanoma paranoid. More awning than head cover. She buys the hat from Jambo Outfitters, surrounded by the sort of jungle attire you see in a Bob Hope/Bing Crosby *Road to Zanzibar* type movie. Rosemary doesn't make the connection between the movie and Bing the boy. She's too caught up in her problems to be on the alert for irony.

After paying with a debit card, Rosemary pushes through the throng of folks who go to a wildlife park for the shopping to the tinted glass doors and on outside where she finds Bing, on his knees, peering into the workings of the Penny Smasher. A pair of exchange students from Bahrain have fed fifty-one cents into the machine. They don't seem aware of Bing, who is enthralled by the belts and great gears flattening the penny into a two-dimensional lozenge with the imprint of a cheetah stamped on the head's side.

One of the exchange students says, "What a waste of spare change."

The other says, "We can collect all four designs for two dollars."

"I'd rather get a henna." And they take their flat penny away.

Rosemary raises one foot to the toe and puts her palm on the back of her head in a vamp pose. "What do you think? Is it me?"

Bing says, "Is what you?"

"The hat."

"You are not a hat."

"Do you think it's my style?"

Bing studies Rosemary's hat, as if he's never seen a hat before. Or he's seen hats but they don't register. Hats, other than his own, are not items Bing feels strongly about.

He says, "I am prepared."

"Prepared for what?"

"To go away. With you."

Rosemary forgets the hat. Her short-term goal is in sight. "You want to leave the park?'

"Today, please."

"What made you decide?"

"I want to reach my potential."

"Wow."

Bing sniffs his armpit to see if he smells. He bathed in the creek this morning, but he doesn't want to go out into the world smelling like an animal. He is choosing people now, over bonobos.

"I don't know what potential is, but if it comes with a phone I will reach for it today."

Rosemary glances at the passing crowd, wondering if they are noticed. She has a creepy feeling that Bing doesn't show up on security cameras and anyone watching her will think she's talking to herself. She saw a movie once about a mathematician who talked to people no one else could see and it turned out those people weren't real. The mathematician was psychotic.

She grasps Bing's arm, as if touch can't be hallucinated but vision can. "Where is your stuff?"

"I have no stuff."

"Everyone has stuff. Clothes. Toiletries."

"Toilets do not grow on trees. I haven't been around humans much, but I'm not stupid."

Rosemary laughs and Bing looks offended. She says, "Photographs? Birthday cards? Sentimental mementos of youth. Objects you think matter."

"Objects do not matter."

Rosemary nods, as if Bing is spouting wisdom. "Sister Starshine says that all the time, but Turk says she's pretentious. I can tell you are not pretentious."

Bing has no clue on *pretentious* so he drops back to the original subject. "I have no stuff. I am prepared to go outside as I am."

Rosemary looks Bing up and down. He's wearing a faded blue sweatshirt with no writing on the front. Bermuda shorts. The engineer's cap. Still no shoes.

"We'll have to buy you shoes before we take you anywhere."

"I tried shoes once. They inflict pain."

"You can't go in restaurants without shoes and you can't live in normal society without going in restaurants."

Bing juts his jaw. Somewhat impressive piece of body language. "I won't go into normal society if I must wear shoes. I'll move into my cave and not talk to you or Dr. Lori. I'll stay alone."

Rosemary wishes she had a lit cigarette in her hand. This would be easier with a cigarette. She could think quicker. "How about I buy you jellies. Jellies never hurt anyone."

Bing pulls his lower lip with his index finger and thumb — his thinking mode. After a bit, he releases his mouth hold and says, "Jelly comes in little boxes on the condiment bar. The boxes are too small to wear on my feet."

Not for the first time, Rosemary wonders about Bing's education. He doesn't know *potential*, but he does know *condiment?* Dr. Lori has misplaced priorities.

"Jellies are squishy shoes. They make your feet feel like you're walking in mud. You like mud, don't you?"

"I enjoy mud."

"They feel just like mud, only they're sparkly and you can go into places that don't allow barefoot boys."

"What kind of world doesn't allow a barefoot boy?"

Rosemary chooses her words carefully. Bing is delicately poised on a balance beam and he could fall off either way. "Do you know the difference between indoors and outdoors?"

"Indoors has a ceiling."

"Well, out there in Greater San Diego, when you go indoors you need some sort of shoes or they'll make you leave, and jellies are as close to no shoes as you can get and still pass. So we'll buy you jellies."

Bing stares at families coming into the front gate. Not many going out this early in the day. Every last one of them is wearing shoes, even the toddlers in strollers. Their other clothes vary considerably based on age, gender, nationality, and proclivity, but footwear is consistent. It's not as if he'll have to wear them always. How much time can people spend indoors?

He says, "I can do those."

Rosemary releases her death grip on Bing's arm. She hadn't realized she was holding so tightly.

"Let's head out, then." She starts walking toward the gate, moving upstream against the crowd. Bing doesn't follow.

Rosemary stops. She turns back. "Bing?"

Bing's forehead has taken on a perspiration shine. His eyes dance, like ponies in a burning barn. "You think I should tell Dr. Lori? She might worry if she can't find me."

"You want to end up back in decontamination?"

"That is not what I desire."

Rosemary says, "In your wildest dreams, can you see Dr. Lori letting you leave here, if she knows you are going?"

Bing pictures Dr. Lori in his mind. Her eyebrows. Her glasses on the chain. The way she crosses her arms over her chest when she is vexed.

"No."

Rosemary eases Bing toward her. Her breath puffs against his eyelids. "It's time for us to go."

CHAPTER TWENTY-TWO

Imagine a mother leading her child into his first day at pre-school. Each atremble — anticipation, dread, terror. That is Rosemary leading Bing through the throng to the front gate. Sweat rivulets run on Bing's face. His hand in hers feels like saturated shammy.

"You okay?" she asks.

Bing nods.

They stop before the turnstile. Bing looks back at the only home he's ever known. More than home, the only place he's known. He sees a formless mass of tourists doing what tourists do. A zoo worker in a gray shirt is cleaning the water fountain in front of Adventure Photo. The only animals in sight are the flamingos. From Bing's point of view, each member of the flock has twisted on the single leg to stare directly at him. They don't bob. No flopping wings. Nothing but the stare of accusation.

"What's this now?" "He can't leave." "This is wrong."

Bing considers Dr. Lori. A lemur rejected her baby a few days ago and Dr. Lori has been on it, day and night. Bing can picture her bent over the tiny body, helping it suck milk off the tips of her fingers. How long before she realizes he's gone?

Rosemary says, "Breathe."

Bing breathes.

Rosemary says, "Let's see what happens next." She pushes through the turnstile, then steps to one side, waiting, watching Bing.

His eyes are on her — the throat, the hair, the eyes. The pull of Rosemary is stronger than the pull of Dr. Lori.

He takes one last, longing look at the flamingos, nods, then turns and follows Rosemary into the outside.

CHAPTER TWENTY-THREE

Bing walks upright, carefully and with purpose, as if crossing a high place on a log. Of course, inside the park he could have crossed a log as casually as a man walks down a hallway on his way to the bathroom in the middle of the night, but, outside, Bing concentrates on breath and balance. He holds his hands away from his body. His head is rigid, eyes focused on a spot in the air, about eight feet to the front. Imagine a man on a tightrope who expects to be struck by lightning. Annihilation as probability.

Rosemary says, "What do you think? You're not dead yet."

Bing doesn't speak. He's concentrating on not falling off the edge of the world, which, in this case, means the outer plaza of the wildlife park. Ticket booths. The information pagoda. Huge signs announcing upcoming events for members only. Parents slapping sunscreen on children who can't stand still.

Rosemary asks, "Is this what you expected?"

Bing raises his right arm up to his line of vision. He cannot lower his line of vision to his arm. Looking down would court disaster.

"I have no boils. No pox."

"You expected to walk through the gate and instantly catch chicken pox?"

Bing stares straight ahead at a bus disgorging Pakistanis bearing cameras and umbrellas. "Dr. Lori said I would suffer from boils and pox."

Rosemary steps off the curb into valet parking. "Face the truth, Bing. Dr. Lori lied."

CHAPTER TWENTY-FOUR

As they cross the street, moving toward the acres of parking, Bing drops to a knuckle-walk. It's easier for the long run. Makes him feel grounded. This being Southern California, people watch Bing without appearing to watch — you don't want to draw the crazies' attention — but some kids skateboarding the lots stop to stare.

Rosemary says, "Must you walk like that?"

"Like what?"

"Like a chimpanzee."

Bing takes offense and, considering how frightened he is, this is no doubt a good thing. "I am a bonobo. Never call a bonobo a chimpanzee. Chimps are vicious and cruel."

"You are human. Say it."

"I am human."

"I know you can walk like a human. I've seen you."

Slowly, Bing straightens up. He is erect. "Is this what is expected?"

"When you are with your bonobo buddies, you can act like a bonobo. In the human world, you should try and act like a person."

"I can do that."

He walks on both feet — no hands — down the long hill to Lot G. Bing has seen cars before, but never more than two or three together. He now faces an immense field of cars, trucks, buses, stretching to the distant horizon, which is another thing Bing hasn't seen before. His views have been short — mostly ending in walls except up by the condors where he is up against a steep hill. He has no concept of distance.

"Do all these come with people?"

"The cars?"

Bing doesn't answer. What else could *these* mean?

"People drive them here from their homes. They usually bring families.

"My family would not enjoy being on the inside of a machine."

Rosemary stops next to her ten-year-old Jetta. Bing isn't expecting a sudden stop, so he bumps her, bounces back, and sits on his haunches.

"That's another thing humans rarely do," Rosemary says. "Sit like that."

"How do humans sit when there is no bench?"

"They don't, as a rule. It's okay to sit on grass, sometimes, on a nice day, but not pavement."

Rosemary pulls her keys from her purse and pushes a button. The car BEEPS. Bing flings himself to the asphalt. He goes fetal.

Rosemary says, "Get up, Bing. It won't hurt you."

"The car spoke."

"I unlocked the door. It beeps when I push this button." She pushes the button again, causing another BEEP when the doors lock.

Bing cowers.

"It's okay. Here, you do it." She holds the keys toward him.

"No."

"Have it your way." She makes another BEEP and unlocks the doors again. "Get up, Bing. People are watching. You're not invisible."

What Rosemary said takes a moment to sink in. She looks around the parking lots. A security guard is watching, no doubt, considering stepping into the situation. A family of blond parents and blond children, all so healthy they could be on a Scandinavian poster are staring. The youngest blond child points at Bing and says something foreign.

Rosemary repeats herself. "You're not invisible."

Bing uncoils his arms from around his head and sits up. Rosemary says, "Why aren't you invisible?"

"I never am."

"You were in there." She motions back at the park. "I could see you but no one ever noticed when you did weird stuff like crawling in the dirt or eating bugs."

Bing makes it back to his feet. "Dr. Lori says I have no aura. People don't notice people with no aura."

"Oh."

"First, she says she doesn't believe that auras exist. They are made up, and then she says I don't have whatever it is people see when they see each other, so she calls it an aura even if that's not what it is." He scratches himself, over the liver area. Then he closes one eye and looks at Rosemary. "Do you know what an aura is?"

"Mine is purple."

He looks at her closely. He doesn't see anything purple. Her skin is pink. Her hair is orange-brown. "Do I have one now, that I'm outside?"

Rosemary stares at Bing who is staring at her. He looks the same to her as he did before. A child in a grown-up body with ape-like posture. "I'm not good at auras. That's Persephone's line. I'll have her meet us for lunch and she can make a study."

Rosemary goes around the Jetta to open the car door for Bing. Bing doesn't move. She says, "I don't see how you could be invisible — hard to notice — in there but not here."

Bing shrugs. "I could always see me."

She motions for him to get in. "Have you ever ridden in a car?"

Bing is haughty. "Of course. All the time."

Rosemary stares at him.

Bing says, "No." He touches the Jetta roof, flinching at the heat. "I've seen people in cars. It appears that the car eats them."

"Watch me." She crosses back over to the driver's side, opens the door, and gets in. She shuts the door behind her and leans over to speak to Bing through the open passenger side door.

"Any questions?"

Bing gets in but he doesn't close his door. He turns to her and asks, "Is this the part where we copulate?"

Chapter Twenty-Five

"Why for God's sake did you expect to copulate the moment we left the park?"

"What sake is that?"

"God's sake."

"Is he bonobo or human?"

"It's a saying. You like these?"

Rosemary points to a pair of green jellies on the rack. They're the closest to masculine jellies she can find, which isn't so masculine.

Bing has no concept of certain clothes being male and certain clothes female. "These are pleasing," he says, touching a pink pair with a flower decoration over the toes. "They're sparkly."

The conversation is taking place at Famous Footwear in Poway a half hour from Escondido off the freeway in San Diego. It's been a tough half hour for Rosemary. First came the seat belt trauma. Bing tried to bite her.

He said, "I won't be tied."

"It's the law," she said. "You have to wear your seatbelt."

"It's worse than decontamination and you said I wouldn't have to do that anymore. If cars are so safe, why tie people inside?"

"You're strapped in. That's nothing like tied up."

Bing refused until she gave up on that one. Rosemary's theory was pick your battles and Bing in a seatbelt wasn't worth major stress. Then, on the access road leaving the park, they met a car coming toward them and Bing shrieked.

"Stop that."

"They'll kill me."

"No, they won't. They're in the other lane."

Lifelong vehicle riders and drivers have certain agreed upon conventions. Right side of the road. Red light means stop. A blinking light on a car is a signal for the intention of turning. Merges and rights of way are accepted norms. Bing has no knowledge of these assumptions, so every car coming toward them is seen as death. Stop lights are random chaos.

"Bing does not enjoy cars," he said.

"You'll get used to it. In a week you'll be begging me to let you drive."

Bing opened the door and tried to jump out. Scared the beJesus out of Rosemary. After yanking him back in she locked the doors from the console in her door, which made Bing feel more trapped than ever.

"I can't breathe with this shut against me. Let me open it."

Rosemary pushed the button in her door that lowered Bing's window. He thought she was able to control glass with her mind. It frightened him.

Famous Footwear is in the back parking lot of a huge Target store nearly the size of the animal park. It is full of aggressive chimp-like shoe shoppers willing to cut you off to get to the desired pair. Bing falls in love with jellies. He licks them, chews them, presses the cool soft plastic against his cheeks.

A passing sales girl sees Bing and says to Rosemary, "Any shoes he eats, you buy."

Bing says, "I enjoy pink sparkles."

"Pink is a girl color," Rosemary says.

"Who made that law?"

Rosemary has no answer so she returns to her earlier line of interest. "Why were you expecting instant copulation?"

Bing holds the pink jellies up to his eyes and looks through at Rosemary. The filer affect turns her a washed purple. Something of a mauve, like a honeycreeper. Her hair becomes the color of male lion fur.

"Dr. Lori said Outies copulate when they are out. It might be where the boils are born from."

Rosemary kneels before Bing to slip the pink flowered jelly onto his right foot. She says, "Listen to me, Bing. Every single thing you've been told about the world is wrong. Every single thing."

She slides on the left jelly. "Your entire life from birth till this morning, you've been given bad information."

She looks up at Bing who has the sad, puckered lower lip look. His eyes droop. "That's not a good thing." Bing stands and bounces on his toes, feeling the plastic heat, soften, and cling to his feet.

Rosemary says, "How's does it make you feel?"

Bing misunderstands the question, or maybe he doesn't. What he says is, "Squishy."

CHAPTER TWENTY-SIX

Bing squats on the passenger side, his pink sparkle jelly-clad feet on the seat cover, knees to his chin, hands stiff-armed against the dash, immediately above the glove compartment. He stares out the window at the passing generic suburban strip made up of optician and dentist offices, muffler shops, hordes of computer repair stores, loan offices, check cashing storefronts, real estate offices, Sam's Club, and, of course, fast food joints.

Next to him, Rosemary is talking about her sister. "Sarah is in long-term care. We'll go visit after lunch, but first you need to meet the people I work with. You'll be on a show tomorrow. I think you'll love Sister Starshine. She exudes happiness."

Bing says, "Exudes."

A gaggle of day care kids shuffle up the sidewalk, clutching a nylon rope that runs to their teacher who is texting. A clown with a red bulb nose and size 60 shoes rides a Vespa past them on the right. The clown sees Bing's gape and flips him the bird. At a stoplight, a grub of a beggar hurls himself at Bing's window and shouts, "Hungry war veteran! God bless!"

"He said *God*," Bing says. "Was that another saying?"

"Don't make eye contact." Rosemary rolls the window up. "If you do he might explode on us."

A wailing ambulance blasts through a light on red, reinforcing Bing's belief that there are no rules and everything is loud.

A bear stands on the corner, twirling a sign on a pole. Bing says, "Can you read what the bear is holding?"

The guy is whipping the sign back and forth like a baton. He appears to be on meth. "It says, 'No money down. No payments for 60 days. O'Meara Cosmetic Surgery.' Are you familiar with cosmetic surgery?"

"Surgery is when they cut an animal open."

"Cosmetic surgery is a thing where you pay some quack to change the way you look."

They pass a grotesquely thin person of indeterminate gender slumped over a parking meter. He or she has peed his or her cut-offs and is trying to smash open the cash box with a brick.

Bing turns to Rosemary. "Are these exhibits?"

She glances at the parking meter felon. "They're people."

Bing doesn't understand. Rosemary says, "This is how real people live. Some of them, anyway. That bear was a kid in a costume, not a real bear. The clown was no doubt on his way to work. This is how people get by."

"I've seen magazines, and outside is nothing at all like this place."

"Magazines aren't real." She pulls into the California Pizza Kitchen parking lot. "Right here is what real looks like."

Bing focuses hard on the yellow sign with the palm tree above the door of the restaurant. "Do I get my picture phone now?"

She whips the Jetta into a parking slot, stopping inches from a vine-covered wall, which is normal if you've driven and parked before. Bing thinks he has cheated death.

Rosemary says, "This is where we eat."

Bing nods. "I enjoy food."

CHAPTER TWENTY-SEVEN

A group of young men about Bing's age are lounging around late model Chevys and Fords that sit close to the pavement. Leaning against hoods, one foot propped on bumpers, smoking unfiltered cigarettes, glaring at pedestrians. Although their shirts and jackets vary, for the most part they wear red pants much too large for their frames, and steel bracelets and necklaces. Recently shaved heads finish the look.

As Bing and Rosemary cross the parking lot, moving toward the California Pizza Kitchen front entrance, one of the young men — a boy really — wolf whistles. "Love the shoes, bro." The others laugh and cut their eyes at one another.

Rosemary whispers, "Don't stop."

Bing stops. He admires the series of blue black tattoos on the kid's bald head, and the Xolos jersey with the sleeves cut off to show more tattoos on the arms.

Bing says, "Thank you, sir. They're called jellies because they feel like jelly between your toes."

The kid sneers. "They make you look sweet."

This time, Rosemary hisses. *"Keep moving, Bing."* She drags Bing away by his arm.

Bing waves back to the boys at the cars. "Thank you for the nice words. I am certain you also are sweet."

The kid takes a couple quick steps toward Bing, but Rosemary has him at the door and is pulling him through.

"Those gangbangers will kill you for looking at them, Bing."

Bing turns his head to look back at the boy who is standing in the lot, staring hard at him. The guys in the background maintain their postures of contempt. "They seem like nice fellas."

CHAPTER TWENTY-EIGHT

Rosemary exchanges words Bing cannot hear with the pretty young woman wearing colorful braces on her teeth at the front of the dining room, then Rosemary says, "They're back there," and she takes Bing through a gap in the tables. Bing hasn't been inside a chain restaurant filled with people before. He drops to a knuckle-walk, then catches himself and comes back up, erect. No one pays him any mind except a toddler in a booster seat who points at Bing's jellies and gurgles.

Rosemary leads Bing through the maze of tables and chairs crisscrossed by waiters, waitresses, and bus people who all seem to find Bing in their path till she stops at a round table where two men and two women sit behind huge menus. The table is made from some sort of hard plastic. The chairs are yellow.

Rosemary speaks to a man in black — jacket, pants, shirt, and hair, all a lustrous black. "I didn't expect to see you here."

The man touches his chin to his pinkie ring which isn't black as he sizes up Bing. "After all the fanfare, you can't expect me to miss a chance to meet the Chimp Boy."

"Bonobo," Bing says. "Chimps are violent. They eat their babies."

The man in black's lips tighten and he nods, as if this confirms his deepest suspicions about Bing's character. The thing Bing notices about the man is how rarely he blinks. His eyes are like the eyes of a lemur.

Rosemary doesn't sit in an empty chair, so Bing doesn't either. She says, "Bing, this is Sister Starshine. You're slated for her show tomorrow."

Sister Starshine — Hawaiian shirt over ample body, Lycra sweat pants, trainer shoes, canvas bag the size of a backpack — says, "You have an azure aura."

She studies Bing so closely he starts to itch. She says, "With silver spikes and golden tendrils. You must be deep."

"Dr. Lori says auras don't exist and if they do I don't have one. That's why people don't see me."

Sister Starshine smiles, as if giving Bing reassurance that contrary to popular opinion, he doesn't have a terminal illness. "You have an aura all right. The aura of a man ruled by a combination of passion and instinct."

"Maybe I grew it this morning."

Rosemary says, "And this is Persephone. Persephone specializes in regressions."

Persephone dresses like a state fair gypsy. A plethora of vibrant scarves. Troweled eye make-up. Earrings the size of yo-yos. She extends her hand to Bing, palm down. Bing looks at it.

Persephone says, "I danced at Woodstock."

Bing looks to Rosemary who says, "Persephone believes each of us defines him or herself by a singular event."

Persephone says, "What event do you feel made you what you are."

Bing considers the question seriously. "I ate cotton candy I found in a dumpster and I threw up. It was blue."

Persephone says, "Now you know."

Rosemary says, "Mitchell here runs the booth. Without him we'd all go to white noise."

Mitchell — very large as in both tall and heavy, cowboy hat, yoked shirt, Wrangler boot cuts, lace-up packers — reminds Bing of the truck drivers who deliver frozen food to the park concessionaires at dawn, so he assumes *booth* is another word for *truck*.

Mitchell forms his hand into a fist with his thumb pointed at the ceiling and says, "Whazup?"

Bing looks at Mitchell's thumb and wonders if it means something that he should know. He mimics the word "Whazup."

Rosemary extends an arm toward the guy wearing black. "And right here is the gifted spirit guide I told you about yesterday. Turk Palisades. Centered Soul exists because of this man's vision."

Turk stares hard at Bing as Rosemary takes her seat in one of the two vacant chairs. She tugs Bing's sleeve and he also sits, all the while watching Turk watch him.

Turk says, "Raised by apes, able to heal the sick and raise the dead. That's some résumé you've put out for yourself."

Bing murmurs. "I don't think I can raise the dead. It looks difficult." At this point, Bing finds himself sidetracked. Jam boxes and cream cups sit nested in a bigger box and cup on the table, beside the napkin dispenser. Bing has wanted to play with these toys for many years, but never had the chance.

Turk makes his fingers into a tent. "Let me tell you up front, the humble savior shtick has been done. So has raised by beasts."

Bing builds a tower made of jelly and cream. It takes all the concentration he is able to muster.

Rosemary says, "Bing, Turk is exchanging ideas with you."

Bing protrudes his lower lip. "Bing doesn't fathom *shtick.*"

That's when the waitress arrives. Turk orders for everyone. "Persephone here will take the avocado egg rolls. Grilled vegetable salad for Sister Starshine."

Sister Starshine makes a grimace face that Bing sees but Turk doesn't. Bing can tell she doesn't want grilled vegetable salad. He can also tell that interrupting Turk to point this out would be considered inappropriate behavior.

Turk studies the menu. "Mitchell needs a wedge salad. Getting a tire around the middle, aren't we Mitch? And Dakota Smashed Beans and Barley for our little Rosemary."

Rosemary isn't happy. "But I want Jamaican Jerk Chicken pizza."

Turk keeps it smooth. He commands from calmness. "Chicken wreaks havoc on your chi, Rosemary. You know that because I've told you more than once. You cannot work for me with an imbalance in your chi. If you are out of balance, the group is out of balance to the detriment of Centered Soul's entire program. We can commit no action that will threaten Centered Soul."

Rosemary sulks.

Turk says, "I value your opinion. Is pizza worth risking Centered Soul's mission?"

Rosemary says, "No."

Turk closes his menu. "Bring me a glass of pomegranate juice."

He turns his attention to Bing. "And what was your diet, while being raised by primates?"

Bing is adding butter pats to the top, only they won't stick unless he unwraps the foil, so he unwraps the foil.

Bing says, "Fruit."

The waitress stares at him under studded eyebrows. She has liver colored hair and fingernails, and a hickey the shape of a map of Wisconsin.

Bing says, "Oranges, grapefruit, watermelon, cantaloupe. Bring all the fruit your gatherers can gather. Limes. I enjoy limes."

Sister Starshine is thrilled no end. "Then you are a fruitarian. How exciting." She explains to the others, who, except for Mitchell, need no explanation. "Fruitarians won't kill animals, like any garden variety vegan, but they take food ethics one step further. They don't kill plants either." She pronounces *either* with a long I. *Ither.* "They only eat food that falls from trees — fruit, nuts. Food they can consume without moving the cosmic footprint. It's a difficult regimen to maintain."

Persephone says, "We know what fruitarian means, Martha —" Martha is Sister Starshine's civilian name. She hates it — "You don't have to rehearse your show at our expense."

Mitchell has been doing isometric exercises with his chair. No one notices except Bing who assumes Mitchell has pain in his digestive tract.

Mitchell says, "So you've never killed a plant or animal?"

Bing finger flips a creamer cup from the bottom corner and his castle tumbles onto the table. "A wild deer came into our compound and my brother and I pulled its front legs off. We didn't mean to kill it, but it died anyway."

Mitchell is charmed to his hefty core. "How brutal. Like pulley bones on a turkey."

Bing says, "I got the big side."

CHAPTER TWENTY-NINE

Lunch grinds to a halt. The radio team sits, almost but not quite frozen mid-bite, watching Bing consume a small mountain of fruit. He has already inhaled a dozen bananas and a watermelon. Now, he's working on cantaloupe. Rosemary leans forward, toward him, transfixed by Bing's fingers. They are long, thin, shimmering in juice. The nails appear worn short as opposed to cut or chewed. The finger pads are calloused, but on the lines of soft calluses, if that is possible, as if more pillowed than ridged.

The palms as they move quickly around the platter also show signs of extreme wear. His wrists are thick as his hands are wide. His knuckles are tough as rhinoceros leather.

Three waitresses cluster together behind Turk.. The girl with the hickey who took their order chews on a lip post. Another waitress rests her hand on the hickey girl's wrist, for consolation. The busboy returns from the kitchen with a pair of cooks and a dishwasher. They stand beside the glittery-mouthed hostess, silent and motionless except for an occasional *catch-that* elbow nudge to their neighbor's ribs.

Conversation has also died at nearby tables. They too watch Bing work his concentrated way through mounds of fruit.

Bing moves into a pile of limes, his favorite. He lifts them up, one at a time, sniffs his chosen lime carefully, then pulls it apart with his fingertips, and pops it peel and all into his mouth. Juice sluices over his lower lip and runs down his chin before dripping back onto his plate. The consumption of one lime takes all of five seconds, and Bing eats twenty.

Rosemary wonders why Bing peels bananas and leaves water-melon rinds behind, yet he polishes off entire lemons, limes, and oranges. There seems to be a system. Bing looks across the table at Rosemary's untouched plate of Dakota Smashed Beans and Barley and points his wet finger at her orange slice garnish.

He says, "You want that? If you don't, I'll eat it for you. I don't mind."

CHAPTER THIRTY

Forty minutes later the Centered Soul crew and Bing pay up and head out. At the cash register Persephone says that since Turk ordered for everyone he should pay. Turk pretends she is joking. Rosemary shows Bing how the toothpick dispenser works.

She turns the knob on the side and a toothpick appears. "See," Rosemary says. "It's like magic."

"Dr. Lori says there is no such thing as magic."

Turk takes offense. His livelihood is based on belief. "Magic is all around us, kid. You have to see it."

Bing turns the silver box over and looks at the bottom. "Dr. Lori seemed certain."

"What did I tell you about Dr. Lori?" Rosemary says. "Nothing she taught you is true."

Bing shakes the box and the top falls off. Hundreds of toothpicks hit the countertop, splattering away in every direction.

The hostess says, "Look what you've done."

Bing says, "It's not magic." He faces Rosemary. "You said it is magic. It's a trick."

"I said 'like magic.' Some things that are not magic look like magic if you don't know how they work. Light switches, for instance. And TV."

Bing gives her a hurt look. He mumbles, "It wasn't magic." As Mitchell pushes through the glass doors, Bing says, "What's TV mean?"

The angry boys await in the parking lot. They've been hanging around all this time, and the leader in the Xolos jersey has lost patience. He stands in the path of our group.

He says, "Nobody calls T.J. Rios *sweet*." The other bangers gather in a clump behind T.J., like coyotes who smell blood. Mitchell steps aside to allow Bing direct access. Turk's face takes on the aspect of a scientist observing a lab rat after its latest shock.

Rosemary whisper-hisses. *"Don't talk to him. Keep moving."*

Bing says, "You seem like a nice boy. You must be held in high value by your mother."

T.J.'s face changes color. His hands form fists. "You fucking with me, chump?"

Rosemary lies to protect Bing. "He's not from the United States. He just arrived, from Lithuania, and he doesn't know our norms."

T.J. says, "If he's fucking with me I'll kill him. I don't care where he's from."

"How can we be fucking from such a distance?" Bing asks.

Rosemary says, "Bing, *shut up.*"

T.J. moves forward, chest-to-chest with Bing, followed by the gang. Mitchell thinks about backing Bing up, but decides it's none of his business. Turk still takes it as a social phenomenon. Persephone blind digs through her huge canvas bag, searching for her phone, which has 9-1-1 on the speed dial.

Bing smiles in T.J.'s face. "Dr. Lori says I should not fuck strangers because I am not a true bonobo. Bonobos fuck strangers." He glances at Rosemary. "But Dr. Lori might be mistaken."

T.J. says, "Not a true boner?" His boys snickers on cue.

Bing says, "Bonobo. We're primates similar to humans only without cruelty and humiliation."

"I don't give a shit who you are. You call me sweet and I cut you." From deep in his oversized pants T.J. produces an evil knife. *Snick.* The blade appears as if from air — much more impressive than the toothpick machine.

Rosemary gasps. Persephone hits the speed dial. Bing smiles.

T.J. growls. "You're dead, meat."

Tires squeal. A 1999 Cadillac DeVille on low riders careens around the turn from Home Depot.

One of T.J.'s lieutenants yells. *"Crips!"*

Windows come down, gun barrels come out, gunfire hails down on the California Pizza Kitchen parking lot.

The bangers dive for pavement. After an instant's hesitation, the Centered Soul crew hits the ground also. Innocent random customers scream and flee or flatten. Glass shatters in the restaurant windows.

Only Bing remains upright. Watching with mild curiosity, a slight smile flickering across his face, Bing stays rooted to his spot as the Cadillac flies up to and past him.

T.J.'s side has their own weapons out and are firing at the receding Cadillac. Mostly out of rage and frustration. Their return fire is too little, too late, although one of them does pop a taillight.

From the ground, Turk snarls. "I don't like your friends, Bing."

Someone screams. *"T.J.!"*

T.J. Rios lies on his back, riddled by bullets. Blood spreads into his shirt from his chest and shoulder, and into his pants above the groin. The boy is conscious, but in remarkable pain.

As his gang runs to his side, Rosemary bounces up and claws at Bing's arm. "Let's get out of here."

Bing looks over at T.J. writhing and moaning on the asphalt. He's fallen next to a rental Hundai. The tourist family still in their car, watches in horror.

Bing says, "The young man is hurt." He walks toward the group around the fallen T.J.

Rosemary shouts, "Stay out of it, Bing."

Bing says, "He needs help."

Turk says, "Let him go over."

Rosemary turns from Bing to Turk. "Why, for God's sake."

"It might be educational."

Bing slips his way through the young men encircling T.J. Most stand, a few kneel. One guy with a shaved skull covered in Aztec symbol tattoos holds T.J.'s head steady. As Bing drops to his knees, the kid holding T.J. barks, "What the fuck you doing, asshole?"

"I am on top of the situation," Bing says so quietly he is hard to hear within the group and impossible to hear out in the second ring of onlookers, which includes Rosemary and her co-workers.

The angry guy says, "Don't mess with my brother."

T.J. coughs a rivulet of blood and fights to speak. "Let the boner try, Martin. You sure as hell can't fix this."

Martin glares at Bing. "You touch him and he dies, I'll kill you."

Bing nods. T.J. looks up into Bing's eyes. "I wouldn't, if I was you."

Bing says, "You are not me. I am not you."

Bing hovers his hands over T.J.'s forehead and the bullet hole in his chest. Rosemary edges closer. Turk still has the interested yet not involved attitude. Two teenagers in the crowd push close enough to aim smart phone video recorders at Bing and T.J.

Bing says, "This should not cause pain."

T.J. tries to laugh at the absurdity of the statement, but instead burps up more blood and a spasm passes through his body like an electric ripple.

There is silence. Martin shifts his weight on this calves, not the paragon of patience. Then, Bing *hums*. The hum starts low, a vibration from his chest, before it escalates into guttural cooing. Rosemary moves forward another step, which blocks one of the filming kid's shot. He mutters, "*Bitch,*" and circles to her side. Rosemary ignores him.

Bing's hum moves from chest to throat and finally his mouth tips open in a full bore bonobo howl. One of the older scary guys steps up to stop him, but Martin holds out his palm.

"Don't."

T.J. sits up, folding at the waist, like a sleepwalker in a horror movie. He bumps into Bing's outstretched hands. Embarrassed at the contact, Bing stands quickly.

T.J.'s face is spooked. It's as if he has awakened from a nap to find the furniture moved. "What happened?"

Bing says, "Some people shot you with bullets. I've never seen one, but Dr. Lori explained bullets to me and that's what is in your insides."

T.J. stares down at the hole in his groin. "What did you do?"

"I stopped the blood flow and glued some of your parts. I suggest your friends take you to a licensed veterinarian now. The wound gash needs attention."

Martin says, "Veterinarian?"

T.J. says, "If this man says veterinarian, that's where I'm going." He stands up. "Who are you?"

Bing says, "Bing."

"I should thank you."

"That isn't needed." Bing turns and walks to Rosemary. The crowd parts to let them through.

Turk meets them at Rosemary's car. His eyes drill into Bing. "I want him in the studio — 9 a.m."

Rosemary opens her door. "Sister Starshine doesn't tape till noon."

Turk's stare is hard on Bing. It makes him feel exposed and that's not something Bing likes to feel.

Turk says, "He's mine now."

CHAPTER THIRTY-ONE

Rosemary drives down a wide boulevard in an upscale part of San Diego — internists' offices, day spas, big houses set back from traffic. She is distracted, but she drives this route so often it doesn't much matter. She could cruise this stretch in her sleep.

Bing plays with the glove compartment, popping it open, then closed, then open. He's taken the CDs, maintenance log, map of Yosemite, and tampon box out and put them on the floor between his feet so he can reach into the box and pretend his fingers are skinks in a cave. It is a deep glove box, as boxes go. Bing has to lean low and peer to see the back.

Rosemary flicks wavy hair from her right shoulder, the side Bing is on. She wants to see his expression when she asks, "How do you do that?"

He points. "You push the button thing and the gate flops."

"How do you make people who are dying not die? You saved that boy's life back there."

Bing finds a barrette in the dark corner of the glove box. He sniffs it, smelling Rosemary. He tastes it and says, "It works, sometimes. Sometimes, it doesn't."

Rosemary doesn't want to hear that sometimes it doesn't take. Still, though, she has to ask. "How often does the miracle thing work?"

"I don't know *miracle?*"

"A miracle is when something that is not possible happens. What you did is impossible, yet you did it and no one can say you didn't. That's a miracle."

"What do you want?"

"I need to know the percentage of miracles to miracle attempts? Fifty? Ninety?"

Bing shrugs. He knows the word percentage as it applies to primate data, but he's not certain what it means to his life.

Rosemary tries a new tack. "So, when was it you discovered your gift?"

The barrette is the spring-loaded kind. When Bing pushes down and releases, it flies into the back seat. "No one has passed me a gift today."

"When you found out you could heal?"

Bing turns the tampon box over in his hands, looking for a way in. It does not smell like food or female, so he tosses it out the open window.

"An ostrich cut her leg kicking a cape buffalo. Ostriches are the meanest animal in the safari field. Listen to me: Never trust an ostrich."

He drifts off, fascinated by the neon sign out front of a Pentecostal Baptist Church.

Rosemary can't help prompting. "And?"

"She was lying in the mud, bleeding, and I went over and made the smooth fluid thick until it clogged the hole."

"The ostrich lived?"

"She bit me." Bing frowns at the memory. "I'm never helping an ostrich again, no matter how long I live or how much she bleeds."

They drive another block and stop at a red light behind a Mercedes with a tiny dog in the back seat shelf. The dog's tongue lolls. Bing lolls his tongue. It feels good.

Rosemary says, "Why do you think it works sometimes and others it doesn't?"

"Sometimes the animal dies because it wants to." The light goes green and the Mercedes pulls away. "Not all animals can live in a town."

Rosemary pretends to concentrate on traffic. In reality, she can barely see traffic. "Do you think you could cure a sick person?"

Bing is dubious. "I'm better with accidents than illness. Illness is complicated. For some ill animals going forward isn't worth the bother and they won't let me fix them. I don't know how it works on humans."

Rosemary punches the radio button and the car fills with the bass voice of Turk Palisades. She lowers the volume quickly, but Bing still hears.

"It all comes down to ego against soul. Are you controlled by your ego or your soul? You can't flash both ways. Do you kick in the doors of opportunity or do you whine. 'Sort of.' 'Maybe.' 'If things line up right.' *Don't wait! Scream Yes to life!"*

Bing twists to look in the backseat.

Rosemary says, "It's the radio."

"I know about radio." He finds the speaker in the door and touches it, feeling the buzz through his fingertips. "That's the man in the restaurant. The man you admire because he visioned Centered Soul."

Rosemary says, "Turk."

"How did he go from the restaurant to the radio place so fast? Is it close by?"

"He's taped."

Bing is confused. He knows the word *tape* is a worm you get from eating food that is not fresh.

Rosemary says, "Recorded this morning, on a digital machine so they can broadcast later. The network runs Turk's show three times a day."

"I demand all you searchers out there, buy a shotgun at your local gun show and I want you to blast your television. Kill it! Blow the Philistines and Pharisees to smithereens. When Jesus said people who pray loudly in public will go directly to hell, he was talking about CBN. Reject the charlatans who preach on television."

Rosemary opens her Droid and touches buttons.

Bing says, "Your friend is angry."

Rosemary studies the phone screen. "Turk's is an enlightened anger. He doesn't suffer false prophets. Listen, Bing, we are going to see my sister, Sarah."

"Is Sarah human?"

"Of course, Sarah is human. She's my sister."

"My brother is not human."

Rosemary closes her phone with a *click*. "Sarah is human, but she's sick. She has pain and the medicine confuses her so some days she wanders or forgets where she is. I use this," — she shows Bing the phone — "to keep track of her."

Bing tries to lift the phone from Rosemary's hand, but she'll have none of it. "Sarah used to be vibrant. She was so alive, standing next to her made me feel stale. But then she got sick and changed."

Bing doesn't know *vibrant*, although he does know *stale* and he knows sickness is to be avoided if at all possible. "I'm sorry your sister is in pain. Pain is never a comfort."

"No, it's not." Rosemary moves into the bottom line, the words she's been leading up to since she saw Bing save the drowned groundskeeper. "I want you to help her."

Bing flips the window visor down. There's a mirror on the back side, which makes him jump. Bing's experience with mirrors has been limited and he never instantly recognizes himself. It takes a moment.

"Bing?"

"How should I help Sarah?"

"Like you did the boy back at the restaurant."

"The boy had bullets inside."

"Sarah has scars inside." Rosemary waves her fingers over her lower abdomen. "I want you to fix them."

As they drive by a green park they pass four middle- to old-aged joggers with headbands, ear buds, and the sleeves scissored from their sweatshirts. They gleam with perspiration and look miserable.

Bing says, "Those men are nervous. They should go to sleep. That's the thing I do when I feel nervous."

"Do you think you can help her?"

"Help who?"

"Sarah."

Bing flips the windshield visor back up. He turns to face Rosemary. He enjoys looking at Rosemary from close up. It is a time he looks forward to.

"I would enjoy meeting your sister."

CHAPTER THIRTY-TWO

Before reaching the place where Sarah stays, Rosemary and Bing have a spat. It happens when she knocks an open Kent 100 pack against her thigh and shakes out a cigarette. Bing starts in mewling before she even lights up.

Rosemary says, "Give me a break."

"Dr. Lori says smoking tobacco is how human people commit suicide."

"What did I tell you –"

"She is not wrong always. Just some of the time."

"This is one of those times when she's wrong. I am not committing suicide. I'm relaxing."

"By taking poison."

"I'm under a mountain of stress. Cigarettes help me stay focused."

Bing tips his head to get his nose into the flow from the window crack. Rosemary relents by giving him a couple more inches of air.

Bing says, "I do not fathom *stress.*"

Rosemary cracks her own window and blows smoke in its general direction. "How is it that woman taught you complicated words but not simple ones?"

"Is *stress* simple?"

"Sure. Between my job and my life I am swamped by insecurity which causes anxiety. You know *anxiety?*"

Bing shakes his head. It causes the wind to blow from one cheek to the other. Kind of cool.

"You know *worry?*"

"That's when you're waiting for a grant to come through. You worry."

"And worry makes for stress. I have a lot to worry over."

"Is that why you are nervous?"

She nods and blows smoke out her nose. She crushes her cigarette out in the ashtray that is almost clean. Only one other butt shows its yellow filter. "You happy now?"

Bing settles back into his seat. "I believe so. Yes. Happy is how I prefer to be."

Rosemary turns into a long gravel driveway flanked by junipers and palms. It circles around a spacious lawn and a water-belching dolphin toward a bone-white building with pillars out front and a long porch on the side Bing can see. The grass is bright green and short. The whole thing looks well tended.

"I'd be thrilled no end if you don't mention the cigarette to Sarah," Rosemary says. "She has enough to dwell on."

CHAPTER THIRTY-THREE

They find Sarah on a glider placed alongside a series of metal chairs that have bent tubing for front legs and no back legs so they rock when you sit in them. There are also wide spaces for wheelchairs to fit between the glider and the chairs. Bougainvillea flower on one end of the porch with yellow roses on the other. Nurses and aides in their color coded smocks and quiet hospital shoes pad back and forth, taking patients inside, tucking blankets around hips. That sort of thing.

Sarah's eyes are closed. They can tell she is awake because the toe of her right foot keeps the glider gently gliding.

Rosemary says, "Sarah."

Sarah's eyes drift open. To Bing, she looks like the doll a tourist child left on the service road behind Nairobi Village. When Bing picked it up, the doll's arm fell off. Her hair had been almost but not quite white, like Sarah's hair. Her ankles had been bent for the child to put on and take off plastic high heels. Sarah's ankles aren't bent. She is different in that respect, although she has taken off her paper slippers so she is barefoot, like the doll was when Bing found her. The slippers lie in a wad on the wood slat deck.

Rosemary says, "Do you know who I am?"

Sarah smiles. "Of course, Rosie. Isn't the afternoon wonderful?"

Rosemary looks around, as if noticing the afternoon for the first time.

Bing says, "The afternoon is wonderful. I enjoy the sun touch on my face."

Sarah graces him with a nod and a smile, as if they both feel exactly the same way. Although thin and vulnerable, Sarah is beautiful in Bing's mind. She is self-contained. There's no need in her. Her skin is the color of concrete yet soft as one of those flowers you blow on and seeds fly away. Her eyes are without qualms.

She shows no surprise or curiosity as to who Bing is or why he is with her sister. "I like the air today. I was just sitting here trying to decide what the air tastes like. Lemon, I think. Or maybe meringue on a lemon pie."

Bing opens his mouth wide and tastes. "Water from the water fountain," he says.

Sarah looks at Bing in what might be called gentle interest. "Isn't it odd, that air can taste like clean water."

Rosemary is floored by the compatibility of thought between the two. Sarah on pain medication and Bing fresh out of the zoo appear to be traveling the same wavelength.

She says, "Sarah, this is Bing. He's the boy I told you about."

Sarah holds her hand out to shake. "I am quite pleased to meet you, Bing." She means it. This woman is way past small talk.

Bing stares at her hand a moment. He knows what to do this time. He grasps her extended hand with both of his, thumbs up, fingers down. "Do you have an IPhone?"

Rosemary is aghast. "*Bing.*"

Sarah says, "I have a Droid. Would that do?"

"I would like you to gift it to me."

Rosemary steps to Sarah's side, protectively. "Sarah needs her phone, Bing. I told you why. It's rude of you to try and take it away from her."

A slight, nearly playful smile flickers on Sarah's lips. "There is no harm in asking."

Bing scowls at Rosemary and says to Sarah. "Rosemary smoked a cigarette. Over there." He motions toward her car in the parking lot.

Rosemary's eyes flash. "Traitor. I told you not to worry her."

Sarah says, "You shouldn't smoke if you don't want me to worry. I always know anyway. My nose isn't broken."

Bing releases her hand and bends down on one knee to examine the glider. He tries to understand what makes it go back and forth.

After choosing not to stick her foot up Bing's ass, even though she would love to do just that, Rosemary says, "I need to talk to the day nurse. Sarah, will you entertain Bing for a few moments."

Sarah speaks slowly, with enunciation. "Of course, Rosemary." She turns her attention to Bing. "How would you like to be entertained?"

"Can you sing? I enjoy singing but Dr. Lori doesn't care for voice music so I don't hear it often. They play loud music through the speakers at the wild bird show, only it's not singing."

"That's not what I mean," Rosemary says. "I want you two to talk. I want Bing to know you better."

Rosemary leaves the porch by a door leading into the building. Bing and Sarah look at one another, shyly. Bing thinks she doesn't have an appearance similar to her sister. The hair and lips are different. The neck is almost the same. Sarah is much thinner. He knows from Dr. Lori that sisters often resemble each other, but then he doesn't look a bit like his brother, Kano. Maybe it's a female trait.

Bing says, "Do you know how the machine works?" He nods at the glider mechanism.

Sarah says, "I push with my foot and it goes back and forth. Sometimes movement hurts, but today it is nice."

Bing leans forward and balances himself with a hand on the glider armrest, next to Sarah's hand. He sees the chair part is connected to the base part by flat, metal pieces that hang between the two. The chair part swivels on something. He can't say what. Machines have never been Bing's strong point.

"Rosemary wants me to make you feel less pain."

Sarah closes her eyes again. To Bing, she seems to be concentrating on her insides. "I know. She told me about you yesterday." She opens her eyes and looks at Bing on his knee by her side. "Or the day before. They run together."

Bing stares up at her a long time. Others would be self-conscious to be stared at from so close for so long with such intensity, but Sarah isn't. She looks back at him, calmly. It isn't one of those who-blinks-first power games people get in when trying to prove they aren't cowed. It is two people exploring what they are seeing.

Bing touches her belly with two fingers. He is listening. He comes up on both knees and looks behind her right ear.

"What do you see?" Sarah asks.

"Pink."

"I've never seen behind my own ear."

"It's pink and very clean. You must wash with diligence." Bing settles back on his haunches. "I don't think I can help you."

Sarah's voice is one of sadness but not surprise. "I didn't think you could."

"You don't have the kind of sickness I can change."

Sarah looks off across the lawn. Two birds are flapping at a birdbath by the drive. From somewhere far away, they can hear a siren.

"Let's not tell Rosemary yet," Sarah says. "She has such high hopes."

He leans back into a squatting position. They are quiet for a while, each lost in his or her thoughts. The siren dies away. One of the birds flies off to the west. The other drops to the ground and hops about, searching for food. Bing watches a fly land on Sarah's foot. It walks up her big toe, but she doesn't flick it off.

She says, "I don't mind dying, you know."

Bing flicks the fly for her. "That's the reason I can't help you. You don't need help."

She looks from the mid-distance back to Bing. "I just feel bad about Rosemary. She doesn't understand that sometimes dying is better than not dying."

They fall back into a comfortable silence. Someone inside turns a radio on — NPR news. Neither Bing nor Sarah cares about the news. They care about the sun on their skin, and the air that tastes like meringue.

Finally, after a long silence, Bing says, "When the time comes for you to leave, do you think I can have your phone then?"

As Rosemary appears from the building, she pushes the door open with a loud *whop* against the wall.

Sarah says, "I don't see why you shouldn't."

Rosemary says, "Shouldn't what?"

Chapter Thirty-Four

"Tell the truth, Bing. What did you think of Sarah?"
"She is content."
"What?"
"Her heart is still."

Rosemary is leading Bing along the sidewalk, past frame houses for families with young children. Starter homes. Her yellow Small House Movement house sits in the middle of the block, but she'd had to park at the end, on the far side of the street. It is one of those neighborhoods where you curb park on one side of the street on Monday, Wednesday, and Friday, and the other side on Tuesday, Thursday, Saturday, and Sunday. Most of the houses have driveways and single car garages or car ports. Rosemary has neither. Her house was built for minimum footprint.

"Sarah hurts," Rosemary says. "All the time. She often doesn't know where she is or who I am. How can you dream she is content?"

Bing stops to study a tricycle on its side. For the life of him, he can't see its use. "She wants nothing."

"She wants to be out of pain."

"Yes, but that's not a crucial want. It's like wanting to go to the bathroom. A person can be content and still need to pee."

Rosemary shakes her head, fairly pulsing with indignation. It's one thing to think like an ape, another to think like a stupid ape.

"Will you help her?"

Bing pokes the tricycle with his foot. The rubber wheel on top circles with a spoke clicking sound. "Sarah does not need help. You are the human person who needs help."

Rosemary turns off the sidewalk onto a series of flagstone ovals that lead across her tiny lawn — no bigger than the dance floor at a corner bar — up to her house. She doesn't much care whether Bing follows or not. He isn't saying what she wants to hear.

At the door, she whirls on him. "Then you better help me by fixing her."

Bing looks down at the flagstone. It is a mottled pink and white, not unlike the seashell he once blew into to make a bottom sound. He has no desire to meet Rosemary's eyes. Bonobos don't operate on the importance of eye contact.

"It doesn't work like that."

Rosemary stares hard at him. "Don't disappoint me."

Bing shrugs. "I will do what I can not to. Disappoint you."

The house is tasteful, urban, cluttered yet not dirty. The nest of a young professional. The furniture is so simple it looks made in a high school shop class. The oak flooring is shined by weekly application of Mop & Glo. The walls are a pale blue with photos of Sarah and Rosemary in Sur la Table frames. There is one print of a Monet water lily painting. The bookshelves are made from stained two by fours and cinder blocks. Bing can't read the titles.

Rosemary says, "You'll stay here till we figure what to do with you."

TV, sound system, microwave, laptop, lava lamp — Bing has no clue as to what does what.

He says, "Is this the part where we copulate?"

Rosemary drops her purse on the kitchenette counter with more force than is needed. "No, Bing, this is not the part where we copulate."

Bing sniffs. Air conditioned air smells off to him, as if a snake died behind a wall.

"Do you have fruit?"

CHAPTER THIRTY-FIVE

The front room lies shrouded in darkness, except for a nightlight plug coming from the kitchen area, and the glow of clocks on various appliances and electrical devices. The lava lamp burps. The curtains are back lit by a security light on the street.

From a pile of blankets on the couch, we hear whimpering. Bing is awake — frightened. He is not accustomed to refrigerator hum. The air conditioner clicks. Water runs through pipes when someone somewhere flushes a toilet. TV sound seeps from next door. Jay Leno. The temperature is wrong. The air is wrong. The couch is pitched at the slightest angle so he feels like he's about to fall off.

There's no mother smell of Betty. No Lola grunts. He thinks he had reasons for running away from home, but now, in Rosemary's small house teeming with strangeness, Bing cannot recall what those reasons are.

He doesn't feel invisible.

Rosemary's bedroom door opens — a rectangle of light framing Rosemary herself wrapped in blue terrycloth. She advances across the room and sits beside him on the couch.

"What's the matter, Bing?"

He looks through tears up at her face and the hair that means so much. Her eyes are warm.

"I have fear."

Rosemary touches his shoulder. He's wearing a never-worn pair of silk pajamas Sarah gave Rosemary for Christmas three years ago. The shirt has panda bears across the front and back. The bottoms are blue. Rosemary has never been a pajama kind of girl, and Sarah knew that. The pajamas were a test to see if Rosemary would wear something she hated given to her by someone she loved.

"You're safe here. The door is locked. I'm with you."

"I have never been away from my family all night."

"Not even in decontamination?"

"I never slept there. Dr. Lori let me out when it was time for nesting. My mother and brother and the others slept together in the compound. This is difficult."

Rosemary is silent while she rubs his shoulder and he sniffles. She says, "This is the first night you've slept alone, in your life?"

Bing nods.

CHAPTER THIRTY-SIX

Rosemary lies on her back, in her double bed, under her flannel sheets and her Grandma Ellie's quilt, staring at the ceiling she can't see up there in the dark. She is as awake as she's ever been. Sleep is but a myth told to children. On one side, the digital clock next to Sarah's revolving photo frame measures the passing of minutes. On the other side, Bing sleeps like a toddler after a hard play day.

He also lies on his back. Only his arms are splayed crucifixion style, so his left forearm hangs dead weight across Rosemary's neck. His legs have kicked the sheets and quilt on his side of the bed to her side. Periodically — an average of twice a minute — he spasms like popping at a hacky sack before going into what, if he were a dog, Rosemary would say was chasing rabbits.

He moans; he snores; he emits little bonobo shrieks.

Rosemary cannot help but wonder what she has gotten herself into. What is she supposed to do with the boy? The plan had been simple — spring him, take him to Sarah so he could cure her, then – then what? What is she supposed to do with the boy/ape after he heals Sarah? Or doesn't heal Sarah, which is unthinkable. She can't keep him like a pound cat. In fairness, she can't return Bing to Dr. Lori. Rosemary takes pride in her fairness. She isn't about to use him and toss him. That would go against her deepest scruples, but she sure can't have him sleeping in her bed the rest of his life.

The thought dawns on Rosemary that she might have worked this out more thoroughly.

Beside her, Bing snorts, then blows drool and other bodily fluids. He rolls onto his side, toward her, and his other arm flops across her belly, like the snake falling out of the acacia.

CHAPTER THIRTY-SEVEN

Bing perches and Turk sits on tall bar stools in front of microphones on the end of swiveling stainless steel poles. The microphones have what looks like golf club socks on them, but, of course, Bing doesn't know this because his experience with golf clubs is just as lacking as his experience with microphones. All sorts of high-tech geegaws are scattered about the room, seemingly left for the purpose of overwhelming Bing. Whatever the geegaws point, Bing is overwhelmed.

Rosemary and Mitchell watch from behind glass. They are in another room full of dials and switches. Rosemary looks up from her laptop to smile encouragement at Bing. Her laptop is linked to a screen Turk can see but Bing can't, not that it would matter if he could. On a normal day, Rosemary would be feeding Turk facts and opinions so he can come across as having a world of knowledge stored in his brain. Today, Turk already knows the questions he wants to ask, so Rosemary is mostly feeding him ideas he does not need.

Mitchell gives Bing a thumbs up — the same sign he gave Bing at the California Pizza Kitchen. Bing still doesn't know what it means, but he has been out of the zoo long enough now he knows he is supposed to thumbs up back, so he does.

They come out of a commercial for CoQ10 supplements and Turk goes into his introduction. "As I speak with my next guest, Bing the Bonobo, I want all of you who haven't seen this to go on You Tube and check out the video entitled *New Messiah at California Pizza Kitchen.*"

Bing twists his headphones this way and then that. He's had them on and off and on again three times. They aren't as comfortable as they look.

Turk sends him a threatening scowl that anyone would know means *Don't screw with the headphones.* "You must see what this kid did yesterday afternoon because there is no way you are going to believe when I tell you."

Bing gums the microphone sock, which causes Mitchell to go into a flurry of sound adjustments. The fuzz sticks to Bing's tongue. He sits there, lolling his tongue, watching Rosemary type on her computer. He knows what a computer is. She explained it to him this morning over breakfast.

She had said, "It's where information comes from."

He had said, "Oh."

Now, in the studio at Centered Soul, Turk says, "I was there and saw the miracle with my own eyes and I still have trouble buying it. A young punk threatened a group of –"

"T.J.," Bing says.

"What's that, Bing?"

"The adolescent male's name is T.J. Not punk."

Turk stares at Bing a few seconds until Mitch makes a roll-it hand motion. Turk says, "Your T. J. is a member of a notorious gang and in my book that makes him a punk."

Bing shrugs, wondering where Turk's book is.

Turk goes on, his lips almost kissing the microphone. "As this T.J. is threatening to stab Bing for having the nerve to call him *sweet,* another gang roars up and sprays the parking lot with gunfire, hitting T.J. three times point blank in the chest and abdomen. T.J. lies on the asphalt, dying, and now you take up the story, Bing. What happens next?"

Bing searches his memory for what happened next. He glances at Rosemary, who is staring at him, intently.

"I fixed the young man."

Turk's voice resonates with mock wonder. "You *fixed* a dying bullet-riddled boy. I saw you place your hands over the wounds and you chanted mumbo-jumbo and *Poof!* All better. No more blood bath. Next thing you're a star on You Tube."

"I do not fathom the word *You Tube.*"

"Bystanders filmed the miracle on smart phones and uploaded it onto the internet. You've had two million hits since yesterday."

Bing ponders this, deeply. He doesn't know *bystanders* either, but he knows Turk thinks whatever went on matters and he is expected to comment.

He makes a chewing motion with his jaws even though he has nothing to chew. "I would very much enjoy a smart phone. Can you please gift me one?"

Turk chuckles, glancing at Rosemary who holds her hands palm up in a *Got me?* gesture. Then she proceeds to type furiously on her laptop. From his side of the glass, Turk reads what she types and says, "Let us backtrack from the miracle."

Bing says, "Back track."

"You claim you were raised by apes and yesterday was the first time you've stepped outside the San Diego Zoo Safari Park. I realize this is Southern California, but that hardly seems possible."

Bing picks a substance from his nose, examines it closely, rubs it off on the microphone sock, and says, "If a thing is, then it must be possible. *Why of the sheep do you not learn peace?*"

Turk blinks. Rosemary types. Mitchell thinks about it.

"How wise you are," Turk says. "Beyond your years and experience. Tell me, Bing, does your power of healing come directly from God?"

Bing looks to Rosemary again, as if asking a question. She points at the ceiling. He looks up at the ceiling and says, "I do not fathom *God.*"

"Who does? But what we want to know is this: What is your personal relationship with God?"

"I heard the word *God* yesterday, in the afternoon, but Rosemary did not define for me. Is this a primate?"

Turk stares hard at Bing. He's done with blinking. "Never heard the word *God.* What are you, some freak of nature?"

Bing puts a finger on his chin, mimicking Dr. Lori. *"Terror in the house does roar, but pity stands before the door."*

Turk allows five seconds of dead air. He's not afraid of silence over the radio. It's how he manipulates his listeners into listening. "Do you know the word *spiritual?*"

Bing shakes his head No.

"Our audience can't see you, Bing. You'll have to speak aloud."

Bing says, "I have not been told that word."

"What about *soul?*"

Bing puckers his lips and lifts himself up and down on the stool. He's got this one. "My friend, Rosemary, works at Soul."

"And you, no doubt, read it on the sign in front of our Centered Soul studio."

Bing stops bouncing. His eyebrows knot. "I cannot read."

"What's this then?"

"I can only see and smell and hear. Sometimes touch. I cannot read."

Turk leans back away from the microphone. He reads Rosemary's notes, shaking his head, rejecting them. He comes back to the microphone, ready to wrap this up.

"Either you have lived an unbelievably sheltered life, or you are the biggest liar I have had the opportunity to come across."

"Most days are used outside of buildings, away from shelter, so I must be the other."

Rosemary gives up on typing. The careful observer, such as Mitchell who is more alert to Rosemary next to him in the booth than the guys in the studio, might notice a change in Rosemary's aspect. It is in the way she regards Bing, a subtle transference of wonder from one man to the other. Bing's lack of defense mechanisms makes Rosemary crave to defend him.

Turk drums his fingers on the console counter. "Tell me truth, Bing," he purrs in his best radio tones. "Are you for real?"

Bing crosses his arms, holding himself by the elbows, and he rocks on his stool. He says, *"Great things are done when Men and Mountains meet. This is not done by jostling in the street."*

Rosemary inhales deeply. This is more than she bargained for.

Chapter Thirty-Eight

Near the finish of the interview, Bing comes to the realization that he should make water. He's never been big on holding past the first urge because he's never had to hold past the first urge. He generally goes where he is. He knows away from the zoo, surrounded by Outies, he can't just go where he stands. Only non-human animals go where they stand.

So, as soon as Turk says, "Stay tuned tomorrow for more on this modern day Messiah," and goes away and Mitchell walks in to retrieve the headphones from his ears, Bing says, "Toilet."

Mitchell tells him down the hall two doors. He also says, "Great job with Turk. I loved what you said about the sheep."

Bing says, "Thank you." He takes pride in being a polite boy. He looks through the glass at Rosemary who is biting her lower lip and peering at her computer. She isn't looking at him.

Bing says, "I must go now."

He stands before the urinal with his pants at his ankles, thinking about Betty and Kano. He wonders if Dr. Lori misses him, or even if she knows he's gone. He wonders what a freak of nature is. He saw a two-headed meerkat once, but it only lived three days. It was baby mouse small and bald. Why would Turk compare him to that?

When he left the zoo, he had no conceptions of outside, so he shouldn't feel disappointed by it, even though he is. True, he isn't covered with boils. No one has killed him dead or forced him to be carnal against his wishes. It could be worse. Yet, he had expected more. Rosemary had been right when she said whatever Dr. Lori told him about outside was mistaken, but, even so, whatever Rosemary told him about outside was equally mistaken. They are either both liars or even though they live there they don't know what outside is like.

The restroom door opens and Persephone enters. She is resplendent. The only word for it, although not a word Bing knows, so he only thinks, *Wow*. Scarves layered over scarves. Long plum-colored skirt to the floor. Silk belt. Enough jewelry to sink a rowboat.

"Bing," she oozes. "I shall now examine you."

When Bing swings toward her his urine stream streaks across her velour skirt.

She looks down at the line across her skirt and says, "I am soiled."

Bing says, "No. Urine. Dr. Lori instructed me in proper indoor voiding." Meanwhile his stream is being spent on the floor tile. "She claimed females would not violate the sanctity of the male toilet, and, in exchange, I must not violate the sanctity of the female toilet. It is a social contract."

Persephone steps away from the splatter. "I need to feel your forehead with none of the others to witness."

Bing finishes his business and tucks. Dr. Lori had been quite frank about the importance of the tuck.

Persephone says, "I wish to determine the physical lineage of your regressions."

"What would be the purpose of doing such a thing?"

"It is of tantamount importance to formulate what bodies you have inhabited before this manifestation. They say you are Chosen. That you have come to California to straighten out the mess."

"I see no mess."

"I was present at the miracle. I know you are a being at a level above commonality and now I must discover how far above. Prophet or savior? John the Baptist or Jesus? We can't have the rabble worshipping a false god."

"There is that word again."

She moves toward Bing and lifts her heavily blinged hand toward his face. Alarmed, he backs into the urinal.

"This will cause no discomfort, Bing. You will feel naught but a soothing warmth emanating from my fingertips."

Bing is so far back his trousers are getting damp. "Do not touch my face."

Persephone advances. "Do not be silly, my young man."

As she reaches to touch his forehead, Bing bites her on the soft tissue between her thumb and fingers.

Persephone yelps. *"Shit fire!"*

Bing drops on all fours. He bares his teeth and howls. As Persephone back away, he bluff charges, stopping before ripping her apart.

She begs. "Please, don't kill me."

Bing realizes his mistake — inappropriate aggression. A crime worthy of shunning. He flops on his back and presents his belly to her.

This frightens Persephone all over again. "What are you doing?"

From his position of submissive exposure, Bing bleats. He says, "Punish me, if you wish. I deserve pain for my loss of civilization."

"I don't want to punish you. I want to study you."

"Can you study me without touching my face?"

Persephone's hands flutter from scarf to scarf, adjusting them into more controllable positions. "I'll do my best."

Bing is cheerful once more. He has avoided punishment. "Okay." He flops back over. He stands up and grins at Persephone. "What would you wish to know?"

CHAPTER THIRTY-NINE

Mitchell and Sister Starshine stand on the walk in front of the radio station. It is evening. The air is cool enough to be pleasant but not cool enough for a jacket. It's that moment when birds seem to take a ten-minute break between the day and night shifts. Mitchell smokes a skinny cigarette that is supposed to be low tar while Sister Starshine drinks Royal Crown Cola from a 64-ounce cup she got for free at a Star Trek convention. Her Hawaiian shirt has perspiration stains in the pits. Her feet are swollen.

"You think these people believed in something else yesterday?" Mitchell says. "Or is this new?"

Sister Starshine regards the crowd gathered across the street — maybe forty-five people in a mix of old, young, poor, not-quite-poor, and sick. Lots of sick. If they represent any demographic group it would be the subset that spends money on lottery tickets.

"They followed a different path yesterday," she says, "and another one six months ago. I recognize a couple of them from my personal appearances at holistic street fairs. They think if they find the correct faith, they won't be miserable."

Mitchell draws deep on his cigarette. He flicks ash to the sidewalk. "Hard to see that bunch as being anything more than desperate."

Turk Palisades slides out the Centered Soul smoked glass door, one hand slapping his breast pocket for sunglasses he wears even in the low light of dusk and the other hand checking text messages.

He glances across at the crowd and says, "What now?"

Mitchell nods to the clump of humanity milling around in front of a Starbucks. "Bing's followers."

Sister Starshine points out a small group on the left, spilling into the Starbucks parking. These folks have lawn chairs and coolers. A dog on a leash is tied to a truck camper bumper. They're here for the long run.

"The ones yonder claim to be chosen apostles. They're more important than the disciples because they were all present at the miracle."

Mitchell says, "I don't recall but a dozen people at the miracle, not counting the bad boys and us. Some of this bunch are lying."

Turk stares at the apostles, thinking all of them are lying. He takes pride in his memory and he doesn't remember any of these pitiful people from California Pizza Kitchen. His mind whirs with possibilities. It only takes a handful of zealots to spark a movement. Turk aspires to leading a movement.

"What's with the wheelchair brigade?" he asks.

"They think Bing can cure them," Sister Starshine says.

The sick clump aren't followers or apostles. They're people whose last hope is a miracle. Those who can hold posters they drew with Magic Markers and Sharpies. THROAT CANCER — PLEASE HAVE MERCY; BLIND SINCE BIRTH; AIDS VICTIM (NOT GAY).

Turk takes his sunglasses back off to see them more clearly. "Didn't they listen to my interview? The ape boy can't read."

Mitchell flips his butt into the gutter where it rests next to a pile of Mitchell butts. He always smokes one cigarette a day, when he gets off. That's because he can't smoke at work and he can't smoke at home where he lives with his mother. Or in the car. Or anywhere but out front of Centered Soul.

He says, "There's contagious terminals over there. I'm afraid to walk through them."

Turk pulls out a comb he bought from Barney's on Wilshire. Combing his hair straight back helps Turk think big concepts. It's a trigger routine.

"Don't be a doubter, Mitchell. If you catch a disease we'll have Bing run his hands over you and make it all well. No problem."

He stares at the crowd, his mind afire with possibilities. He loves the feel of the comb passing through his hair. This is the inspiration he's waited for.

"Miracles are good," he says. "I can use miracles."

CHAPTER FORTY

The next morning Rosemary awakens alone under her grandma's quilt in her double bed in her room in the small house. She stretches, admiring the soft sunlight on her lemon-colored wall. There are many ways to divide humanity into two groups and many people would perform that operation — those who love Disney World and those who hate Disney World, for example. We have hundreds more examples. Those who drink coffee; those who don't. Those who watch "American Idol;" those who would rather snort Drano. One way of dividing humanity is those who wake up feeling okay and those who wake up feeling like crap. The two sets often switch out within a half hour, but there's a fairly deep gap in that first five minutes between glad-to-be-alive and not-so-sure.

Rosemary tends to wake up feeling refreshed and hopeful. It must be genetic because there is little in her life that should motivate morning happiness. It's only a couple minutes later when she recalls her sister's condition and global warming and dying sea mammals that her heart plummets. But, that first few breaths after awakening is enough joy to keep her going.

On this morning, Rosemary awakens alone and it takes a short time to recall that she didn't fall asleep alone. She fell asleep next to Bing in her dorky pajamas, hogging the bed and acting out dreams with his limbs.

Rosemary gets up, throws on her flowered bathrobe, and moves out into the living room separated from the kitchen by a sternum-high counter. The open area theory of design.

She sees no Bing, but the front door is open wide. Rosemary clinches her robe tightly to her waist and steps out onto the porch. The dawn is cooler than she's used to — Rosemary isn't an outside at the first crack woman — and the light is gentle, as if seen through several layers of Saran Wrap. She looks both ways up and down the block, seeing no movement. A car idles in the driveway two houses down, but no one is in or near it. Someone, somewhere out of sight, is mowing their lawn at first light, which always pisses Rosemary off no end.

She steps from flagstone to flagstone until she reaches the street, then she looks back at her own house. Bing is on the roof, still wearing the silk pajamas.

Rosemary walks back toward the house. She shades her eyes with her hand, looking up at him.

"What are you doing on my roof?"

Bing leans over the edge to see her. His legs dangle. He has on the engineer's cap and her coral necklace that he didn't ask to borrow. "You can see me then?"

"Of course, I see you."

"In the zoo, you wouldn't have seen me."

Rosemary does a 360 to check if anyone is watching. Across the street, a woman with her hair in electric curlers opens her door and picks up a newspaper from her flowerbed. She glances at Rosemary and Bing but she doesn't react. This is an American suburb. If your neighbor does something weird, you ignore him. No judgment calls here.

Rosemary waits for the woman to go back inside, then she says, "You're in plain sight. How could you think people will look at you and not see you."

The concept saddens Bing. Invisibility has always been a constant in his life. "I don't know. I'm used to people not noticing."

"Maybe it's the pajamas." Rosemary doesn't believe this but she doesn't want Bing upset either. "They stick out."

Bing starts to unbutton the top. "I'll take them off."

"Don't do that. People will notice if you sit on my house naked. They'll call the police."

"Oh." Bing looks up and down the street, as if expecting the police. He's seen police before. The come into the zoo and handcuff drunks and pocket pickers. He avoids them.

"What are you doing up there? Rosemary asks.

"I'm thinking."

"You had to go up on my rooftop to think?"

"I think better above dirt."

"What are you thinking about?"

"I'm thinking about Dr. Lori."

Rosemary doesn't want to hear this. She is afraid Bing will get homesick and ask her to take him back before he's fixed Sarah. She wouldn't blame him for being homesick. The world must be strange to someone raised in a zoo.

"What about Dr. Lori?"

Bing pokes at bugs in the rain gutter. They're dead. He prefers live. He isn't yet reduced to eating dead bugs. That's only for when he is extremely hungry.

"I'm wondering if she uses the toilet."

"Yes, Bing. Dr. Lori uses the toilet."

"Persephone disturbed my toilet time yesterday and I concluded I've never seen Dr. Lori use the toilet. I've never seen any female human void. Dr. Lori taught me proper procedure, but she didn't show me how females do it." He stares down at Rosemary, as if picturing the process. "They don't have penises, you know."

"I know that one."

"I'm wondering if they go."

Rosemary almost smiles, picturing the woman in the hot curlers sitting at her window, eavesdropping. What would she make of the conversation? No doubt she is working out the words for posting it on her blog.

"Everyone uses the toilet, Bing. Even females. Even Dr. Lori."

Bing considers. "How do you know? Have you seen Dr. Lori go?"

"I have not seen Dr. Lori go, but she eats food and drinks water. Anyone who eats and drinks has to get rid of the extra somehow, and they do it by pooping and peeing. Everyone, Bing. It's the law of nature."

"Even fish?"

"Even fish."

Bing stares off at the horizon he can see between houses. The sun is fully up now. He can hear freeway noises in the distance, although Rosemary can't, or at least, she isn't aware of them. She's heard the far-away freeway too long to know she's hearing it.

Bing appears lost in deep thoughts. He says, "I wonder if Dr. Lori does."

CHAPTER FORTY-ONE

R osemary's doorbell rings. Insistently. Several times — although chimes might be a more exact description than rings. Whoever is punching her button is not accustomed to killing time in front of closed doors. There's little to distract the mind from Rosemary's porch. No doubt whoever is punching the doorbell has, by now, pulled out an electrical device and is checking messages, news, or scores. People in a hurry can no longer be expected to suffer more than five seconds without input.

Rosemary crosses from the bedroom, fresh from the shower, towel drying her hair. She's wearing oversize sweats and fluffy house shoes. She waves her hand through the air to disperse cigarette smoke that she imagines wafts about her person.

She opens the door to Turk Palisades, who, sure enough, is checking his screen. He clicks to sleep mode and charges past her into the house. No pausing for pleasantries. "Our podcast has had twenty million hits in two days, and that doesn't count the million and a half who heard the original show. That You Tube miracle footage is up to fifty million."

Turk is wearing black. Silk shirt, jeans, ankle boots, he's a Johnny Cash impersonator. "Your monkey boy is the break we've been praying for."

Rosemary tucks her hair into the towel in a maneuver women are genetically programmed for and men aren't. "He's not mine and he's not a monkey."

Turk turns on her. "What's that?"

"The boy is Bing. He's not really a bonobo, much less a monkey."

Turk advances on Rosemary, studying her for signs of weakness. "You're not emotionally involved with this ape, are you?"

Rosemary sniffs and looks at Sarah's photo above the false mantel. It's Sarah in her field hockey uniform, alive in victory. She'd scored the winning goal while Rosemary was stuck in the penalty corner. "Of course not."

"He's our ticket to the stars. One cannot get emotionally involved with ones ticket. You understand the subtext?"

Flustered and uncomfortable, Rosemary retreats to the kitchen where she fusses with the Cuisinart coffee maker.

Turk follows. "I've got him booked on San Diego Now. First thing Monday."

Rosemary stops, mid-reach for a mug she got free at a radio producer's convention in Las Vegas. "But that's TV."

"If he behaves himself and doesn't scratch his nose or pick his butt on camera, we'll place him on The View within a week. That's your mission from now to Monday. Teach him how to sit in a chair without being disgusting."

Rosemary pours herself coffee. Assuming it is for him, Turk takes the mug from her hand.

Rosemary says, "TV is the enemy. The false prophet. Why don't we keep him for ourselves?"

Turk squeezes a stream of honey into the mug. He likes his coffee sweet. "Your limits amaze me, Rosemary. It's hard to believe how much time and energy I've invested in giving you the benefits of my wisdom."

Rosemary recalls what *benefits of my wisdom* means. They are the same benefits all the interns receive. When Rosemary first came to Centered Soul she saw Turk as the mentor she'd always craved. She was wild in her devotion to him. She was badly hurt when she went from intern to full-time and he cut out the personal instruction. Too much risk of a lawsuit, should her job end in bitterness.

"TV is not the enemy," Turk says. "Being common is the enemy. You want to be exceptional, don't you?"

She chooses another mug, this one a cup hand-painted by her mother at one of those paint-your-own ceramics shops in Encinitas.

Her mother had painted the cup black with tiny silver stars. Rosemary's mother was out of the picture now. Supposedly she'd moved to Denmark to farm. Before Rosemary can pour herself a second cup, Turk takes her wrists in both his hands. He turns her arms so the wrists face up, toward him.

"Listen to what I have to say." He leans in, close to her face. "If every searcher in America who is interested in life regressions, Transcendentalism, or inner balance tunes into my show, I still won't have the numbers of a brainless bimbo batting false eyelashes on Home Shopping Network. Spiritual radio has a ceiling and I intend to smash through to the infinite."

"By switching to TV?"

His tone is that of a sage speaking to a simple peasant. "We put the boy on TV, build this thing into a national frenzy, then have him perform one more brilliantly marketed public miracle, and I'll be the most powerful personality in entertainment."

He sees disappointment in Rosemary's eyes. "Us," Turk says. "Bing. You and me. Centered Soul. We'll reap a fortune."

Rosemary unlocks her wrists and steps away, toward the refrigerator. She speaks with her back to Turk. "Reaping a fortune isn't why I followed you into spiritualism."

Turk touches her shoulder, swiveling her into eye contact. He knows she can't get away so long as he maintains eye contact.

"We'll heal your sister."

Rosemary blinks tears. She stares at the floor. As if escaping from captivity, a long lock of spiral curls pops free from the towel apparatus covering her head. The word might be *Boing*, the way it pops out.

"Isn't that the reason you rescued him from the zoo?" Turk asks. "You're not out to give this boy a centered soul of his own."

Turk turns to take in the living area. The house is so compact he can see most of it without walking around. Only the bedroom and bathroom are behind doors, and those doors are open, now. Bing's absence is obvious.

"Where is Tarzan anyway?"

"Bing went outside to play. Said he wanted to be under the sky."

"By himself?" Turk retrieves his coffee mug from the counter. He looks into it as if deciding whether to drink or not, and decides not. "You sent our star outside without a handler?"

"Bing doesn't need a handler. He isn't an animal." Rosemary considers this statement. While Bing is not an animal, he certainly isn't a grown up who can fend for himself. Handler is a nasty word, but if a nice synonym can be found, Rosemary would use it.

"He's worse. He's a celebrity," Turk says. "You can't send a celebrity out with no handler."

"Why not?"

"You have no control. He might start thinking."

CHAPTER FORTY-TWO

B ing is in a park. Not a park, really, more of a triangle formed by three streets that cross one another but don't intersect. Besides badly cut grass, there are two Japanese black pines and a bench made of moldering concrete with a weak attempt at a Greek design on the back.

Bing crouches on his haunches beside the root hump of one of the trees, next to a mid-sized red anthill. He strips a needle cluster through his teeth until he is left with a single, long needle. It's not a maneuver most men his age can do cleanly, but Bing doesn't view it as exceptional. He sights down the needle to gauge straightness, then he inserts the tip of the needle into the top hole of the anthill.

Red ants don't like objects stuck in their holes. They swarm up the needle, soon coating it with wriggling, crawling, antennae thrusting red bodies. Bing cocks his head to one side. He studies ants climbing over ants. Some circle the needle, most head up the blade toward his fingers. After thirty seconds or so, when Bing judges the needle about as ant saturated as it's going to get, he withdraws the needle from the anthill hole. He holds it upright, to the sky, then he licks it like a kid on a Popsicle.

As he slurps ants, he thinks about Rosemary's eyebrows. Her eyelids. Her lashes, top and bottom. Her eyes. He wants to lick her eyelashes. They might feel like licking ants.

That's when Bing hears a squeal of brakes, a *Yelp*, and a curse — *Fuck!* He looks up from his ants to see a motorcycle on its side in the street and a leather-clad motorcyclist pulling himself to his feet, cursing again and again. The motorcyclist rights the bike, climbs on, and kick starts the machine. He glances down at a clump of fur beside the curb, then he drives away, swerving his body left, then right, before straightening up and speeding off.

A boy — maybe ten, shorts, white t-shirt with nothing written on it, untied sneakers — shrieks his fury and runs into the street. He kneels next to the clump of fur, which is a Springer spaniel with broken back legs. The boy cradles the dog in his arms. The dog is near the limit of what the boy can carry, especially crying. He brings the dog to the only grownup in sight — Bing.

Bing moves from haunches to knees as the boy gingerly places the dog on the ground. Bing can tell it's a fairly old dog. The muzzle is gray. The teeth are worn. His mud red collar looks as if it hasn't come off in years.

"The fellow on the motorbike ran into your pet and drove away."

The boy gasps through tears. "Bastard jerk."

"Maybe he was afraid."

"He wasn't afraid." The boy touches the dog behind its ears. The dog looks up at the boy with an expression of infinite depth. He doesn't appear to be in great pain, although he can't breathe properly and blood dribbles from his nostrils.

The boy's lip trembles. "He's an asshole."

Bing and the boy kneel on opposite sides of the spaniel, watching him gulp for air. His tongue lolls from his mouth. He makes no sound that Bing can hear. Bing wonders why the man on the motorcycle would be a body part.

"My mama's had Spanky since before I was born. I said I would take care of him if she let us go for a walk." The boy's tears drip onto the dog's fur. "She's gonna kill me."

Bing looks from Spanky to the boy. He sees a leash coiled in the boy's hand, a leash that should have been attached to the red collar.

"I shall try to help."

More sniffles and a snort, as if the boy is pulling tears back in. "What can you do?"

Bing leans forward over Spanky, who looks up at him. The dog's eyes skitter, as if he sees things in the air Bing and the boy can't see. He moans — once.

Bing places his hands, palm down, over the dog's head and mid-section. He closes his eyes, but not tightly closed. Fluttery closed. He *hums*. The hum is a monotone, neither up pitch nor down. It continues a full thirty seconds. Around them, the world is silent, as if the air has been sucked away.

The boy says, "Spanky died." Bing opens his eyes and looks down at the clump of fur that used to be a dog.

The boy says, "You told me you would help."

"I am filled with sorrow."

They both stare at the dead Spanky. An SUV drives past. A crow caws. The ants from the anthill crawl across Bing's ankle. They bite him but he doesn't react.

Finally, the boy reaches over the body and touches Bing on the shoulder. Bing's first impulse is rapid withdrawal, but he stops still. He's grown accustomed to touching in the last few days, mostly from Rosemary. He doesn't mind so much now.

The boy says, "You did what you could."

"I failed."

"Spanky doesn't hurt anymore."

Bing tastes salt in his mouth, from his tears.

CHAPTER FORTY-THREE

Bing comes in as Turk is going out. Turk has finished not drinking the coffee and he's explained the social impact of Bing picking his nose on TV.

He said, "Don't blow this, Rosemary."

She said, "I don't want Bing hurt."

Statements like that bring out the worst side of Turk Palisades. He falls back on sarcasm, and, while no one comes across as noble when they're dripping sarcasm, Turk comes across as worse than the norm. Maybe it is the poofy lips. Or the slicked-back hair that makes him look like a futures and options investment banker. Whatever the cause, it is not pleasant to witness.

"No one's going to hurt your little pet."

The door opens and Bing drags into the room. He looks discouraged. His pants are dirty. There's a visible tear streak down his face.

He says, "Hello, Mr. Turk."

Turk stares at Bing like he's an exhibit.

Rosemary says, "Where have you been, Bing?"

"Outside."

"What have you been doing to keep yourself busy?"

"Nothing."

Turk goes into friendly uncle mode. "Rosemary and I were just visiting, Binger. We're wondering how you would like me to put you on TV?"

Bing looks from Turk to Rosemary to the floor. "That would be nice."

"Nice?" Turk kind of blows out the word. "That would be *Great!*" He does a Tony the Tiger on the word *Great!* "We'll make you the most famous boy raised by apes in the world. You'll make George of the Jungle look like an assistant night manager at Arby's."

Bing blinks rapidly, which is not something Rosemary has ever seen him do. "I do not know this George person."

"My point, exactly." Turk laughs at his own joke. "Nobody who counts knows about George of the Jungle, but by next week, they will know about Bing the Bonobo."

Bing's eyes search out Rosemary. "Is that good?"

Rosemary says, "Yes, Bing. It will be easier for you to get the things you want when you're famous."

"I don't want things."

Turks laughs like Bing is being hilarious. He points an index finger at Rosemary. "Have him ready by Monday." Then he pretends to shoot her with his finger pistol and leaves. He shuts the door with more force than is necessary.

In the sudden silence after the door closes behind Turk, Bing says, "What is TV?"

CHAPTER FORTY-FOUR

"TV isn't radio. You can't simply talk and act anyway you want because people can see what you're doing. You have to behave."

"I would very much like to view TV."

"You've never seen TV?"

Bing twists his left foot up to his face and bites off the ragged cusp of his big toenail. He tastes the nail a moment, then spits it into a glass dish Rosemary has provided for just such an event. She's starting to know Bing and plan ahead.

Bing says, "Your TV in there looks like a security monitor."

"So you've seen security monitors."

"Everybody has seen security monitors." He switches feet. "But monitors can't see me, except for Dr. Lori. She has a special monitor that can follow me all over the park."

This is part of Bing Rosemary has never figured out. "Why is it that security cameras don't pick you up?"

"Except Dr. Lori's does."

"All security cameras except for Dr. Lori's. How is it they don't capture you?"

He shrugs. "Do you think this TV I'm going to will be able to see me? What I can and can't do has changed since I left the bonobos."

A picture comes to Rosemary's mind of the TV host sitting next to an empty chair. "It would be freaky if they stuck you in front of a camera and your image wasn't in the shot. Your disciples would go ape shit."

Bing looks at her.

"I don't mean literally. No one would turn into ape waste."

"Then why say they will?"

"It's a metaphor. Means their brains would have the alertness of poop on the ground."

"I don't know metaphor."

"We'll work on it."

They are in Rosemary's small kitchen, which is divided from the living area by a rib-high counter. Rosemary's kitchen has a nook table with benches on two sides, so they aren't face-to-face. They have to turn slightly to see one another full on. Rosemary sits on the trapped side of the table. She can't get out unless Bing stands up and moves. His legs are turned to the side in a way where he can see them while hers are under the table.

"You can't go twitchy on TV," Rosemary says. "No scratching or eating bugs during the interview."

He examines his foot closely. There is blood between the third and fourth toes. Using his tongue for floss, he cleans it out.

"You must sit perfectly still while the host asks a question. Then you answer, but you still can't move anything except your mouth."

"What question is that?"

"We'll worry about the questions after we establish a demeanor of calm control."

"I can do control."

Rosemary turns on her ever-present Droid and scrolls to the stop-watch function. "Let's see how long you can go without movement."

"Your phone will explain that?"

"I'll touch this spot and say, *Go,* and the clock will start. I'll touch it again when you wiggle and we'll see how much time has gone by. You understand?"

"I'm not comfortable with time."

"No one is, Bing. But we need to see what you can do. Ready?"

Bing nods. He leans back with his right ankle over his left knee. His hands rest on top of his head.

Rosemary says, "Go."

Bing's foot flutters.

Rosemary says, "Stop."

Bing says, "What?"

"You moved."

"I deny it."

"Your foot's like a dry-humping rabbit."

He looks at his foot. "But I didn't go anywhere. I'm still right here."

"You don't have to go anywhere to move. Let's try again."

This time, Bing sneezes. Rosemary leans over with a paper towel to blot the snot train. "Two seconds."

"TV is hard. I don't think I want to be on TV. I'd rather eat at that fruit place."

Rosemary falls back on a technique she learned from an Atman master who manifested on Turk's show. It seemed to work well for the Atman guy. "Think of it this way. Pretend a blue band of light is entering your body at your belly button."

"The proper word is *navel.*"

"Right. Your navel. And the band of light travels up your body and comes out at your Third Eye where it has turned a rosy red."

"What defines a Third Eye?"

"Your forehead."

Bing touches his forehead. "I have no eye in that place."

"It's invisible."

"Like I used to be only I'm not any more."

"Stay on task, Bing. The blue light goes in, that rosy light comes out, and your body is focused and solid. No tremors."

"How am I supposed to answer questions with light going in and out and my body frozen?"

"We'll worry about questions after we stop the fidgets."

CHAPTER FORTY-FIVE

After twenty minutes of blue light in and rose light out — and a terribly failed experiment with duct tape — Bing finally focuses enough to move onto the question and answer part of training. By now, Bing and Rosemary are sitting on bar stools on opposite sides of the counter. Rosemary is using a pepper mill with a Knot's Berry Farm logo on the side as a pretend microphone. Bing chews gum. Rosemary knows gum will never fly as TV etiquette, but it's the closest she can get him to calm.

"The show host will sit across from you, like this, and there will be a microphone hanging above your head, out of the frame."

"I don't fathom."

"It doesn't matter, I'm explaining too much. The audience will be out that way." She waves vaguely toward the refrigerator. "Ignore them. Pretend they don't exist."

"Why pretend people who do exist don't?"

"You're talking to the host who is this dippy woman and you're playing to the camera. Ignore the audience."

Bing starts to ask what he plays with the camera and Rosemary knows he's about to ask. She jumps in before he can. "The dippy woman will tell the audience your story."

"How will the dippy woman know my story?"

"Your publicist with have e-mailed her. Me, actually. We don't have a full-time publicist and the guys in marketing only work up spots for our in-studio shows."

Practically every word she says flies over Bing's head. He focuses on the part about Rosemary. "You are my own publicist?"

"Until you get so big we hire someone." She considers the concept of Bing getting big. It might change him. Turn him into a jerk, which would be sad beyond belief. She's starting to enjoy his naïve comments, and the longer he's out of the zoo, the more his innocence will go to pot. She's not sure that's a good thing.

"So the host will ask a question, like Turk did, only they won't care about your spiritual journey so much as your human interest side."

"I am interested in humans."

Like that. Six months out of the zoo and he either won't say stupid stuff like that or he'll be self-conscious of cuteness. Cuteness is obscene when it knows it's cute. Observe the seven-year-old beauty queen.

"Let's try one," Rosemary says. She holds the peppermill to her mouth as if it's a microphone even though on the actual TV show there won't be a handheld. She thinks it will make Bing think harder on his answers. "You were raised in the San Diego Zoo Safari Park and have never been outside before a week ago. Do you recall how you came to the zoo?"

Bing chews hard. He still can't understand why he isn't supposed to swallow the gum, but Rosemary said it would make her feel better if he just chewed but didn't swallow, so that's what he does. "Dr. Lori says I came in a box."

Rosemary raises a skeptical eyebrow. "Did she tell you the stork brought this box to the zoo?"

"UPS."

"UPS brought you to San Diego?"

"I have seen them often. Brown shorts. Tan legs. They carry objects. Sometimes they carry animals but usually they bring paperwork. Dr. Lori hates paperwork."

"Did Dr. Lori give you information about your birth mother and father?"

"I don't fathom."

"If the host asks a question you don't understand, you nod your head and say, 'That's a very good question,' and then don't answer it. I've produced hundreds of these things and that's how the experienced people handle it."

Bing nods his head, slowly. "That is a very good question."

"Okay, not for TV but just for me. What do you know about your birth mother and father?"

"No information."

"Dr. Lori never told you where the box came from?"

"She said it came from UPS."

Rosemary pours herself a glass of water from a carafe with a carbon filter in the top so the water is more pure than what comes from the sink. Bing's glass is still empty.

"Tell me about the California Pizza Kitchen."

"I ate limes."

"I mean, tell me about the boy who'd been shot. How did you save the boy?"

Bing nods. "That is a very good question."

Rosemary laughs. "You're funny. You know that. When you aren't being disgusting, you're funny."

Bing revels in her laugh. It is what he looks forward to the most. "Is that a positive or a negative?"

"Definite positive, so far as I'm concerned. Okay what's your earliest memory of life at the zoo?"

Bing closes his eyes to make it easier to bring up a memory. He's never had much use for remembering. He knew where things he needed were located, and what he could eat. Otherwise, there wasn't much reason to think of the past.

"When I was small, I ate a yellow candy bar. I found it outside the snake house. Someone had left it on a ledge, before you go into to see the snakes. And I ate it."

"Was the yellow candy bar good?"

"It was good, but not positive. Dr. Lori told me eating found food is improper. I also remember a mountain gorilla stepping on my foot. That hurt and it was the first time I went to decontamination."

"Why punish you for being stepped on by a gorilla?"

"I was not allowed in the habitat but I went in to play. Dr. Lori said I might be killed. She was angry. Before that, I didn't know about killed."

Rosemary takes a drink of water. She thinks about the moment she realized she would someday die. Backseat of her parents' car, driving across Arizona, she and Sarah were naming roadkills. Sarah named a dead coyote Rosemary. Sarah must have been three, which made Rosemary five when she discovered death.

"What does Dr. Lori look like?"

Bing opened his eyes. "Old."

Rosemary likes the sound of that. "How old?"

"Dr. Lori is female, but she's maybe a hundred and fifty years old. She's been at the zoo since before time."

"Why do you think she hid your existence from the world?"

"To protect me from people like you. She said I would shrivel and my penis would fall off without her to shield me and I must always do what she says. She said Outies would ruin my skin."

Rosemary stifles a smile. No matter how tough this Dr. Lori is, only a woman would threaten a child with ruined skin. "Your skin looks smooth to me. Has your penis fallen off?"

Bing glances down as if for reassurance. "Dr. Lori lied. I don't know why. Is the interview over?"

"Do you want it to be over?"

"I do not enjoy thinking about Dr. Lori."

"Do you miss her?"

Bing nods. "That is a very good question."

CHAPTER FORTY-SIX

The black man's head is bald, shiny. He wears a frilled shirt so white it's uncomfortable to look at, and black trousers that glisten like his head. He may only have one eyebrow. It's difficult for Bing to tell. He stands behind a woman who has strips of white cloth swaddled over her body covering the parts Bing knows must be covered by Outies. Her skin is lighter than the man's, more the shade of a hairless coconut.

The man bounces on his toes, up and down to loud music while the woman rubs against him like a bear scratching its back on a tree. The music goes into a *beat, beat, break.* The woman slides to the floor with her legs split, front and back. She slides between the man's legs, then comes erect as he spins to face her.

Bing tries the split move and falls. He gets up quickly, his back curved, his shoulders forward, then he holds an arm out from his body and tucks the other arm forward, just like the woman on the television screen. He bounces to the music, which isn't similar to music he's heard at the zoo or since he got out. This music *thumps* like someone slapping his ear holes.

The couple faces each other, not pressed together but with a gap between them bridged by the touching of one hand and the grasping of torsos with the other. They skip in a circle around the floor. The woman throws her head way back as they sweep through a turn. Bing throws his head way back as he sweeps through a turn.

The observer will note Bing is aping the woman's motions, not the man's. Bing has no concept of gender roles. He was raised in a matriarchal society — two parallel matriarchal societies if you count both Betty and Dr. Lori. He knows nothing of the shame of femininity.

The music pounds three beats, then ends and the two people hug for a few seconds as the unseen audience goes wild with joy. Bing pretends to hug Rosemary, but, of course, his arms surround air. The black man and lighter woman smile at some other people sitting behind a long table. The man and woman bow.

Bing turns and walks into the bathroom where Rosemary lies soaking in the tub.

She says, "Bing!"

"Explain to me the TV. A male and female faced and touched with their hands and gyrated to music."

"I could have sworn I locked the door."

Bing realizes Rosemary has no clothes. Her wet hair is draped over the end of the tub. Her hands are balanced on the sides. Her knees are slightly bent so the kneecaps rise above the water surface.

Bing steps forward to look down at her body under the water. "You are shaped strangely."

"Bing, why don't you wait outside while I dry off and dress. Then we'll talk."

"I want to understand what the male and female were doing. Was it courtship?"

"They were dancing. I could hear the 'Dancing with the Stars' theme through the door. You had it too loud."

Had Bing been a detective, this would have blown Rosemary's claim that she owned a TV she never watched.

"What is dancing?"

"You've never seen dancing?"

"I have heard the word, but do not know the meaning. A zoo interpreter told her group the ibises danced before mating. Were the two about to perform copulation?"

"I doubt it, not on national TV, anyway." Rosemary gathers herself and leans forward. Her hair comes across the tub end to hang down her back. "You poor boy, how could you grow up and know gyrating and copulation but not dancing? Dr. Lori should be in jail."

Rosemary reaches into the water and pulls the rubber plug from the drain hole. "If you'll give me ten minutes of privacy, I'll show you what dancing is."

Bing frowns. He likes Rosemary's hair, but he wanted a clear view of her bare back and now he doesn't have one. He says, "I do not fathom privacy."

CHAPTER FORTY-SEVEN

Rosemary pats herself dry, careful not to rub, and puts on white shorts, a gray spaghetti top, and sandals — the San Diego at-home-on-a-Saturday-night look. She can hear Bing in the front room slapping bongos on his belly. Sounds like a fairly complex six/eight jazz solo on alternately tight and relaxed abs, not something he would have heard in the bonobo habitat. She knows Bing's belly is hard as a barbecue grill. Rosemary feels queasy when she pictures it. Sleeping next to the man-child has been not difficult so much as not easy. She's never been one for tasteless lust, but. But.

She leaves the bathroom to find Bing standing in front of a commercial for term life insurance for seniors, a universally trusted actor whose name Rosemary can never remember explaining what will happen to your wife should you croak.

Bing's shirttail is tucked under his chin, so he can slap bare belly. He bends his upper body toward the commercial without moving his chin off his chest. "What?"

Rosemary has no capacity for deciphering the purpose of life insurance — *You wager money you'll die* — to Bing, and even if she could she doesn't know term from not term.

"It doesn't matter." She turns off the TV. "You ready to dance?"

Bing lets go of his shirttail. "Is it appropriate?"

"Dancing is always appropriate." She flips on her MP3 player hooked up to speakers and scrolls through her list. "Here's a waltz. You know waltzes?"

Bing doesn't bother to say No. Of course, he doesn't know waltzes. He knows tabla when he hears it, with the sitar and wooden flute. The music they blasted at the Frequent Flyers bird show would be classified as movie spectacular if anyone had ever classified it for Bing and no ever did.

Count to three," Rosemary says. "One-two-three, one-two-three."

"One-two-three."

"Sarah and I taught each other how to waltz to this song in our room. We'd start out arguing over who got to lead and end up laughing so hard we fell down. Sarah threw up once from laughter."

"Is that a positive?"

"You bet your butt it is."

Rosemary flips a switch and after a few seconds "Home on the Range" bursts from the speakers.

Rosemary faces Bing — stomach in, chest out, back stiff — and holds her right arm out, slightly bent, palm down. Her left arm curls before her body, like the woman in the white cloth strips.

Rosemary says, "Assume this position."

Bing does, which means his right hand sticks out the wrong way.

"Other hand out. We have to match up." She wiggles her right hand fingers. "And hold one another with this hand."

"Oh."

"Now, count. One-two-three. One-two-three.

Bing counts simultaneously, "One-two-three," what the kids at the zoo called a *jinx*.

Rosemary shuffles her feet — left-right-left, right-left-right. "See what I'm doing. Copy that."

Bing copies. He nails it right away.

"Perfect." Rosemary left-right-lefts and Bing right-left-rights and they move toward each other till they almost but not quite touch.

Rosemary says, "You got it."

"I know."

Rosemary fits her hand into Bing's. Her other hand rests on his shoulder. "Put your free hand on my hip."

He does.

"Lower."

He does that too.

"Now, move about the room."

Bing looks perplexed.

She says, "What's wrong?"

"Deer and antelope are serious. They don't play."

"It's just words to the song, Bing. Listen to the beat."

"Baby antelope might kick some, but mostly antelope eat grass."

"Ignore the antelope and dance. We're going to start moving now."

Two false starts later, Bing finds the flow. The song ends, Rosemary runs over to push Replay, and they begin again.

"You lead," she says.

"What does that mean?"

"Move around the room in a circle. Just keep your feet moving one-two-three."

"Like the male and female on the television?"

"Only slower, I imagine."

Bing takes off and they are dancing. Rosemary is amazed. She smiles straight into Bing's face. She can see from his eyes that he feels no awkwardness.

"You are a natural."

"Dancing is natural. I wonder why Dr. Lori didn't teach me dance?"

"Same reason she left God and love out of your education. She's a dipshit."

Bing tries out the word. "Dipshit."

"I mean it, Bing. You must have dancing in your genes. You know genes?"

"Pants."

"No, genetics. Genetics are the traits we get from our parents."

"Everyone knows what genetics are. You have no need to explain them."

Rosemary leans into the centrifugal pull of waltzing. It's a bit like flying and a bit like floating on your back in a slow river. "In your world, everyone knows genetics but no one knows dancing."

"Is your world separate?"

"Now, let's move a little closer to each other."

"Like so?"

"You were born to dance, Bing."

"I wondered why I was born."

And Bing and Rosemary spin around the room together. *"Seldom is heard a discouraging word, and the skies are not cloudy all day."*

CHAPTER FORTY-EIGHT

The bedtime ritual. White tea and whole grain Wheat Thins in a mandala. Rosemary calls it a mandala. It's more a pattern. Ten crackers that could be taken as an atomic bomb mushroom but in Rosemary's mind are a baobab with a single cracker like a star hovering over the bare limbs.

Bing stands nearby, watching, drinking chocolate milk from a mug. Rosemary has never shared the ceremony before. She feels the need to explain.

"Growing up, my parents were obsessed with these role playing games, mostly Dungeons and Dragons."

"Dragons do not belong to a real species."

"Sometimes I think my parents weren't real parents." In a white cotton nightgown and blue terrycloth robe, she touches each cracker once. "They would be playing games half the night and leave me to put Sarah to bed. I invented this routine with Wheat Thins. They weren't whole grain back then. Just regular."

Bing — wearing a royal blue jogging outfit that's been hanging in Rosemary's closet for three years — swishes chocolate milk around his mouth. He's had whole milk before, but never chocolate. He likes the crisp feel on the sides of his tongue. Dr. Lori wouldn't allow sweets. He had to scavenge whatever sugar he ate, so he's always connected the taste to being naughty. It seems odd to drink sweet milk indoors.

"Then Dad died from breast cancer. Did you know men can get breast cancer? They hardly ever have it treated in time cause they're embarrassed or clueless or something — men don't check themselves for lumps — so the survival rates are way lower than they are with women."

"I have seen cancer on elephants."

"After Dad died, Mom fell off the deep end. Discovered Kaballah. Swore off personal intimacy. Gave away our money. It's a wonder Sarah and I didn't starve."

Rosemary picks up the ten Wheat Thins, then she shuffles them four times.

"Mom's off in Denmark now, raising vegetables, tending goats, and servicing the needs of her master. She's renounced her family — that's us."

Rosemary re-deals the crackers in her pattern, tapping each one twice as she sets it on the table. "I think that's why Sarah and I are so much closer than sisters from normal families." She quarter turns each Wheat Thin clockwise so there are no horizontal or vertical edges. Only diagonals. "Sarah had trouble sleeping there for a while, and I started laying out the crackers in a certain way. I told her it was an antennae and Dad could read our minds when we spread them out just so. He knew our thoughts while we ate the crackers. Knew if we brushed our teeth or put on dirty underwear. It's shameless what I did to get her to behave. Don't you think?"

Bing steps to the table, picks up the single Wheat Thin floating above the tree, and places it dead center, within the branches.

"It works better as a bird than a star."

Rosemary is shocked. Her pattern of over fifteen years is shot to hell. Bizarre as it sounds, she thinks her life will never be what it was. "I invented the mandala. How can you tell if it works or doesn't work?"

"You want dead people to hear your thoughts, put the piece there. The way you had it nobody knows what you're feeling."

Rosemary stares down at the new pattern. It does have symmetry. She always thought of the star cracker as her father's one-breasted soul, hovering over the sisters. Having him right down in the midst of the tree is more of a comfort. The first few years she practiced the ritual, it was a habit. Sometime in her teens she started to believe it brought stability and continuity, but she always knew she created the pattern randomly. It was like a bedtime prayer, what you say doesn't matter so long as you say the same words every night, giving yourself permission to sleep.

And now Bing tells her she's been doing it wrong. The mandala isn't random. How is she supposed to absorb that?

"Are you sure?" she asks.

"Yes. Then you dip them in tea from the outside in. That one first." He points to the cracker on top.

"I always ate from the bottom up."

"Try it the other way. You'll feel nicer.

Rosemary sips her tea.

CHAPTER FORTY-NINE

A woman child named Krystal Lee stands before Bing, staring at his head. Or maybe his nose, Bing isn't certain. Whatever she is staring at, she seems perplexed by the sight. Bing — in long pants and a tuck-in shirt from Target, and jellies — sits on what looks like an old-fashioned barber chair, the kind that twirls and can be cranked up and down to adjust height. Or course, Bing doesn't know it looks like an old-fashioned barber chair. Dr. Lori's always cut his hair with a pair of scissors designed for castrating lab rats. Because the chair spins and pumps up and down, Bing sees it as a toy.

"Be still." Krystal wears a green smock. She looks professional. "I can't work with you fidgeting."

"Good luck on that one," Rosemary says. Rosemary — in casual skinny jeans and a jersey — stands behind Bing, her fingers lightly resting on his shoulders as if to calm him down. She can see his face in the mirrors behind and to the sides of Krystal Lee. They are in what the TV people call the Green Room, which every TV station has even though most of them are not green. Rosemary doesn't know why Green Rooms aren't green, so she can't explain it to Bing.

"Hold the chair," Krystal Lee says to Rosemary. "I can't make him up if he keeps spinning."

Rosemary holds the chair steady. So far, Bing has behaved himself admirably, but Rosemary is so antsy her ears itch.

She says, "There's no call to be nervous, Bing."

He grins at her in the mirror. "I am not nervous."

Rosemary says, "Be yourself," as Bing pulls faces at himself in the mirror. He has amazing individual control of his eyebrows. She says, "Whatever that is."

Krystal Lee leans in to peer at Bing's forehead, actually his Third Eye, if you buy such things. Krystal is twenty-four, straight out of community college where she trained in theatrical make-up. She dreams of moving to Hollywood and doing Meryl Streep's eyes.

"What brand of moisturizer do you use?"

Rosemary snorts a giggle and Krystal Lee gives her a look. Bing is trying to see if he can open his mouth wide enough to engulf an imaginary cantaloupe.

"Bing isn't into moisturizer," Rosemary says.

Krystal Lee sighs. "I didn't think so." She picks a powder puff. "We can work with this."

"Thank you." Rosemary tries to make up for the inappropriate giggle. "I know he's a challenge and I appreciate you giving him your best."

"No need to lay it on too thick," Krystal Lee says. Rosemary isn't sure exactly which way she means that. Krystal Lee moves the puff to Bing's face. He jerks away.

She says, "What?"

Bing bares his incisors and growls.

"Listen, sweetie, this is my job."

"Do not touch my face."

"You can't go on camera without make-up. You'll look like a drowned corpse."

"Stay away."

"It's nothing personal." She moves back in for the puff.

"I can bite the hand off your arm."

Krystal Lee recoils. She bumps into the mirrors.

"What?"

Rosemary says, "He can."

Bing hums a little song.

CHAPTER FIFTY

Jazmine DuMont is slinky. Not precisely the quintessential daytime TV talk show host in a major market, but close. She's got the hair, the teeth, the blouse starched and pressed. Poised, confident, a hint flirtatious. The only thing off is her ears. They hang too low, as if she started wearing heavy danglers at an early age. Her ears are distracting. She also has the scratchy voice of a former high school cheerleader. Jazmine is proud of her voice in the way celebrities are proud of the facet that makes them less than perfect.

Bing slumps in a brown leather chair with his shoulders up at cheekbone level. In the lights, on camera, his skin looks just the way Krystal Lee said it would — drowned corpse. Or soggy cardboard. There are various ways to describe Bing's TV complexion and none are flattering.

The commercial of a local day spa ends and the audience claps for no reason that Bing can see. From her own leather chair that sits a tad higher than Bing's Jazmine flashes lips and teeth at the proper camera.

"I'm here today with Bing." She turns slightly toward Bing. "Do you have a last name, Bing?"

"Bing is the last name I have."

"What's your first name then?"

"Bing."

"Oh." She smiles back at the camera, as if giving her viewers a nudge with her eyes. "Like Madonna. Or Cher."

"I do not fathom those words."

"They're examples of women with only one name. So famous they don't need two."

Bing rocks slightly. He wishes he could see Rosemary. She must be able to see him, but bright lights are in his eyes. He is aware of people without being able to make them out properly. It is unpleasant.

Jazmine goes into her spiel. "Mr. Bing. Raised in the San Diego Zoo Safari Park. Able to perform miraculous feats of healing gun-shot wounds. Hailed on spiritual radio as the new Messiah. I could hardly get in the door when I came to work this morning for all your followers outside." She looks to Bing for comment, but doesn't get one. He's waiting for a question.

"Is there anything you can't do, Mr. Bing?"

Bing considers. He starts to speak, then stops. Then he starts again. "I cannot fly like a bird or swim like an eel."

The studio audience goes wild in response to an APPLAUSE sign that Bing can't see and couldn't read if he could see it. He has no idea why the people out beyond the lights are so thrilled with his answer.

Jazmine continues. "Before we get into your miracle and the whole Messiah legend, I'd like to hear about the zoo. I understand you were raised by bonobos, often called the missing link between chimpanzees and humans."

Bing pushes himself up with his hands until he is hovering two inches over the chair. "Chimpanzees are cruel and vicious. Like people. We cannot link two species if they are alike and we are not."

The audience claps. Bing nods.

Jazmine says, "So you are saying humans are cruel and vicious."

"Compared to my family, they are. Bonobos do not take money from each other. I have watched humans take money. I have seen humans throw electrical batteries at the cheetahs. Bonobos do not throw batteries at cheetahs."

Jazmine's legs are crossed and her right foot rocks up and down. Her toe is stuffed in her shoe, but her heel swings loose while the shoe heel hangs below her foot. Her shoes are red as a Coke can with three-inch heels. She keeps her feet off camera.

"Tell the truth, Bing. Do you think you are you an actual bonobo?"

Bing blinks. He views the question as stupid. Does he look like a bonobo? Does he smell like a bonobo? "My family is bonobo. My mother and brother. I am human, but they do not know that."

"Are you a virgin?"

Bing's face is a marble slab. A sheet of unused yellow legal pad. Rosemary told him not to answer questions he doesn't fathom, that silence makes the TV host nervous, so silence is power over personality.

The audience snickers, on cue.

Jazmine fills in the noise void. "Our research shows that bonobos are the most sexually active and diverse members of the animal kingdom. Homosexual, incest, oral, positions only found in the Kama Sutra — if you were raised by bonobos you must have been exposed to a wide variety of experience."

"Dr. Lori told me the wise boy does not touch genitals, nor is he touched in the genitals. I avoid that."

"And Dr. Lori is?"

"My second mother. She tells me the difference between what is right and what isn't."

With an edge of smirk, "And sex isn't?"

"Sex is correct at the proper time with the proper species."

Jazmine ignores the camera to look Bing full in the face. He sees that her long earlobes are changing colors, growing a deeper pink. The vein on her forehead pulses ever so slightly. "Then you are a virgin. How intriguing is that?"

Bing has never heard of a question that is not a question. He answers as honestly as he can. "I do not know how intriguing that is."

"The girls must be all over you."

Bing views this as another stupid question, if it is even a question at all. He falls back on a smile. Better silent than sorry.

Jazmine moves on to a new subject. "How does it feel to have people calling you the new Messiah?"

Bing wants to help. Instead, he says, "That depends on what happened to the old Messiah."

The audience laughs and applauds. Bing nods his head, wisely. Jazmine winks at him.

CHAPTER FIFTY-ONE

Back in the Green Room, Bing has turned his eyelids inside out and he is looking at himself in the mirror. He's familiar with mirrors, of course, but he's never sat on a bar stool in front of one with nothing to do and nothing to eat. He flips his lips from string to overinflated inner tubes and back. He tries to pull his lower lip over his nose, but fails. He can't do everything.

Between faces, Bing coos happily.

Krystal Lee sits on her own four-legged stool and stares at him. Nothing at San Diego Mesa Community College prepared her for Bing. Nothing in her background of MTV and reality cable prepared her for Bing.

"Can I bring you some water?" she asks.

Bing says, "Am I dirty?"

"To drink. I thought you might like a drink."

Bing drops his head into a 45-degree angle so Krystal Lee appears to be standing on the wall. "Water would be nice."

But before Krystal Lee gets his paper cup, the door flies open and Jazmine blows in. Her hair is down and her color is up. Her nostrils flare. She says, "Leave us alone, Krystal Lee."

Krystal Lee says, "Bing asked for water."

"He's not thirsty. Go."

Krystal Lee sends Bing a look that might convey pity. Then, she leaves. As the door clicks shut, Jazmine advances on Bing.

"You have fun on the show, Bing boy?"

Bing doesn't stand, but he does flick his eyelids back down. "It was an experience I never had at the wildlife park."

"No doubt it was."

"I enjoy new experiences. They stimulate inside my head."

Jazmine standing puts her chest at Bing's eye level. "You want something stimulating in your head, look at these," and she commences to pull off her starched and pressed blouse. Her bra is red frills.

"Do you like my breasts? I think they are nice. I had a breast reduction a few years ago and I've never regretted it."

She snaps off the red bra. Bing's eyes go circular.

"I was an ass double in Hollywood and I wanted more of myself on camera. You'd be amazed at the stars whose asses you've lusted for in the movies that are actually mine."

"I've never seen a movie."

"That's interesting." Jazmine plows on without breaking stride. "Even you would know the women whose dimples I've replaced. Some of the most desirable stars in the world I could name have cellulite like a Baggie full of wet sand. They had me sign a non-disclosure contract, or I could tell you stories would curl your pubes. Do you want to touch them?"

Bing says, "Me?"

"Who else am I talking to here?"

Shyly, Bing reaches out and touches the tip of his index finger to the tip of her nipple. Jazmine emits a tiny moan.

Bing says, "I thought it would be soft."

"Would you like to suckle my breasts, virgin child? I'll just bet they're nicer than the tits on that ape you call Mom."

"Betty's droop to the left."

"If you suckle me, I might suckle you. You'd love that. All my adult life I've wanted to break in a virgin. You know how hard it is to find a legal age virgin in California? Like searching for unicorns."

Bing has heard of unicorns. Dr. Lori told him they are mythical, impossible beasts. He wonders if virgins are mythical beasts and, if so, how it is that he became one.

"How often do you figure Tarzan and Jane did it?" Jazmine doesn't wait for an answer. "They never show squat in the movies, but come on. Apes raised him, for God's sake. How could he not be stiff as a tree under that leather thong thing?"

"George of the Jungle was raised by apes," Bing says. "Turk told me. He says there are more of us."

Jazmine's tits hover an inch from Bing's eyes — or to be precise, her left breast is an inch from his right eye. Her right breast is a bit off the edge from his left eye, in the peripheral vision. Still, her nipple and his eye — basically equal in diameter — front each other.

Jazmine reaches over to tousle his hair.

Bing says, "Don't touch my head."

"How about down there then. You think Dr. Lori would mind if I zipped your zipper? You think she'd approve of me as a species?"

She fumbles with his new pants. Since Bing is still seated on the stool, it's tricky. The mechanics take her attention off Bing and onto the zipper.

She says, "Some cooperation here."

That's the point where Rosemary enters. Neither Bing nor Jazmine hear the door, but they both hear her.

"There you are, Bing. I've been searching all over. How'd the TV gig go?"

Bing blinks in the face of the nipple. "It was a new experience."

Rosemary brushes past Jazmine's boobs as if they're cobwebs. She grabs Bing by the upper arm. "Show's over, Bing. Let's hit the road."

Jazmine pouts. She doesn't like being pushed to the side. "What are you, his zookeeper?"

Rosemary looks Jazmine in the eyes, as opposed to the other pair of orbs facing forward. "That's right. I protect Bing from predators."

As she leads Bing away, he looks back at topless Jazmine. Her arms are crossed, covering her nipples. Her eyes flash fire.

He says, "It was nice to meet you, Jazmine."

Chapter Fifty-Two

Various TV station employees who come off more as support staff than on air personalities loitering in the hallway part for Rosemary and Bing, almost but not quite pressing themselves against the walls. Imagine a pack of teenagers at the mall moving aside for a mumbling schizophrenic. No direct looks. No friendly nods or unfriendly obstacles. Just get out of the way and it will pass.

Rosemary notices the attitude. Bing doesn't. He walks on his toes, his jelly heels brushing the carpet. If a smile really can be an umbrella, Bing stays dry.

Rosemary says, "Are you okay, Bing? Did she frighten you?"

"The television woman exhibited outward signals of aggressive behavior."

Rosemary glances at Bing, whose head bobs with each step. She is never certain whether he knows more or less than he says. "The slut tried to jump your bones. God only knows what would have happened if I hadn't saved you."

"There's that word again. Everyone says it but no one tells me what it means."

"God?"

Bing stops to kick off the jellies. "Jazmine and I might have consummated sexually." He walks on down the hall, barefoot. "I've never consummated sexually. I have seen others often. Some days bonobos consummate all afternoon. They appear to enjoy themselves, and I think I too might enjoy myself, but Dr. Lori said I would writhe in pain if a being touched between my legs. She said I would

162

grow hives if I even touched myself between the legs except to make water. I did once without telling her."

"And did you grow hives?"

"A pimple, maybe. I never was sure."

Rosemary goes back for the jellies. Bing waits, patiently. Rosemary says, "Do you still believe Dr. Lori?"

"She said I would die if I left the zoo and yet I still live."

"And yet."

Bing cocks his head to the side. He likes the way this makes him look at things from a new angle. "I feel Dr. Lori was mistaken. When I first left the zoo I looked forward to behaving like an Outie, which meant constant consummation. Do you think I might have died, had we let the female jump my bones?"

Rosemary hands Bing his shoes. Their fingertips touch for a moment, spontaneous as a dream. "Not likely."

Bing doesn't put them on. "So what fate did you save me from?"

As they cut through the waiting room Rosemary pulls a banana from her bag. She peels it and hands it to Bing, who inserts the banana whole into his mouth. The receptionist drops her cell phone, the back pops off, and the battery slides under her desk.

Bing speaks through a mouth full of mush. "I might have had a treat."

Rosemary says, "Jazmine felt no emotional attachment for you. She wanted to use you for her amusement, like you are a freak in a circus. You don't want to evolve into a circus act."

"Would consummation with no emotional attachment constitute a negative outcome?"

"Sex is only mutually pleasing when it happens between two people who are in love."

The receptionist on her hands and knees groping under the desk snorts. Neither Rosemary nor Bing realizes the snort is meant for them.

Bing says, "I do not fathom *love.*"

"How is it you know *constitute* and *exhibited outward signals of aggressive behavior,* but not *love?*"

"I know only words Dr. Lori spoke?"

"And *God.* You don't fathom *God* either. You know all this biological gobbledygook but not *love* or *God.*"

"Gobbledygook?"

Rosemary holds the door open for Bing. "The more I hear about Dr. Lori the less I like her."

CHAPTER FIFTY-THREE

Bing walks out of the TV station directly into a melee. Right off, a kid in his late teens, maybe twenty — clunky glasses, shoes, and belt buckle — falls to his knees in Bing's path.

"Father, forgive me, for I have sinned."

Black guy — skinny as a fence post in a black velour jogging suit — cries out. "I sinned more than he has. Forgive me."

A third grade literary arts teacher from Mission Bay shouts, "I have early onset Alzheimer's. You are my only hope."

A full tilt cacophony of begging for forgiveness, miracles, and money bursts forth. Bing stops short; Rosemary walks into his back side.

She says, "Shit."

Bing says, "Why now?"

"I don't mean *shit* literally. It's a word people say when they've faced with unexpected crap."

"Crap?"

An older man who hasn't shaved in a week walks toward Bing, hands extended, Ping Pong ball eyes aimed at the sky. "Help me, prophet. Restore my sight." His hands clutch at Bing's face, which makes Bing go bonobo defensive — teeth bared, throat growling. The rest of the crowd sees the old blind man fondling Bing and they want a piece of him also.

Rosemary shouts, *"Leave him alone."*

Fat chance of that. There must be twenty of them, all desperate for what they think Bing can do. The litanies of pain and humiliation are too much even for Rosemary. Bing appears to have frozen up. Arms reach for him, grabbing, pushing. Men weep. Women mumble. The kid on his knees will soon be crushed.

Bing emits an ear splitter of a shriek that brings the mob to silence. Rosemary, who was next to him, fighting to protect him, takes a direct hit to the eardrum. In the white whine of after noise, she hears Bing speak.

"I am invisible!"

The kid on his knees says, "I can see you, master."

"No, you can't." Bing turns to the blind guy with his hands out. "Can you see me?"

"No, sir, I cannot."

"That proves it. I'm not present." The crowd backs off a step, understandably confused. Bing goes on. "I want all of you to accept that I am not visible even if you think you see the real me. You are seeing my shadow, not me, and my shadow cannot perform your tasks."

This draws a few disgruntled mutters but for the most part this crowd lacks cynicism. If a man tells them he is invisible, it must be true.

"I need you to act as if the real me went away a few minutes ago. You do not know where I am.

The black guy says, "Where are you then?"

"Somewhere else."

Rosemary says, "This won't work."

Bing doesn't answer Rosemary. He continues to speak to his followers. "I am going to leave now, with my friend, and you will ask yourselves where I have gone. That is my wish."

"Your wish is my divine order," says the kneeling clunky kid.

"Not my divine order," says the blind man.

"You cannot see me," Bing repeats. He motions for Rosemary to follow him and they pass through the crowd and on across the street toward her car.

CHAPTER FIFTY-FOUR

Rosemary says, "Why leave? Why not heal the whole bunch, one at a time?"

Bing seems distracted. All that touching from strangers has thrown him off balance, as if he actually is his own shadow. "They would not have reached satisfaction."

"I think the Alzheimer's woman would have been plenty satisfied with a good healing."

"Even if I grant them what they asked for, I can't give them what they want."

Rosemary stares into her Acai Super Antioxidant smoothie. Smoothies aren't meant for looking into and thinking things through like coffee, green tea, or all forms of alcohol. Smoothie contemplation takes place on the surface. "I like you better when you're eating bugs. The glowing love from your followers thing gives me the willies."

Bing slurps his smoothie — a Mega Mango. He also has a plate of limes on the side. They are in Jamba Juice, after leaving the TV station and the confusion of the street. Rosemary didn't want to go home quite yet, but she didn't want a bar or café either. Her needs were specific. Bright light, pastel colors. Cleanliness. Short of a Laundromat she knew about in Torrey Pines, Jamba Juice was the one place to fit the bill.

"I have heard young ones say *love*," Bing says, "In the animal park."

"So you do know what it means."

"They say it at the beginning of a longer word — *loveyou.*"

"I love you?"

Bing shakes his head. "When they speak on their phones and they want to do something else. They say *loveyou.*" Bing says it flat, quick with no inflection or emotion. "It means they want to stop using the phone. *Loveyou* means *goodbye.*"

"*Love you* doesn't mean *goodbye,*" she says. "That's just what kids say to dismiss their parents. *I love you* means almost the opposite of goodbye."

"Hello?"

"More like *let's be together.*"

Rosemary and Bing are the only customers sitting at the round, high tables. A jogger had come in for a shot of wheat grass, but he did his business and left. Otherwise, it is Rosemary and Bing and the staff who doesn't have any interest in Rosemary and Bing at 10:30 on a Monday morning.

"Love is when two people care deeply about what happens to each other," Rosemary says.

"Like you and Sarah or me and Betty."

The new name causes Rosemary a jolt of alarm. She didn't know of another woman in Bing's life. "Who is Betty?"

"My mother. She's a bonobo, not my birth mother. She protects me."

"Oh." Rosemary reaches across to wipe a smoothie mustache from Bing's upper lip. He lets her.

She says, "Those are family love, which is the most important kind, but we're talking about romantic love. That's when you care about someone you aren't related to, so there's no logical reason for caring. You just do. You want to touch them all over all the time."

Bing bites a lime in half, thinking about being touched all over. It might not be so bad if the toucher was Rosemary.

Rosemary says, "Romantic love is when the other person's happiness is more important than your own."

Bing inspects the remaining lime half. He turns it in his fingertips, admiring the shine on the flesh. "I care about what happens to you more than I care about what happens to me."

"No shit?" Rosemary studies Bing's face. She searches his eyes for the hidden meaning. People don't say stuff like that without hidden meanings, not in her life, but one thing Rosemary likes best about Bing is the lack of disguised motives. He means the words he says. A boy raised by apes does not have an innate sense of irony. That strikes Rosemary as an amazing scientific discovery.

Bing says, "I care about you, personally. Not just as the pretty girl with nice hair who took me from the zoo. I cared about you from the minute I saw you burn the letter."

"You were there?"

Bing nods.

The letter was from her mother at the religious group farm in Denmark. Rosemary would rather not think about her mother, just now, so when Bing doesn't push for an explanation, she doesn't give one.

Instead, Rosemary says, "Me too. I care about you, Bing. I don't want you to be unhappy."

"Is that the same as wanting me to be happy?"

Rosemary thinks, then she decides. "That is what I want."

Bing swallows. His Adam's apple visibly rises up, then down. "Love is us. You and me."

Rosemary stares at Bing a long while. He tries to stare back but can't match her intensity. He wants to. Since leaving the zoo he has discovered humans put emphasis on the mutual line of sight. They take it as an outward sign of something inside that matters.

To Bing, Rosemary's mind seems to be whirring. He imagines he can hear it going round and round, although there's a chance he might be hearing a refrigeration unit back where the juices are made.

Finally, Rosemary says, "Like us."

CHAPTER FIFTY-FIVE

Rosemary pulls the Jetta up against the curb on the Monday side of the street, which is the side opposite her place. The Jetta is black; the curb is concrete. The sky, as usual in the San Diego metroplex, is off-blue.

She gets out, locks her door, and walks across the street toward her small home house before she realizes Bing isn't at her side. Bing is still in the car. She goes back and opens the passenger door to find Bing bent forward peering into glove compartment.

She says, "Bing?"

He says, "What?"

"That's what I was going to say. What?"

Bing looks from the glove compartment to her. "This cave is different now that we are love."

She looks past him into the glove box. Looks the same to her. "How so?"

"Whatever I see has changed. Things I knew what they were, I don't know anymore."

Rosemary studies Bing. He seems dead serious. "Don't analyze the deal to death, Bing. Time to go inside."

"That's proper."

He gets out and they cross the street, holding hands. Bing has never walked, holding hands with the fingers intertwined before. It's different from when she led him out of the zoo, grasping his hand by the palm. He isn't certain of the significance. There must be significance. What he can tell is that it feels okay.

At the front door, Rosemary releases his hand to fish for her key. She sticks the key in the lock and says, "Are you ready, Bing?"

"Yes, I am ready," he says. Then, "What am I ready for?"

"To go inside."

"Okay. I am ready to go inside."

Inside, Rosemary crosses to the kitchen bar to drop her keys into a small ceramic bowl kept there for the very reason of holding keys. She kicks off her sandals.

Bing stands just inside the doorway, watching.

Rosemary walks back to him, drapes her arms across his shoulders, and pulls him into a kiss.

Bing is floored. He's seen couples press their faces together at the zoo, sometimes for as long as they could possibly hold breath in their lungs, although usually it's shorter. He's tried to imagine what they are doing and how it feels, but the reality is nothing of a sort what he imagined. He imagined pushing his mouth against a slightly bald tire hanging in the enclosure. Rosemary's lips are different. Soft and firm at the same time. They taste Tic Tac sweet. They seem to pull him in to her, not as if swallowing him or even sucking his face into hers, but more of a melting into one another sensation. She absorbs him.

That's when Rosemary puts her tongue into play.

Bing is lost, nauseous, elated, tingly, afire, and coming out of his skin, more or less in that order. After what feels like a week but probably is only a half minute, Rosemary draws her face back away from Bing. Her green eyes cast a challenge straight into his.

Bing says, "I do not know what is expected."

Rosemary cups his face in her hands. "This is the part where we copulate."

Chapter Fifty-Six

First, a scuttling sound, like mice in the trash, or as if paper bags are brushing together. Then a *coo* followed by air movement in, then out of lungs under stress. The *coo* volume increases, more guttural as it passes from mouth to throat to chest to gut and on below.

An odor wafts. Sweat in a dry sauna, only sweeter, as if someone has thrown sage on the heating element. Not an unpleasant smell or even a strong smell. In light we might not even be aware of it, but in darkness when senses expand we smell this sagey sweet sweat.

The *coos* rise to *glottal grunts*. Speak the word — *glottal*. These are not grunts picked up in urban decay but sub-Saharan sounds and below the jungle snorts we hear gasping, holding-onto-yourself breathing, and a rhythmical whisper of *Yes, yes,* then again *yes.*

The air pulses and blows like a fan set on High, but this is no fan only a clapping. The sound of one hand clapping. A *squeal*. Loud. Insistent. The *squeal* grows and grows and grows layered over a *howl* building up and up until the darkness is torn by an all-out SCREAM OF RELEASE.

Darkness again. Silence, only now we think we can make out a hiss of exhalation followed by inhalation.

Then, Rosemary: "Bing."

More silence.

"Bing? Are you there?"

CHAPTER FIFTY-SEVEN

Fireworks and a national holiday would have been appropriate in light of the way Bing feels, but there are no fireworks. No day off with pay for a grateful nation. Instead, Bing has triggered a worldwide internet frenzy. For centuries mankind has searched for proof of the impossible and here it is — presto — on YouTube for all to see and marvel at.

Of course, a sizeable portion of the population doesn't believe. They claim fakery or scientific explanation. The cynics stew in the juices of denial. Conversely, the believers believe too well. If Bing can heal, he must know secrets. He must be wise. He must be able to heal anyone. He is the genie. He is Lord.

Bing isn't aware of any of this. All he knows is he and Rosemary copulated and it was fine.

Friday finds him in Turk's mammoth office where Rosemary dropped him off while she works in her cubicle down the hall. She said Turk wanted to get to know Bing, but, so far, Turk has been on the land line telephone while Bing plays a game on an iPad connected to a flat screen TV wide as Rosemary's bed.

Bing is playing a game Rosemary found on Nick.com. The game is an electronic version of what used to be called paper dolls. A bald girl in her underwear stands on the screen while the game player mix and matches from a near-endless supply of hair colors and styles, clothes, shoes, accessories, the works.

Bing loves it. He gives the girl short black hair with long earrings, then long straight hair parted in the middle around cat eye glasses. He tries a two-piece bathing suit followed by a ski bunny outfit. Then he moves on to nail polish.

Turk idly watches Bing play as he gives someone on the other end of his phone grief. "We don't perform miracles for under ten million, plus agent fees, plus lawyer. Non-negotiable. Bottom line. End of day."

Turk's feet are propped on an aircraft carrier of a desk. Besides the desk, three chairs — one behind the desk and two facing it — and the flat screen TV, there is also a high tech espresso machine from Italy and a free-standing mirror from Turk's grandfather who financed Centered Soul Network.

Turk studies Bing while Bing giggles to himself. It's hard to call Bing anything but smug.

Turk says, "If I didn't know you, Bing, old sport, I'd say you're getting laid."

Bing glances from his game to Turk and grins. *Laid,* in this context, is beyond him.

"I just got off with Oxygen. They want you on a reality series."

Bing returns to the game. He's on shoes — cowboy boots, ballet slippers, he can't find jellies.

"There's this show where they find some poor out-of-work loser with autistic kids and a wife in a wheelchair and they build him a house. As if that will make it all better."

"I have no need for a house," Bing says.

Turk rises and walks to the tinted glass wall. He looks down on the gathered mass of sick and searching people who wait for Bing to save them. A few have sleeping bags. One guy is selling Bing Bonobo t-shirts.

"Oxygen wants to run through four sob stories and the home audience votes on which one you should heal. You cure the most pitiful contestant and the others get lovely parting gifts."

Bing settles on slightly used penny-colored hair, somewhat long. "When I help someone, it does not always help."

"I doubt that. You wouldn't have tried to save the gangbanger if there'd been much chance of failure. His home boys or whatever they're calling themselves these days would have carved you into strips."

Bing shrugs. He chooses green eyes.

Turk says, "Anyway, no one would believe Oxygen didn't rig the deal. For a real miracle to convince, it can't be done in the studio."

Bing goes back to shirts and skirts. Whatever Turk is talking about is outside of food or Rosemary, so he is not interested enough to follow it closely. Turk leaves the window and comes over to stand behind Bing where he can see both Bing's thumbs on the iPad and the paper doll on the flat screen.

"Bing, son, the time has come for another miracle. Your hits are flagging. We need something big and public. Something that can't possibly be faked."

Bing tilts his head so he's looking up and back at Turk. His primary view is of nostrils. "Why call me *son*? Are you my father?"

Turk hasn't thought along those lines, but it can't hurt. "I am your spiritual father. You are the new Messiah and I guide you by word and deed. You may call me *Father* if you wish."

Bing sighs. He doesn't know exactly what *spiritual* means, although he's closer than he was a week ago, but he does know *spiritual father* isn't the same as *father*.

"I would enjoy knowing my father."

"That's me," Turk says. "And I'm the man to make you famous beyond your wildest dreams."

"I do not dream of famous."

Turk frowns. This isn't within the norms of his value system. "Everyone wants to be famous. You were in that zoo too long. You got your values turned upside down."

Bing puts a yellow sundress on the girl.

Turk says, "We're going to have you heal Rosemary's sister. That should raise your profile."

"My profile is high enough, I think."

Turk tries another angle. "Saving the sister will make Rosemary happy. You want Rosemary happy, right?"

"That is correct. Rosemary's happiness must be placed before my own."

"Right." Turk isn't certain where that came from. "We'll do it in Balboa Park, with a media circus bigger than the O.J. trial."

Bing gives her sandals. "Rosemary doesn't want me to evolve into a circus act. She said so."

"Rosemary talks too much. We need to put a muzzle on that."

"She is my friend."

"But I'm your father. I'm the one you listen to."

Bing gives the paper doll girl's hair a permanent. She is the image of Rosemary the day he spotted her from the acacia tree.

Bing says, "I win."

CHAPTER FIFTY-EIGHT

Rosemary is driving. This being San Diego, there's going to be driving in any story set here. Rosemary is driving back to the Rose of Sharon Extended Care facility and Bing is hand surfing out the passenger window. Not that he's ever seen a surfer. Bing hasn't seen an ocean. He's spent his life within thirty miles of the Pacific but he has yet to see it.

Bing holds his right hand out, parallel to the highway. He tilts the thumb side up and the wind blows his hand up. He tilts the pinkie side up and the wind blows his hand down. Flipping back and forth is fun and it's even more fun when he makes a *bloop bloop* sound as accompaniment.

Rosemary turns off the freeway onto an access road with stoplights and the game ends. Not enough wind.

Bing says, "Phooey," which is what Dr. Lori would say if a monkey pooped during an examination.

Rosemary flicks her turquoise blue lighter and fires up a Kent 100. Bing pretends to gag.

"It's my car, Bing. I can smoke in my own car."

He coughs to the point where hacking up a piece of lung is a possibility.

She says, "*Shit,*" and stubs out the cigarette. Bing smiles. They pass a pet mortuary next to a Coffee Bean. Ralph's Grocery. A hot dog stand that looks like a hot dog. Legal Limit Tanning and Massage (PARKING IN REAR).

Rosemary says, "So what did you and Turk find to talk about?"

"He wants another miracle."

"I knew that would come up soon."

"He said I should fix Sarah."

Rosemary glances over at Bing who is biting the plastic off a huge pickle they bought at Trader Joe's. This pickle is big as a bread loaf. "What did you say?"

"I didn't say." Bing sucks juice from the pickle. It makes his nose wrinkle.

"Do you think you can make Sarah well?"

Bing nibbles the tip. It's not like fruit he is accustomed to. He is filled with suspicion. "Turk says I can. He's certain beyond doubt, but I don't know. She doesn't seem to need fixing."

"Sarah is in terrible pain, Bing. Listen to me. She needs fixing and if you can do it, you should fix her. It's right."

Bing takes a bigger bite. "Turk said I should not listen when you talk. You need a muzzle and I should listen to him." Pickle juice runs down Bing's chin and drips onto his shirt. "I don't fathom *muzzle.*"

"It's a cup they strap on a dog's mouth to keep it from biting."

"You don't bite. I bite."

At a stoplight, Rosemary holds a dollar bill out the window so a dirty man in shorts and a sleeveless army shirt with a sign Bing can't read can take it. He says, "God bless."

Rosemary says, "Yeah, right." She rolls her window back up quickly. "Did Turk say why you should listen to him and not me?"

"He said he is my father."

The light changes and Rosemary turns off the boulevard onto the side street that leads to the Rose of Sharon circular drive, but instead of going on to the extended stay facility she pulls into a parallel parking slot. Bing can see the intersection beggar watching them, wondering why they stopped.

Rosemary shifts around so she is almost facing Bing. "Turk told you he's your father, as in he's the one who impregnated your mother? You know what impregnated means?"

Bing nods. "Impregnated happens often at the zoo. It's all the animals have to do."

"And?"

"Turk says he's my spiritual father. Spiritual father doesn't need impregnated mothers, I think. Spiritual father means *boss.*"

Rosemary starts the car again and pulls back into the street. She drums her long fingers on the steering wheel. "Turk Palisades is a teacher. A wise man, a mystic, hell, he's a genius. But he cares first about his network and second about his network. Do you understand?"

Bing throws the pickle out the window. This isn't what he wants when he wants food. He says, "It's love. He cares about the happiness of Centered Soul instead of human people."

"That is correct. Turk will use you and me both if it helps the ratings. Ratings mean more than people."

"He thinks more of ratings than Sarah?"

"You got it."

Bing looks down at the pickle stain — which is shaped like the Virgin Mary — on his shirt, although that is not really what he's looking at. He's trying to figure out Outies. "How does this make him wise?"

Rosemary thinks. She never looked at it quite that way before. Would Jesus or Bill Clinton or Curt Cobain or any man she admires put popularity over the personal relationship? Probably. World savers tend to be lousy family members.

Rosemary says, "Just don't let him make a clown out of you. You are a person, not entertainment."

"Some days we have clowns at the zoo, in the Safari Base Camp."

"You are out of the zoo now." Rosemary pats his leg. "How about if I do some research? Maybe we can figure out who your birth parents are."

Bing wipes his juicy hands on her wrist on his leg. "That would be interesting."

She pulls up to the Rose of Sharon verandah. "You're okay here while I go back to work?"

Bing unfastens his seat belt. It is his newest skill for dealing with the outside world. "I like Sarah. She reminds me of my mother."

Rosemary has no idea how to take that. "Now I am confused."

"My mother at the Park. Betty." Bing opens his door and gets out.

Rosemary says, "Sarah is like a female bonobo?"

Bing leans down to look across the seat at Rosemary. He nods. "Bonobos are more alive than humans. Sarah is not like other humans. Neither are you."

"I'll have to think about that one."

CHAPTER FIFTY-NINE

Rosemary's Centered Soul cubicle is the same size as the other cubicles in the building because the free-standing eight-foot high walls bought in bulk from Home Depot are all standard length. Each cubicle is a square — an actual cube — and the walls are covered by a dark green material, mostly cotton with some Dacron thrown in for texture. Rosemary's walls are dominated by large twelve-month calendars. Really large. Many of the day boxes have writing in them. Today's date reads: CAT WHISPERER. CLEOPATRA. This indicates to Rosemary that the two guests she is in charge of producing today are a cat whisperer and a woman who used to be Cleopatra. The word CLEOPATRA shows up five or six times a year on Rosemary's calendar. It's the second most popular reincarnation, after Elvis Presley.

What makes Rosemary's cubicle unique compared to other nearby cubicles is not its size or the texture of its walls, it's the window. One wall is actual, permanent, and midway across this wall is an inset window overlooking the employee parking lot, which isn't great shakes as a view, but what makes it great shakes is that it lets in natural sunlight. That window has been the object of much inner-office intrigue over the years. It causes rampant envy among the spiritual workers who gossip that you have to sleep with Turk to get it. To Rosemary, the window is worth suffering through the jealousy. She loves her window.

There are three photos of Sarah on the desk next to Rosemary's computer: a close-up of her face, a hugging a Scottish terrier shot, and a drinking Dos Equis photo in which Sarah's arm is draped over an obviously soused Rosemary.

Rosemary nips and tucks from web site to web site, writing down pertinent information in a notebook, the paper kind, not a small computer. Every so often she leans back in her chair and tugs at her right earlobe in silent contemplation. After a half hour of this, she leans forward to peer into the computer screen. She breathes out. "*Jesus.*"

Mitchell fills the open doorway. There is no door, only a doorway. Turk doesn't encourage closed doors.

Rosemary says, "What?"

Mitchell comes into her cubicle. In his yoked shirt and cowboy hat, he's too big for cubicle proportions. When Mitchell is in a room, there isn't much space left over for air. This time, it's not only Mitchell. His ham-sized hand is wrapped around the upper arm of a tall woman in green Army pants and a shapeless white turtleneck. Her hair is cut-short gray. She wears glasses hanging from a chain around her neck. She has a tan you rarely see outside the California desert or Arizona.

"This woman's been roaming the halls," Mitchell says. "Says she is looking for you."

Rosemary and the woman stare at one another in distaste. At least, the woman stares with distaste. Rosemary stares with curiosity that intends to turn to distaste as soon as possible.

Rosemary says, "I'm assuming you are Dr. Lori."

The tall woman blinks, once.

Mitchell says, "Should I remove her from the building?"

Rosemary glances down at the website on her screen, as if confirming information. "That's okay, Mitchell. Let her stay."

Mitchell doesn't want to leave. "The Bing disciples have been sneaking in all day. I caught one pretending to deliver a pizza to Turk's office. Pepperoni."

"Turk would starve before eating pepperoni."

"That's how I knew the guy was fake."

Dr. Lori shows no interest in this exchange. She's not impatient. She's not amused. About all you can call her is haughty.

Rosemary says, "Dr. Lori and I have things we need to discuss."

Mitchell releases his hold on Dr. Lori's arm. "Call out if she turns whack job on you. I'm close by."

"Thank you, Mitchell."

Mitchell huffs off and the old woman and young woman observe a period of silence, as if waiting to make certain he isn't hovering before ripping into each other. Or perhaps it's that span of silent measuring before an Old West gunfight.

Rosemary breaks the impasse. She nods at her computer screen. "There's no Dr. Lori working with primates at the San Diego Zoo Safari. No Dr. Lori anywhere out there. I've got a first name Laurie in concessions and two Lauras in the ticket booths. A Larry the clown in the Frequent Flyer Bird Show, but no Dr. Lori."

Dr. Lori advances into the room, her eyes behind the glasses on scan, checking out the calendars, taking note of the Sarah photos.

"Everything you've ever told Bing is a lie," Rosemary says. "Even your name. You knew he would talk someday and you covered your butt."

"Where is my boy?"

Rosemary puts her computer to Sleep. "He's with my sister." She nods toward the photos. "They take care of each other while I'm here."

"I had hoped to speak to you anyway." Dr. Lori moves over to the desk and stands towering over Rosemary. The desk faces a moveable wall, as desks tend to do in cubicles, with the window on her left, and Rosemary has no second chair to offer. She realizes Dr. Lori intends to intimidate from on high. There's not much Rosemary can do but arch her neck backward and look up.

"And I've been looking forward to talking to you. Tell me, Dr. Lori." She puts a touch of smirk on the words *Dr. Lori*. "How did you come to take possession of Bing?"

"That is none of your business."

"Fair enough."

"He was hidden in a crate from Zaire, in with a female bonobo and her offspring." Dr. Lori's nostrils quiver as she stares down at Rosemary. "The box contained a note: *The baby's name is Bing.*"

Rosemary absorbs this. It's fairly close to her wildest theory, although the details are too strange to actually buy. "And you didn't report this to anyone?"

Dr. Lori turns and walks the two steps to the window. She stares blank-eyed out at the employee parking lot. "There was no point."

Rosemary is extremely glad Dr. Lori moved out of her personal space. The staring up at nostrils thing was hard to maintain, but looking away would have been a sign of failure.

"Most people would not see it as pointless," Rosemary says. "Most people who find a baby tell someone."

"I'm not most people."

"Did you research the crate? You must have known who sent it, couldn't you ask why they dropped a child inside?"

Dr. Lori turns from the window, her arms held tightly across her basically breastless chest. "Mobuto's army was slaughtering all the whites south of Congo River. I believe his parents put Bing in the box before they died."

"You believe?"

Dr. Lori shrugs.

Rosemary says, "Bing was wondering who his birth mother might be one night recently. He didn't mention the slaughter part of the story."

"He doesn't know. What good could come of him finding out his parents were killed?"

Rosemary stares at Dr. Lori. Her hair is cut like a wrestler Rosemary dated in high school. A total control freak, she really hated that guy.

Dr. Lori takes her glasses off and lets them drop on her chain. "I want you to send him back to me."

"Send him back? Like a dress that makes me look fat?"

A black cloud appears to settle on Dr. Lori's already too-tan face. She looks capable of violence. "This is a game to you, but you'll destroy Bing and then go about your merry way without a trace of guilt."

"I'm taking care of Bing."

"He's a child. He will always be a child. Are you prepared to take care of his needs for his entire life?"

Rosemary would love to stand in righteous anger, but there isn't room in the cubicle, not without risk of contact. "He's a child because you kept him a child. There's nothing wrong with Bing's brain or body. You forced him to remain the way he is, so he would need you."

"You have no idea what you are talking about."

"So tell me. Tell me why Bing knows more about genetics than I do, but he can't read. Why he's never heard words like *love* and *God*. Explain to me why it's for Bing's own welfare to keep him locked in a zoo."

Dr. Lori starts forward, then she turns back to look out the window again. She sees a white dog peeing on the back tire of a pickup truck. She sees two of Bing's disciples smoking a crack pipe. She speaks without looking at Rosemary.

"Have you ever seen an exhibit animal turned loose? Of course you haven't, but maybe you've read about it. Every so often some well-meaning idiot opens a cage."

Dr. Lori makes her voice go pitiful. "*Wild animals must be wild. We must rescue the tigers and gorillas.*"

She spins to glare at Rosemary. "Most stay put, but the animals who escape have a life expectancy in hours. Not days."

Rosemary runs through any number of comebacks she could say or should say, starting with, "If every parent felt like you they'd handcuff their kids to their beds," and going on to more forceful yet biting comments. She doesn't say any of the things she could say. Rosemary instinctively knows that biting sarcasm bounces off this woman.

"Bing is not an animal," Rosemary says. "He's human."

Dr. Lori uncrosses her arms. Something other than barely controlled fury shines in her eyes. It's almost as if she is pleading.

"Bing is a precious child, with gifts you cannot fathom. Living outside will destroy all that is good and pure in the boy."

She steps toward Rosemary who recoils. "You care about him," Dr. Lori says. "I can tell. I trust you care about him enough you don't want to see his life ruined."

Rosemary holds her hands in her lap. She lifts her chin just a bit, and says, "I'm not ruining Bing. I'm setting him free."

Chapter Sixty

Sarah lies in an antiseptic hospital bed with the guardrail up on her left side so she won't roll out in her sleep. The rail is down on the other side. Maybe no one thinks she'll roll right. It would be difficult on account of the IV tether running from her left arm to bags of saline solution and morphine drip, so if she rolled right she'd have to tear out the IV needle taped to her wrist.

Her bed machinery is set so her head is up, in theory so she can eat her tray lunch. The reality is that between the pain and the morphine, Salisbury steak is the last substance in the world Sarah wants in her body.

Bing leans in over the bed to study her face from extremely close up. "Your eyes are not how eyes ought to be."

Sarah picks up a hand mirror from the bedside swing-in table, next to her untouched tray. They keep the mirror nearby to encourage her to take pride in her looks. The head of the facility once wrote an article for an extended care magazine that connected pride in appearance with not giving up.

When Sarah views herself in the mirror, she sees pale, dry skin with flake splotches. She sees cheekbones that weren't visible a year ago.

Her voice is so soft Bing has to lean forward to hear. "What's odd about my eyes?"

"The black hole in the center there. Dark makes it big and light makes it little, but your hole is tiny small. It should only be that small if you're looking at the sun."

She sees what he means. "It's the medicine. I don't understand why, but morphine makes your eyes think you are staring into the light."

Bing draws his face to within an inch of Sarah's eyes. He first studies the right, then the left eye. He notes that the whites are boiled egg white white. Between the black pinprick hole and the whites, her eyes are blue, as opposed to Rosemary's green. He's always thought birth sisters should have eyes that match.

"Dr. Lori gave morphine to a lemur after another lemur tore out his testicles and he hurt."

Sarah almost smiles. "I don't have testicles, but I can only think that if I had them and someone tore them out, it would hurt."

Bing tries to imagine what torn out testicles would feel like. He imagines it would be uncomfortable. "The lemur died." He settles back into the guest chair and points to a monkey dish holding three forlorn peach slices floating in lukewarm fluid. "May I eat this please?"

"Knock yourself out."

"I don't –"

"Go right ahead."

As he slurps peaches Bing looks at Sarah who seems to be looking inside herself. Just like on the porch, she is still the most remarkably pleasant to look at person he has ever seen, including Rosemary who is also remarkably pleasant to look at but in a more active way. Looking at Rosemary makes him want to lick behind her ears. Looking at Sarah makes him want to look at Sarah longer.

Bing says, "Rosemary told me you sometimes forget where you are."

Sarah rubs her nose. Itchy skin, dry mouth, pinprick eyes — she hasn't been here but a few times, but it only takes once to know what to expect. "I find that nice, sometimes, not knowing where I am. I'd rather be somewhere else than here even if I don't know where the somewhere else is. It's like going on vacation." She nods a bit. "Do you ever have times you'd like to forget where you are?"

"Sometimes," Bing says, although at the moment he can't recall a time like that. "I usually know where I am. I haven't been enough different places to forget them. Mostly just the zoo and Rosemary's house."

"How is my sister?" Sarah asks. "Rosemary fakes cheerful when she comes to visit. She thinks she has to be strong or I'll collapse in a heap, so I don't know how she truly feels."

Bing tips the monkey dish to suck down the sticky fluid. "The slut jumped my bones."

Sarah — who wasn't actually paying close attention to the conversation, due to brain slog and concentration on her insides — catches on to what Bing is saying. She makes the mental leap that the boy heard the word *slut* somewhere but he doesn't know the insinuation. Same with *jumped bones*. Bottom line, though, is this guy is sleeping with her sister.

"Good for her," Sarah says. "Good for you too."

Sarah watches Bing at an angle, as if she knows things about him that he doesn't know and she finds those things humorous. It makes Bing self-conscious, which isn't a state of being he recognizes.

"Her boss the great man wants me to heal you. He said it will raise our profile."

"What does that mean?"

Bing shrugs the way bonobos shrug — with his entire body. "It has to do with famous."

Given the situation, Sarah would rather float away, but Bing is igniting hope and hope is something she needs to pay attention to. "Are we going to cooperate with this? You told me before you didn't think you could cure me."

"Turk says I can, and he's a genius with vision." He picks up the mirror and spins the handle between his palms, causing a strobe-like reflection. "What do you think?"

Sarah motions toward the IV bag. "Whatever happens has to be better than being tied to that."

Bing stops the twirling mirror and studies his lips. Being raised with bonobos, Bing has always found his lips lacking expression. He makes a kissing shape.

Sarah says, "Bing?"

"Sarah, what's a messiah?"

She wants to follow his thought process, but it isn't straightforward and she needs straightforward. "A wise man. A healer and savior. It's religious."

"I don't fathom *religious* but Rosemary wants me to make you better. She told me the day she took me from the zoo. We are love now. Her happiness is what matters."

Bing sits in his chair and Sarah lies on her bed in silence for a while, each thinking their own thoughts and wondering what the other is thinking. Sarah can't tell if Bing is thinking about the implications of being a messiah or he's simply admiring his lips. He thinks she might be asleep with her eyelids half closed and half open.

Bing says, "I think Rosemary is love with you. She cares that you are happy more than herself. I am love for her." He drifts off.

Sarah says, "And?"

"Rosemary comes before me for me and you come before Rosemary for her, so what matters is what you want. Not Turk or Rosemary. You."

"I have no clue what you just said."

"If I help you feel less hurt, it would be good. Yes?"

"I would do anything to feel less hurt."

Bing stops playing with his face. "Anything there is?"

Sarah nods and this time it's a *yes* nod and not a nodding out of reality nod. Even Bing can tell the difference.

"I did not know you want this so much."

Sarah reaches her hand with the IV in the vein across to touch Bing on his wrist. "Pain is no fun at all, Bing. None."

Bing stares at her. She stares back. A world of communication flows between them. It would be awkward if she wasn't stoned and he was more than two weeks from living with apes. As it is, they both understand.

"We'll do what Turk and Rosemary want," Bing says.

She watches him closely. Even though he is in soft focus, she knows what he is thinking and what it means to her.

Bing says, "I'll be famous for them. You won't hurt."

CHAPTER SIXTY-ONE

The miracle is set for next Saturday. Tuesday, Rosemary takes Bing to a movie — *Harry Potter and the Half Blood Prince*. Bing has more experience with Impossible Shit than special effects, so, naturally, he believes it's all real and he makes such a racket they are escorted from the theater before Harry finds out whether or not Draco Malfoy is a death eater but not before Bing discovers popcorn.

Wednesday, Bing borrows Rosemary's Jetta keys without permission. He has observed closely, so is able to stick the key in the ignition and he does know how to put the car in gear, and he knows at least the theory behind steering. What he hasn't observed is Rosemary's feet as she drives. The accelerator and brake are unknown elements, which is why Bing tops out at two miles an hour before he high centers on a lilac bush.

Thursday, they go shopping at the mall. Bing drinks from the reflecting pool. His followers spot him and two hundred people follow Rosemary and Bing into Nordstrom's. Bing bites a paparazzi. Later, he eats his first plate of nachos and the onslaught of grease on his system culminates in vomit at the height of a romantic moment with Rosemary.

Friday night, Sarah goes for a walk.

CHAPTER SIXTY-TWO

George Levinson, C.P.A., battles his lungs. He concentrates on his abdomen because he's been told raising your abdomen will bring in more oxygen than raising your chest. He sucks air and counts — *one, two three* — then he exhales — *one, two, three.*

George is dying. He's known this since yesterday when his wife Anita brought toiletries and an overnight case of clothes to the hospital. She's in for the duration. Right now, Anita sleeps next to his bed in a hospital chair so uncomfortable it must have been designed as punishment for loved ones.

George it trying to memorize Anita as he counts each breath. She's lost weight. Her collarbones are bookends. Her hair is flat. George and Anita have been together fifty-two years, yet she won't tell him he's dying. She won't call hospice. His fear is that caretaking him might finish her. Her heart isn't up to living on coffee and sleeping in a chair. He should die and let her get some decent sleep, but his other fear is death.

Blackness and forever nothingness. To George, people who aren't terrified by death haven't put any thought into the matter. Every tortured inhalation beats the alternative of disappearing into the blank room.

Outside his window the horizon behind the avocado field shows a line of light. He's survived one more night. George doesn't want to die at night. He doesn't want to die. A finch lands on the feeder Anita keeps stocked outside George's window. George blinks, watching the bird twitch at the seed. He loses focus on breathing and his chest throbs, then he sucks air with a rasp of the tubes that dip into each nostril.

Without knowing how he knows, George is aware someone else is in the room, someone other than Anita. With effort, he turns his head from the window to the door where he sees a beautiful young woman — white hair, white nightgown, blue eyes, soft mouth. She is at peace, looking at him.

George's voice is raw. "You an angel?"

Sarah smiles. "Yes."

"You here to take me?"

She tilts her head a touch to the side. "Not now. Soon."

George blinks rapidly, processing. He always wanted to believe, but no matter how hard he tried, he couldn't. But, now, with her standing before him – "Will it hurt?"

"Of course not." Her voice is what he always imagined an angel's voice would be. "You will feel better than ever before. You will have no pain, and you will breathe without effort."

"Will I know who I am? Where I am?" This matters to George. He's read about belief systems where you go on but you don't remember your life or what you did or who you loved, which, to George, seems an awfully lot like not going on at all.

"Yes, silly. You will still be you after you are no longer pinned to your body. You'll just feel good."

"I don't understand how that can be."

Sarah lifts her hand, as if bestowing her blessing. "The only thing to understand is this: There is nothing to be afraid of. That is what you need to know now. Nothing to fear."

George feels the terror lifting, like a wet, heavy net rising from his body. He can accept this. "What is it like, on the far side?"

Sarah seems to be listening to someone outside the room. After a long moment, she says, "Do you recall the dog you loved, as a child?

"Toby?"

"Toby is waiting. He will be just as happy to see you now as he was when you came home from school."

George pictures the dog he hasn't thought of in years. Toby was Australian shepherd and whenever George returned from anywhere, even if he was only gone five minutes, Toby would explode with joy.

Sarah goes on. "You will be fine. The change is easier when you aren't frightened. It'll be like slipping into a warm bath."

"Okay." George glances at his sleeping wife, then back to Sarah. "I'm ready."

She gives her head a small shake. "Not now."

"When?"

"Later today, after you have said goodbye." She leans toward Anita. "Don't change without telling her you are content. That you love her. That she is not to blame."

"Not to blame." George draws a breath. *One-two-three-four.* He nods again, slowly. "It'll be good to see Toby."

Sarah slips away.

CHAPTER SIXTY-THREE

The day arrives.

Bing curls fetal in darkness. A true darkness without form. None of this various shades of black you find on moonless nights on the savannah at the Safari Zoo. This is a darkness your eyes will never grow accustomed to. In darkness, Bing nests on and under warm, wooly material. Like being untethered in space, he feels buried in softness and he trembles with fear.

He moans. He would wonder what he ever did to reach this place, but that was earlier, now he has moved beyond thought to white emotion.

From far away, he hears a voice. "Bing?"

It is Rosemary, calling him. "Bing, where are you?"

Bing curls deeper into himself. He holds his breath, no moaning now.

"I need you, Bing."

Part of Bing, the part past memory, feels the way he did in the box with Betty and his brother on the long trip from Africa. It's the dark, soft odor of being inside the warmth of breathing fur.

"Bing." The closet door opens, flooding the pile of dirty and clean clothes with light. Rosemary can see Bing's bare foot, peeking out from under her sweats. She says, "It's time to get ready."

She reaches in and pulls her winter coat that she hasn't worn in three years — since Yosemite with Sarah — off Bing's head. His eyes are clenched on the theory that if he can't see her, she can't see him. He's naked.

"What are you doing?"

Bing says, "Decontamination."

"You self-imposed decontamination?"

He nods without looking up.

Rosemary says, "You're not contaminated, Bing. You're pure as bottled water."

"Are you sure?"

"Get up and get dressed. It's time we put this show on the road."

Bing opens his eyes, but he doesn't move.

Rosemary says, "Bing. Pull it together here. I can't let you flake now."

Bing turns his face to look up at Rosemary. Backlit by the bedroom, her hair appears to be smoking, about to burst into flame. He says, "Too late. I am flake."

CHAPTER SIXTY-FOUR

Bing sleeps under a big damn fig tree. One of those trees so big and old they rate a name. The afternoon is blue and open in a way fairly unique to San Diego County. There is a crispness, a mix of humidity, sunshine, and breeze. Even for a city whose primary distinction is its weather is better than the weather in Los Angeles, days like this are not taken for granted.

A hundred yards from Bing, across an immaculate lawn, lies a scene of orchestrated chaos. The crowds are held back by yellow rope. They have naturally divided themselves between God seekers and the afflicted. Network and cable news trucks have their satellite hookups mounted like antlers. One truck has the sole purpose of dropping off and picking up Port-A-Potties. Earlier in the afternoon, Bing volunteered to help unload the blue plastic outhouses, but he was rejected on the grounds of no union card. He didn't understand and not understanding flustered him to the point of sleeping in the fig roots.

A temp stage has been set up on risers at the end of the picnic area, behind a huge flat rock that costs Turk $3,000 for the day. This is a rock straight out of *Narnia*. Waist high, flat as a Ping Pong table, you could easily envision tying a lion down on it.

Turk — in upscale, urban black, with silver jewelry off his neck and right wrist — stands next to Sarah's primary physician explaining Sarah's health problems and the impossibility of faking a healing to a pool of reporters. They've passed around x-rays. Turk uses a laser stick to point out scar tissue on an x-ray blown up the size of a movie screen behind his podium.

"This is Dr. Aurelio Chavez who will explain the disease better than a modest radio personality such as I am ever could."

Turk steps aside and Dr. Chavez takes his place at the microphone. Dr. Chavez has been in long-term care for thirty years, first as a doctor then as an administrator. He sees this as his fifteen minutes in the spotlight and he doesn't intend to waste the moment. As the doctor pontificates — no other word will do — on the subject of tubal scar tissue, Mitchell edges under the spreading fig leaves to awaken Bing.

"Hey, Binger, they're about ready for you."

Bing blinks awake. Bonobos don't go from asleep, to sleepy to gradually awake. They go from full sleep to full alert. It's a jungle thing based on predator and prey. Lions can afford morning grogginess. Bonobos can't.

Sticks in hair, Armani suit, Givenchy black t-shirt, jellies, he plucks a cocoon off a fallen twig, pops it open, and eats the white thing inside.

Mitchell settles in beside him. "Can I ask you a question, Bing?"

"Yes, you may, Mitchell. I would enjoy answering a question." The ground is littered with dry fig husks and a visible root system you mostly see in hot weather trees, making it awkward to sit or lie on. Mitchell shifts around, settling his great bulk. He leans forward, like a man about to fart, but instead he pulls a fig husk from under his bottom.

"Do you think I should move to Africa?"

Bing says, "That is a good question," because Rosemary taught him to say that when asked a question he can't answer.

Mitchell takes off his cowboy hat, revealing a tan line like a bowl across his forehead.

"I'm thirty-four and I live with my mom and step-dad. You know what that's like?"

"I am not thirty-four, I don't think."

"I haven't been laid in two years. The last time I brought a girl home the next morning Mom brought us oatmeal in bed." Mitchell snorts a mirthless laugh. "With raisins and brown sugar. That was the last I saw of that chick."

"Turk said *laid*. I thought I could fathom *laid* but I don't anymore."

Mitchell edges toward Bing, in confidence mode. "I've been told by a fella who should know that African women go ape-shit for cowboys."

Bing considers the picture. "In what part of Africa do women go ape-shit?"

Mitchell frowns. He hadn't considered parts. "Is there a difference? It's desert at the top and jungle at the bottom, but the girls are all the same. My friend said a cowboy in Africa is like a kid at 31 Flavors of Ice Cream."

"Is that the number of ice cream kinds? I only know two."

"He said you point at your choice and enjoy. Then when you're done, you point at a new choice. I figured since you came from Africa you would know the mores."

"I do not know mores."

"About the girls."

"Pointing and enjoying does not sound like what Rosemary showed about being love."

"We're not talking love. That won't come till girl number three or four."

"I may have been born in Africa, I do not remember. Rosemary is the first girl I met and she is from somewhere else."

"I figured you know something about leaving home and going in search of your bliss. How's that working out for you?"

"I would not compare my friend Rosemary to ape shit." Bing pops another fig worm. "She says I am to reach my potential and that is positive."

Mitchell stares hard at Bing, trying to catch the message he is sure Bing has hidden beneath his words. "That is positive?"

"Correct. Potential is good. Staying stuck on the wrong side of the cage is bad."

Mitchell slaps Bing on the thigh. "I understand you, brother."

Bing slaps Mitchell on the thigh. "I do not understand you."

Mitchell motions to the media mess across the picnic grounds and lawn. "Soon as this is over, I'm packing for Africa, and if anyone asks, you get the credit."

"Rosemary has a credit card."

CHAPTER SIXTY-FIVE

K rystal Lee — on loan from *San Diego Now* — does Sarah's makeup while Sarah sits in a director's chair, her eyes closed and her hands resting on a knit bag in her lap. Rosemary paces.

Krystal Lee says, "I never get to make people look worse than they are. This is good training for when I move to Hollywood." The women are set up outside because the light in Sarah's trailer isn't adequate. The miracle will be outside; Krystal Lee wants to see Sarah's face under miracle conditions.

As she works, Krystal Lee chews Spry gum, careful to keep her lips pursed so she doesn't smack. "You have naturally luminous skin," she says. "Too bad you're sick."

Sarah says, "Too bad." She is wrapped in flowing white Egyptian cotton. The Goddess look. She is barefoot and her hair is pulled back behind her ears. Naturally luminous or not, Sarah's bruise-colored eye bags hang dark on her pale skin. Krystal Lee has orders to make her already sickly pallor worse. Rosemary can't handle looking at her sister. She appears dead.

"God only knows you can bail on this is you're not comfortable," Rosemary says. "Are you comfortable? I wouldn't blame you if the whole thing came across weird."

As Krystal Lee applies white lip gloss over dark lip gloss, Sarah opens her eyes. "Turk Palisades would murder us both if I bailed now."

Rosemary's eyes go slick. "I don't care about Turk. I care about what is right for you." She circles clear around Krystal Lee, glances at Sarah's face, kind of shivers, and then circles back the other way. "When I dreamed up this plan it seemed perfect. You know, perfect."

Sarah starts to nod but Krystal Lee stops her. "Freeze."

"But now I don't know," Rosemary says. "I won't be able to bear it if something goes wrong."

"That's a wrap." Krystal Lee takes a photo of Sarah with her cell phone. She plans to put this job on her web site. "Don't touch your face. You look dandy."

Rosemary says, "Dandy?"

Krystal Lee gathers her makeup in a large box that was originally sold to hold fishing tackle. "For a girl who is supposed to look like she's on death's doorstep, she looks just the way she should." Krystal Lee heads back to her car. She has no interest in sticking around for the miracle. It's almost time for *Say Yes to the Dress* on TLC and if she hurries she can catch the fight with the sister-in-law.

Sarah watches Krystal Lee walk away, then she turns to Rosemary. "I don't want to bail, Rosie."

"I'm just saying you can, I'm not saying you should."

"I am sick of being sick."

Rosemary kneels in front of Sarah and takes her hands. "Since Dad died and Mom went nuts, you've been mother, father, sister, and friend to me. Without you I'm meaningless. You're what keeps me from flying apart and splattering across the universe." She starts to weep quietly.

Sarah touches a tear at the outer edge of Rosemary's left eye. "I had a dream last night that Mom was here, wherever here was in the dream. She'd cut her hair short." Sarah nods, picturing their mother as she looked in the dream, which wasn't the same as she'd looked when they last saw her. "Did you ever tell her about all this?"

Rosemary blinks quickly, the sign that she is choosing between lies and truth. She goes with truth. "I wrote Mom, right after your second operation, at that religious farm in Denmark. I told her about your illness." Rosemary is quiet for a moment. Sarah waits, without the need to prompt.

"Mom wrote back to say her true family at the farm practices no contact with their random, earthly relations in order to find God free of distractions. She told me not to bother her."

Sarah gazes down at Rosemary. It's more or less the way she had it figured, but it's a relief to finally know for sure that the sisters are on their own.

Rosemary says, "I didn't tell you because you had enough trouble. I thought I was protecting you."

"I wish you didn't protect me all the time."

"You're right. I shouldn't do that."

"So why tell me now?"

"I don't know why now. I guess you deserve to know everything I know, before you go up there." She tips her head to indicate the rock, the risers, cameras, and the ever-swelling crowd. "I was so hurt by the bitch I burned her letter."

The tears are flowing freely now. Rosemary doesn't even try to wipe them off as they drip down her face, running her eyeliner.

Sarah cups Rosemary's face between her palms and draws her close. "You'll be fine, Rosie. You are strong."

Rosemary sniffs. "Could have fooled me."

"Besides, you have your boy. He won't allow you to fly apart."

Rosemary is so surprised, the tears stop. "Bing?"

"Bing knows what matters and what doesn't. If you get confused, ask him"

Rosemary repeats herself. "Bing?"

Sarah smiles for the first time in several days. "Here he comes now."

Rosemary turns to see Bing approaching in a knuckle-walk, which is a posture he hasn't used probably in as long as Sarah hasn't smiled. The Armani is wrinkled and dirt spotted from his nap under the fig. His hair is all over the place.

"You look handsome today," Sarah says.

Bing stops beside Rosemary. He looks down at himself, checking to see if he is handsome. He doesn't buy it, but he knows Sarah is incapable of a lie.

Sarah speaks to Rosemary. "Doesn't Bing look handsome, Rosie?"

Rosemary says, "Stand up straight."

Bing stands.

"Where's your shoe? And your cap?"

Bing raises first one foot and then the other. He's only wearing a single jelly. He feels the crown of his head, like a dodderer searching for his glasses.

"I must have left them over there."

"We'll have to find them soon, before your disciples steal them for souvenirs." Rosemary brushes off Bing's shoulders. "Turn around."

Bing turns. She slaps at his back, raising a dust cloud. "Are you certain you know what you're doing?"

Bing turns full circle, back to face her. "I am not."

"I mean with Sarah. Are you certain you can fix her?"

Bing looks to Sarah in her flowing white gown. He is awestruck at the fragility. "No. I don't know. I will try as hard as I can."

"You better do more than try. If you fail, I'll cut off your leg and beat you with the stump."

"Is this true?"

Rosemary eyes take in the by-now huge crowd. "And if I don't kill you, those people over there will."

Sister Starshine — out of her radio togs and into the Starshine look she stole off a 1965 Cher — breezes over from the direction of the reporter clot. Her voice is more mellow than usual, the result of a double Xanax dose. "Rosemary, dear, Turk wants you on camera."

Rosemary exhales a puff of air. "Oh, hell."

"He says the concerned sister will add pathos."

"I've had about all the pathos I can stand." She touches Bing on the lower arm. "Go find your cap and shoe. You look lost."

CHAPTER SIXTY-SIX

Rosemary follows a semi-stoned Sister Starshine off across the lawn into the media circus. As they walk along the roped off God seekers, people reach out across the line, hoping to touch them without knowing who they are. Rosemary and Sister Starshine are on the inside, so they must be somebody.

Sarah stands to watch her sister move away. Rosemary is wearing a short, black skirt and a sleeveless light blue shirt, both from Gap. Toms shoes. From the back, she looks younger than she is.

"Poor Rosemary," Sarah says.

Bing is also watching Rosemary's backside. "She is filled with tension."

"This is harder on her than it is on you or me. She feels responsible."

"What for?"

"That's how love works. The hurt intensifies as it passes from the person in pain to the one who loves the person in pain." Sarah turns back to Bing. "Take care of her."

"I will if she will allow it. I don't think she will allow it." Bing points to the fig tree. "My hat is there. Will you walk with me?

Sarah touches her fingertips to his arm. "I'd love to walk with you."

Bing takes off his lone jelly so now they are both barefoot. They promenade like kids going to the dance across the grass. Near the tree, they pass a line of concrete picnic tables on each side. Behind them, people shout Bing's name and hold up signs he can't read. Far off to the side, Rosemary is at the microphone, answering questions they can't hear.

Sarah says, "It is a lovely day."

Bing says, "I don't know *lovely*. Is it the same as *love?*"

"It means nice. A good day to be alive."

"But then all days are lovely days. I never saw a day I wanted to be dead."

"I have."

"That is sad." He thinks hard about a day where he might want to be dead. A day in decontamination maybe. He says, "A bad day would be night, I guess."

Sarah speaks without looking at Bing. "I had a baby, you know. A girl."

"I did not know."

"She died trying to get out of me. The doctors performed a Caesarian and something went bad. That's why I hurt so much now. They made a mistake."

Bing has no idea on *Caesarian*. "That is sad."

Sarah touches his arm. "When you stop my pain, it won't stop hers."

"Rosemary, or your baby?"

"Rosemary. My baby is in no pain now."

"No, she's not."

"Rosemary won't be better unless you make her better."

"She says she'll be happy, after you are well."

At the tree, they come upon the hat and jelly, right where Bing left them. Sarah stops and turns to stare into Bing's eyes. Unblinking, he looks back into hers. He's growing accustomed to human eye contact. He likes the feeling it brings.

"I don't see how this can turn out the way Rosemary wants it to," Sarah says."

"Maybe."

"No. It won't be possible."

"That is what a miracle is. Rosemary explained it to me. It's when I do a thing that is not possible."

They stare at each other for a few moments. Bing sees her eyes are still pinpricks so she must be taking medicine. Sarah sees he is a frightened boy.

"I almost forgot." Sarah digs into the knitted bag. She pulls out the Droid phone. "I promised you this."

Bing slips the phone into his pocket without looking at it. "Thank you, Sarah. I will return it. After."

As he reaches down for his engineer's cap and the lost jelly, Sarah says, "I wish I could give you more."

Bing places the cap square on his head. He says, "Me too."

CHAPTER SIXTY-SEVEN

The young man from the acacia tree who had been seen by one person in his life now stands behind the sacrificial stone with the whole world watching, or at least a sizeable portion of the whole world. Bing wears Oudry's engineer's cap, and both pink, sparkly jellies. Sarah lies on her back with her head to Bing's left. She closes her eyes against the sun.

Behind Bing, on the risers with a view of Bing's back and partial view of Sarah, range Rosemary, Turk, Dr. Chavez, Sister Starshine, Persephone, Mitchell, and a couple more guys in suits that aren't known to Bing. Rosemary is positioned on the end so she can see her sister's face. Turk has a monitor to catch the CNN camera feed. Rosemary can see the monitor too, if she wants, but she doesn't want. She sees nothing and no one except Sarah.

Out past the cameras, the crowd spreads across the lawn into the picnic area and the trees. People stand on picnic tables. A few have climbed trees. To Bing, it is the largest gathering of humans he's ever seen, somewhat like a field growing faces and heads for a crop. Considering the numbers, the lawn is eerily quiet. It's like waiting for first serve at a tennis match.

Sarah flickers her eyes and looks up at Bing. "You okay?"

Bing places his hands in position over her forehead and womb. He says, "Do you know what will happen?"

"I think so. Do you?"

"No."

Sarah tilts her head back to look at Rosemary standing at the edge of the riser. Sarah winks at her sister.

Rosemary blanches.

Sarah looks back at Bing. She says, "Go."

In the silence, Bing moans. A whisper of a moan, almost empty of sound. The moan of awakening from a long sleep.

Sarah closes her eyes again, and breathes a sigh.

Bing mumbles words, or, to be specific, syllables. Bonobo, African syllables. The hair on the back of his neck lifts. His palms grow warm, then very warm. He tastes metallic saliva. He smells burnt hair. Bing closes his eyes and sees a rusted crack running across corrugated tin. The room is hot, humid. He hears scratchy music. A man and woman are slow dancing. The man's hand is cupped to the woman's lower back. The woman's chin leans into the man's throat. The woman glows like the sun behind Rosemary's hair. Bing hears a tone, more than a hum. The tone is mid-range and constant, and he sees pink. The entire world is flat pink. The woman turns to him and nods. Bing knows who she is.

He *howls!*

It's over. He doesn't need to open his eyes. He says, "Sarah left."

Behind and to his left, Rosemary's voice: "What?"

"She's gone somewhere else."

Dr. Chavez jumps off the riser and pushes Bing to the side. The doctor feels Sarah's neck for a pulse. He doubles his fist and slams it into Sarah's chest.

He shouts, "Defib!"

A woman Bing hasn't seen before rushes forward with a blue box that she opens to reveal a machine.

Rosemary strikes Bing on the back of his head. "What have you done?"

"Sarah's pain is no more."

"You asshole."

Rosemary's eyes are red wild, more animal than Bing has seen in a lifetime with animals. She throws Bing a look of hatred, then shoves him out of the way and runs to Sarah's body where Dr. Chavez is hooking up wires from the machine.

Bing watches them shock Sarah, knowing it is past the time of bringing her back. The cameramen are in a scrum, pushing, shoving, shouting obscenities at one another in their rush to film Sarah's death. Behind them, the crowd surges forward, or much of the crowd surges and the rest goes dormant in sadness. The ones moving forward and the ones not moving cause a clash. People fall. People scream.

Someone grabs Bing's arm and spins him. Turk: "You killed her."

"Yes."

Turk is in a fury, ready to strike Bing down, but he doesn't. Instead he barks. "Mitchell, get the car."

Mitchell says, "How's that?"

"The car, dammit. We're leaving."

Persephone strides forward and slaps Bing in the face. She says, "You are a charlatan."

Bing doesn't fathom charlatan but he says, "Yes," anyway. He knows he deserves whatever charge anyone can bring.

Turk pulls his arm. "Let's go, Messiah."

Bing looks at Rosemary and Sarah. The crowd is moving so fast Rosemary has to fight to stay with her sister. Between shocks, Dr. Chavez breathes into Sarah's open mouth, so Bing can't see Sarah's face. It doesn't matter.

He says, "Rosemary might need me."

"You've done enough for Rosemary," Turk growls. "You're mine now."

"Is that proper?"

"Mitchell," Turk yells over the melee. "*Go!*"

Mitchell runs interference for them as they fight through the crowd. Turk drags Bing away from Sarah. Bing doesn't resist.

CHAPTER SIXTY-EIGHT

The car isn't a car. It's an Infiniti SUV. Big, black honker with tinted windows and fat tires. Mitchell drives, although Bing can tell the car isn't Mitchell's. It belongs to Turk or the radio station or somebody, but Turk wants to sit in the passenger seat where he can keep an eye on Bing in the middle line of three rows of seats. He has Mitchell push a button that locks both Bing's door and window. Even the seatbelt locks. No chance for escape.

Because they are parked in, Mitchell drives off one curb and up another before he hits a driveway leading to a real street. No one speaks as he tries to race to the radio station. It would be a ten-minute drive only they get stuck behind a two-tier cattle truck driving right through San Diego on city streets. When they finally pass Bing can see runny dung dribbling down between the truck slats. He wonders how they got cows on the top level.

He wonders where Sarah is now. She's not in her body. He knows that much. Dr. Lori had nothing but contempt for those who buy into existence after death. She told Bing it was the same as belief in the tooth fairy, although she never got around to telling him who the tooth fairy is supposed to be.

Bing listened to Centered Soul radio at Rosemary's small house and in her car, so he is familiar with afterlife terminology — heaven, reincarnation, transmigration, the Great Whatever, Nirvana, Happy Hunting Ground. He isn't certain what this means other than people don't want to stop when their bodies do, but Rosemary puts stock in it, so it must be worth thinking about. The whole coming back again idea is a comfort.

"Don't you look smug," Turk says. "I trust you are proud of yourself."

"I don't think so," Bing says. "I have caused Rosemary distress. We didn't intend that."

"Forget Rosemary. She hates you."

"I hope that is not true. I don't see how love can hate."

Mitchell parks in the employee lot and he and Turk hustle Bing through the back door. A crack addict who has been living in the station Dumpster for two weeks because he wants Bing to cure him sees Bing's arrival and scurries around the building to the street to alert the smattering of followers who have already started arriving and are pissed off.

Once through the door, Turk says, "Set up the booth. We're going live."

Mitchell peels off one direction. Turk yanks Bing the other.

Turk says, "Let's see how you handle damage control, kid."

"Am I damaged?"

CHAPTER SIXTY-NINE

B ing doesn't lick the microphone this time. He's experienced with studios now, especially this one, so he knows what is expected. The host talks. He listens. He answers. Sometimes the host listens to the answer but usually not. Usually the host is working on the next question and doesn't care what the answer is.

Mitchell is in the booth. Bing can see him flipping switches, turning knobs, adjusting his headset. They are interrupting a Sister Starshine pre-recorded show about foods in the fourth dimension. Sister Starshine is interviewing a woman with a loud voice who claims macadamia ice cream soothes the soul and brings a person into the bosom of the Godhead. That's the word — *Godhead*. Bing wants to ask Turk how a Godhead relates to God. He's been learning about God by listening to Rosemary's radio, and, as Bing understands the theory, God has no body, much less a bosom, to stick a head on. He wants to ask, but Turk is too intense to approach. His eyes crackle. It isn't a time for questions.

After the next commercial — body salve for the restless chi — Turk jumps in with no words as to why Sister Starshine and the ice cream woman stopped in mid-conversation. Turk says he is bringing a special report on the death of young Sarah Faith in Balboa Park this afternoon. He explains a bit of background — Bing, the zoo, the miracle of California Pizza Kitchen — but mostly he figures his listeners know who Bing is and what happened at the park. Turk assumes the audience up and down the network has turned off their televisions by now and is awaiting word as to what to believe.

Turk wraps up the introduction and jumps right into it with Bing. "You told the world you are the coming of the new Messiah, and we believed in you. I believed in you."

Bing has been turning his cap inside out and back again, but he stops. "You said *Messiah*, Mr. Palisades. I didn't know the word –"

Turk cuts him off. "And now you've killed Sarah Faith. Here's what I want to know — why? Why did you cause the death of an innocent, beautiful girl? Her condition was painful, yet not life-threatening. She might have lived for years had you not told every-one you could cure her."

Behind Mitchell, the booth door swings open and Rosemary enters, followed by Persephone and Sister Starshine. They stand at the soundboard, staring through the glass at Bing. Rosemary's face is splotched with purple streaks. Her eyes are wet red. She's a mess. Persephone and Sister Starshine appear to be holding her upright.

Bing looks for a connection between himself and Rosemary. He doesn't see one.

Turk says, "Stop picking your nose, Bing, and answer the question."

"I do not recall a question."

"Did you plan to kill Sarah, before you put on that circus act out at the park?"

Rosemary leans forward. Her face is a brick wall.

"I did not plan Sarah's death," Bing says. "I planned to stop her pain."

Turk snorts derision. "You chose a hideous method of stopping pain."

Bing tries to smile at Rosemary. She doesn't respond. He would give whatever he has to get a sign of recognition from her, but she gives no indication she has ever seen Bing before. Mitchell reaches up to touch her shoulder. She doesn't react to him either.

Bing says, "I did what Sarah wanted."

Turk writes a note to himself on a pad of paper. He brought a sheaf into the studio before the interview. Now, he shuffles through the pages, as if looking for a clue. "You expect us to take on faith that Sarah asked you to kill her."

"I don't fathom *faith* except as her name. And Rosemary's."

Turk's hand slams the console, making Bing jump. "I am sick of your false stupidity. You know what faith means. You know much more than you ever let on. From the beginning, I suspected the innocent animal shtick was nothing but an act."

"Sarah wished to be cured of her disease. If that was not possible, she wished for the other."

"Death?"

Bing nods.

"I told you before, our listeners cannot see you, Bing. Did you or did you not know Sarah would die from your *miracle?*" He sneers the word *miracle.*

"We thought she might."

"We? You and Sarah or you and someone else?"

"Sarah. She thought she had to leave. I thought she might get to stay, she might be okay after, but I was wrong. She had to go to get better."

Rosemary blinks. Bing wants to speak to her, to be with her without glass between the two of them. He is afraid that she doesn't want what he wants and that she might not want it for a long time. She hasn't taught him enough about being love for him to know if it can be taken away. It doesn't seem possible, but he doesn't know. Dr. Lori never taught him about love.

Turk shuffles through the papers on the table. He pretends to be looking for something, but he isn't. He knows where he will go next.

"I want you to listen to these lines from William Blake's notebooks. You are familiar with William Blake's notebooks, I take it?"

"I do not read."

"We'll see about that." Turk reads. "*Why of the sheep do you not learn peace?* Sound familiar?"

Bing remembers. "I said that on your radio program."

"You admit it then." Turk flips to the next page. *"Terror in the house does roar, but pity stands before the door. Great things are done when Men and Mountains meet. This is not done by jostling in the street."*

Turk looks up and over at Bing. Bing waits.

Turk says, "Well?"

Bing says, "That's an interesting question."

"The Gospel According to Bing Bonobo was lifted from William Blake. Every word of it," Turk says.

"I did not know."

"How can that be possible? You *did not know.*"

"I have not met Mr. Blake."

"You expect us to believe that you and the great English poet from over two hundred years ago just happened to say the same lines."

Bing twists his cap back right-side out and puts it on his head. He crosses his legs at the thighs, then he twines his arms together like two snakes. "I heard someone else say those things."

"So you admit you stole your entire spiritual philosophy?"

"Is it stealing to repeat?"

"It is if you pass the wisdom off as your own." Turk rests his weight on one elbow and pivots on his microphone to move physically into Bing's space. "Face it, monkey boy, you are a fraud. A swindler. A false prophet and now a murderer."

CHAPTER SEVENTY

Bing's eyes never leave Rosemary. Does she believe the words Turk is speaking? It's important to Bing to know. Does Rosemary believe? By watching closely, he can see a quiver in her nostrils. She's only five feet away, even if there is soundproof glass between them. He can make out the pupils in her eyes. He can see a faint rise in her chest. Rise and fall, in short breaths. Her hair covers her ears. Bing wishes he could see Rosemary's ears. He could tell something of her thoughts by the color of the top arc. That's the spot where Rosemary hides her true emotions.

Turk continues the onslaught. "Your obsession with being a religious mystic turned you into a monster."

"No."

"You wallowed in the glory of disciples and apostles. I saw you watching yourself on You Tube. The insatiable craving for attention. You are nothing but a cheap clown."

"That is true." The word *clown* strikes a memory. "Rosemary said I should not allow you to use me as your clown, but I did."

Turk glances into the booth at Rosemary. "Yes, Rosemary Faith. The victim's sister."

"Rosemary and I are love. She said you might use me to increase your numbers."

Turk's mouth twitches, somewhat like a jaguar on stalk. He looks from Bing to Rosemary and back. He runs his fingers through his hair.

"Here's the truth." Turk's voice drips sarcasm. He is a master when it comes to dripping sarcasm. "*Son.*" He pauses to let that word sink in. "Rosemary sprang you from the zoo for the single purpose of healing her sister. Rosemary never cared for you. She never even liked you. You are nothing to her but a medical device. A medical device that failed."

Rosemary stands rigid in time. Persephone rests a hand on her arm now, and Sister Starshine is watching her instead of Turk, but Rosemary herself has the lifeblood of a wax figurine. Bing wants to scream and run to her like a child to its mother when the car door is slammed on the child's fingers. He can't. Rosemary is both the mother and the car door.

"Rosemary used you a hundredfold more than I did," Turk says. "I promised to make you famous. She promised love. Well, now, Bing, old sport, you're famous. I came though on my end of the bargain. You are famous for being a fool."

Bing stands up.

Turk says, "I delivered my promise, and, if you dream Rosemary loves you, you're an even bigger fool."

Bing walks away. As he opens the studio door, he hears Turk go into his purr voice.

"This is Turk Palisades, coming to you from the Centered Soul Spiritual Network, where we bring you the truth and nothing but the truth, twenty-four hours a day."

Bing goes out and quietly closes the door.

CHAPTER SEVENTY-ONE

Bing can't find the proper door. The booth is right next to the studio, so it can't be but one door away, only there's a corner in the hallway and when he goes around the turn he gets his sides mixed up. The first door he opens looks like a decontamination chamber. The second, a toilet. Then, he gets it right.

Persephone still has her hand on Rosemary's arm. Mitchell is standing instead of sitting. Sister Starshine is digging into her huge bag of a purse. Rosemary has slumped forward to rest her forehead on the glass. When Bing enters, they all turn his way.

He steps toward Rosemary, hoping to touch her. One look at her eyes puts a stop to that idea.

Bing says, "Are Turk's words a true statement?"

Rosemary crosses her arms over her ribcage. "That you are a fraud, a swindler, and a murderer. Yes, I would say those words are true."

"That you do not like me. That you took me from Dr. Lori for your own use and not because you care what becomes of me."

Rosemary hesitates, as if weighing her answer. "I took you from Dr. Lori for Sarah. Do you think I was nice to you because of the charming way you scratch your anus?"

"You jumped my bones."

Mitchell clears his throat.

Rosemary says, "I did what I had to to save Sarah."

"You said we are love."

"I thought you could help Sarah. I was wrong."

Bing holds his hands to the sides of his head, like the monkey in the hear-no-evil poster. "We are not love?"

Rosemary lifts her chin. She stares straight into Bing's eyes. "Of course I don't love you."

Bing drops his arms and slumps to the floor. His face loses color. He feels nausea as the room swirls.

"You are not human," Rosemary says. "No woman is going to love an ape."

CHAPTER SEVENTY-TWO

Bing lies on the studio floor, more or less fetal. His trunk, arms, and head are fetal, but his legs are splayed like a blown hairpin. He isn't weeping. He is trying his best to be invisible. He misses invisibility. Where did it go? All he wants is to disappear.

Cowboy boot steps cross the room and stop before his eyes. Mitchell says, "Get up, man. You're embarrassing yourself."

Bing makes it back to his feet. The women haven't moved. Sister Starshine still has her hand in her bag. Bing tries to picture what she was digging for when he came in, but he fails. Rosemary still stares at him, a blank, unblinking slate.

Bing sniffs loudly, like snorting up his life, and turns for the door.

In the reception area, he sits on the tile and takes off his jellies. He sniffs them both, one at a time. They still smell like warm rubber, only now they've absorbed a salty, dirty foot odor. Bing licks the right shoe. He wants to chew it and he would have two weeks ago, but now a secretary has come out of an office and is staring down at him. Bing has changed. He no longer feels comfortable chewing dirty shoes in front of strangers.

Bing gets up again. He passes the jellies to the secretary who holds them away from her body, as if he has handed her a dead rat. He walks outside where he is hit first by a spotlight and second by trash.

Tuna fish on pita bread bounces off Bing's neck followed by a cold Starbucks venti to the chest. Blinded by the light, Bing raises his hands to cover his eyes. The crowd takes this sudden arm movement as aggression and falls back, jeering. Cat-calling. *Killer. Judas. False prophet!* Only in California would a mob cry out *False prophet!*

Bing spins away from the light to face the door. He scrapes tuna off his Armani collar, but he can hear them closing in again. A woman yells *Asshole!* Rosemary called him *asshole* back at the park. The boy with the dead dog called the motorcycle rider *asshole.* What can it mean in this context? He knows an asshole is the place feces comes from, but why he should be one is mind boggling. He takes a half brick to the back. It doesn't hurt, but it does stun him into action.

Bing turns left and walks. The spotlight follows, as do his disillusioned disciples. The ones that aren't furious are weeping. A woman in stiletto heels and a fur vest has tears streaking black down her face. It's hard to say which group — angry or sad — troubles Bing most. He's never considered that any action of his would affect strangers. The emotion strikes him harder than the trash.

After a few steps, Bing drops his knuckles to the sidewalk. He can cover more ground this way. A TV reporter — not Jazmine — appears at his side. Male, tucked-in dress shirt and pressed trousers. Canvas shoes. Haircut close on the sides and back but spiked on top. He holds a wireless microphone in his right hand.

"How must it feel knowing you are the most hated man in San Diego?

Bing stops moving.

"Or all Southern California. Heck, we might be hard pressed to find a human in the United States more reviled than you tonight." The reporter glances back at his cameraman and spotlight holder, giving the audience a confidential smirk. "Do you have a statement to make?"

Bing grunts and bares his fangs.

The reporter says, "Whoa, there."

Bing bluff charges. The reporter holds the microphone like a light saber, Bing rips it out of the reporter's hand and spits it out on the sidewalk. The reporter backpedals until he falls off the curb onto his back, exposing his mid-section to attack.

Bing growls. The crowd clamor goes frenzy.

That's when a 1987 Chevy Impala painted with a Frida Kahlo-esque mural of snakes in the eyes of a skull smoking a cigar squeals to a stop, missing the reporter's odd haircut by inches.

T.J. Rios leans out the open passenger window. "Jump in."

Bing drops the primate rage. "What is that?"

"Get in the damn car. Quick."

The back passenger door swings open and the guy who opened it scoots to the middle of the seat, making room for Bing who steps over the reporter and into the car.

T.J. barks at the driver, who happens to be his brother, Martin, "*Go!*"

Martin goes.

Chapter Seventy-Three

T.J. and Martin sit in the front with two other gang guys in back with Bing. The one in the middle of the back seat hates Bing because he hates sitting in the middle. He wants a window. Besides, T.J. was rude when he ordered the back door opened for Bing. He didn't have time for niceties and he cursed. Said, "Open the fucking door."

The backseat guy by the far window isn't friendly either although his surliness is not Bing specific. It's aimed at an old gnome on El Cajon Boulevard who called him a *punk*. The old fart was ninety at the least and he stood in a crosswalk, shaking his fist, and didn't care if the kid killed him or not. He showed disrespect and the kid — Manny — can't live with disrespect. He should have beat the crap out of the old man, but then they'd have revoked him and he would have gone back inside for beating a ninety-year old. You can't win with people older than your grandparents.

Bing sits, hands on thighs. He stares straight into the back of T.J.'s head. He asks no questions. He feels no curiosity as to the timing of the rescue. He still can't get over what Rosemary said.

T.J. twists around to face Bing. He says, "We saw on TV where you let the skanky one die."

"Rosemary is disappointed."

T.J. snorts. "No, duh. You were set up to heal the woman and you smoked her."

Bing was lost on *skanky*. He has no notion of *smoked*. He supposes it is a cigarette thing.

"So we turned on that piece of shit radio station," T.J. goes on, "to see what they had for you."

"I do not feel Centered Soul is excrement."

"He sure as hell did a number on your ass. A firing squad would have been sweeter. Soon as we heard what the dickwad put out, we drove over, see if you need a hand."

Martin laughs a bitter, dry rumble. "You need more than a hand. That crowd would have ripped out your heart and eaten it."

Bing says, "I do not fathom why they are angry."

T.J. goes philosophical. Most people don't realize, but gang leaders can be deep as a regular person. Deeper sometimes. The specter of daily death will bring out abstract thoughts in even the violent.

He says, "Nothing worse than people think they was scoring good shit only to find themselves dumped on. The ones whose dream was to stick their tongue up your butt after what you did when I was shot are the first to call for your nuts on a stick when you don't do what they thought you promised. Where can we drop you?"

Bing finally looks out the window. They're passing through a neighborhood he doesn't recognize, which would be almost any neighborhood in San Diego. Many of the signs don't have letter combinations he has seen before. The store lights are bright and yellow and the stores sit close to the street. There are more people outside than he's seen at night when he travels with Rosemary. He knows now what *drop you* means, and this isn't a place he cares to be dropped.

"I have nowhere to be," Bing says. Two women fight by a car next to a partially burned building. The one woman pulls hair and the other woman bites. T.J. and the boys don't seem to notice. Loud music comes from somewhere behind the storefronts.

"Where I lived before Rosemary, I used to hide," Bing says. "I should like to find a new place to hide in."

T.J. and Martin exchange a glance. The two in back look out the windows. T.J. says, "We're going to a place. You can hide there."

CHAPTER SEVENTY-FOUR

Bing does not understand what it is to feel numb. For as long as he can recall, he's felt something — joy, interest, fear, excitement, hot, cold, prickly, hunger, lack of hunger, sometimes boredom, which isn't the same as numb. Even in decontamination, he felt alive. His fingers could touch. His nostrils could smell. After Rosemary said she doesn't love him, he stopping touching and smelling. He feels nothing.

At the border, they crest a hill to see a city spread out in lights. There's a major traffic jam with some cars going through and some being directed into a parking area where dogs sniff wheel wells. T.J. tells Bing that these dogs are nose dead or they'd be on the other side of the border, sniffing cars coming out of Mexico, not cars going in.

"Who's going to smuggle anything in?" T.J. asks, and Bing says, "In what?"

Martin pulls the car into a parking space and the four boys get out. T.J. motions for Bing to follow. They cross an asphalt span to a man in a gray uniform and a hat, sitting behind a card table. A tall man drinking from a paper cup joins the man at the card table, but the second man doesn't sit. He stares at Bing.

T.J. speaks a language Bing doesn't know. It sounds somewhat familiar. He's heard it at the zoo, but he doesn't connect the words to meaning. The sitting man laughs loudly and talks, and T.J. laughs, as if to say, "We're all buddies here," but the standing man doesn't laugh. Martin smiles and bounces on the balls of his feet. The other two boys stare into the mid-distance.

T.J. talks for a full minute and as he talks, the man behind the table leans forward to look down at Bing's feet. The Armani is worse for wear, by now, but it's still an Armani. The man isn't certain what to make of Bing.

He and T.J. exchange comments until the standing man spits on the pavement. He says, "You speak Spanish?"

T.J. answers before Bing can say anything. Bing doesn't care.

T.J. turns to Bing. "Get back in the car."

As they wander back to the car, Martin says, "They believed you?"

"No shit. Let's go."

The boys and Bing return to the car and drive into Mexico.

CHAPTER SEVENTY-FIVE

The boys and Bing pass under a huge white rainbow and enter a courtyard. Bigger than a courtyard — a plaza. Bing sees it as a habitat with no grass. Around the sides there are bars and game centers and places for changing one kind of money into another kind. Martin shows Bing a bail bonds store with the sign in English. Not a lot of people in the plaza. Three flags atop poles. A shirtless red-haired woman sits on the bricks and smokes a cigar.

T.J. says, "I told the guard you are my cousin who went to Imperial Beach to a wedding and got drunk and white boys hit you. Took your shoes and money and papers. We're here to carry you home."

"Idiot believed he's your cousin?" Martin says, although it is closer to a mumbled grunt than articulate speech.

T.J. shrugs. "Too much hassle to ask questions."

The painted Impala crosses a bridge over a dribbly, weedy irrigation ditch. Bing can see people below, burning trash. They appear to sleep in a box.

"I am where?" he asks.

T.J. says, "Tijuana. Nobody finds you here. You can hide the rest of your life."

They drive around a road kill black dog being picked at by crows. Bing thinks about trying to save it, but he knows he can't.

He says, "This is proper."

Manny gives him a look that says a life spent in Tijuana is not proper and Bing is stupid to think it could be. It's a complex look.

"We're meeting girls." T.J. rolls his window all the way down. He rests his arm on the ledge with his fingers drumming the roof. "You like girls?"

Bing's nose twitches at the smell of burning tires and hot food. He is no longer numb. Parts of him are coming back, in spite of what he wants. "Dr. Lori says girls are a pox on the land."

"Our girls are clean. She's talking about L.A."

"The only girl I know says I'm an ape."

T.J. laughs. He's in a good mood. Has been ever since he didn't die. "These girls we're meeting go for apes."

After the bridge, the streets get crowded and loud. Traffic is more stop than go. The sidewalks are crammed with people not moving but blocking the horde of people who are moving. There's music and color. And horns. Cab drivers drive with one hand on the wheel and the other pressing their horn, a cigarette they don't touch between their lips. Men and women in khaki pants and solid color tops carry possessions on their heads. Bing has never seen people with stuff balanced on their head. A pizza delivery guy wearing an insulated pizza case like a hat reminds Bing he hasn't eaten since bagworms at Balboa Park.

T.J. turns the radio to a local hip hop station broadcasting in a mix of languages. He cranks the music to the point where the bass thrums Bing's head. Other cars also blast thrumming bass beats so his brain is overcome. The stimulation onslaught pushes Bing past the reason he is here. What he thinks about now is finding a place to hide. He needs to curl up.

Martin slows as they drive by a woman in a tank top with ragged cut jeans shorts. Her legs are black and her face a blotchy tongue color. Her white hair is cut short as a putting green.

Martin says, "Now there's a pox on the land."

Even Manny snickers at that one. Only Bing and the nameless kid in the middle are silent.

Twenty minutes later they pull into a lot next to the Cinépolis multiplex. The front lights are blue and pink and brighter than daylight. The smell is rancid French fry oil.

Martin honks the horn — one long, two short — and a gaggle of girls gathered under the Coming Attractions poster separates itself from the wall and shuffles a few steps closer without actually coming close. Bing tries to count them, but they're dressed in similar fashion and he loses track at three. There aren't many. They shouldn't be difficult to count.

The four guys pile out of the car, laughing and cursing and behaving like young men anywhere. The sulker from the middle acts tough, probably because he has to, while T.J. and the ones who are tough can act anyway they want. Bing emerges last, somewhat stunned. Imagine a gazelle in headlights.

The girls in black shorts and tight jersey shirts haven't embraced the Mexican look at all. They could be from Billings, hanging out at the mall on a Montana summer night, except these girls tend to cover their teeth with one hand when they laugh and their earrings are striking beyond what you see at the Billings mall.

T.J. nudges Bing in the ribs. "Merelda there is mine, but you can have your pick of the others."

Martin says, "What the fuck?"

T.J. hangs his arm around Bing's neck, as if they are cousins raised together in an extended family. "You bring me back from the dead and we'll see about you having first shot at the chi-chi."

Bing has no idea which one is Merelda and T.J.'s hand is dangerously close to his face. "I should hide now."

T.J. looks from Bing to the girls. "But check out those sweet bitches."

As if they can hear him even though they can't, the girls pose along he curb. Bing checks out, as ordered. He is able to distinguish individuals, based on shape as opposed to clothing and hairstyle. One girl stares big-eyed at him as if he's the one in the zoo and she's the school kid on a field trip.

T.J. grins and squeezes Bing's neck. "I can fix it with Tonia there. She don't speak a word of English. You'll love her."

Bing studies Tonia, working out the word *love* with respect to a stranger. It doesn't fit. "I am not enthusiastic about chi-chi tonight.

I think I will go this way." He points toward a narrow street leading off from the metroplex.

The other three boys have sauntered into the girl gaggle and are culling individuals from the herd. Only T.J. hangs back and he's ready to move on. "You sure?"

"That is correct?"

Manny is leaning toward the girl named Merelda, speaking quietly into her ear, making T.J. anxious. "I have to go."

"Thank you for aiding my escape."

"No prob." T.J. walks away, then stops, obviously nagged by doubts. "You okay? Tijuana isn't always sweet to white boys."

Bing looks down the narrow street where he plans to find a hiding hole. It doesn't appear threatening, by his standards anyway. There's people and lights and smells. Couldn't be worse than the hyena habitat.

"I will stay on top of the situation."

"See you around then." T.J. walks to Merelda, shoulders past Manny, and swings his arm around her neck in the same gesture he'd used on Bing a moment before — more possession than affection.

He calls back to Bing. "We're even now."

"We are even."

T.J., his gang and their girls move in spurts and stops with friendly shoves and insults toward the box office. Only Tonia stays behind to send Bing a seductive smile.

Bing waves to her.

She hesitates, then waves back.

Bing misses the invitation.

CHAPTER SEVENTY-SIX

Forms push in and out of Bing's bubble of awareness. Strangers bump him. Noises assault. Voices come but Bing can't say who is talking.

"Viagra." "Cialis." "Black tar." "Marry me."

The pavement beneath his feet is sticky. Warm, like blood. The air smells similar to the elephant habitat. Bing turns right, then left, and within a short time is lost with respect to backtracking to T.J. He's on his own, looking for a tree or a cave or any place without people who can see him.

His path is blocked by a very old, very short woman, pushing an umbrella stroller full of trash. She rams him with the stroller and barks a word Bing doesn't know yet he does know it is not meant with grace. A cat sees him and reacts violently. The cat was cleaning itself, ignoring all the other bodies on the sidewalk. Why arch and *Yowl* at Bing? He does not understand.

He hears gunshots. At least, Bing thinks they are gunshots. He's heard them before on Rosemary's TV, and once at the zoo keepers put down a broken legged okapi with a gun. Always before, they helped animals die with syringe shots, not gun shots. Something was unique about that okapi.

A thin man with black teeth, wooden crutches, and rank breath hisses at Bing. "You want crank. You strike me as a boy looking for crank."

Bing says, "I could use a drink of water."

"Three dollars. I'll supply good water. No bugs."

Bing thrusts his hands in his Armani pants pockets. "I do not have money."

"Why you wasting my time?" The black teeth man spits on Bing's leg. "Move from my way."

Bing steps aside. The man humps a crutch on Bing's foot and swings his weight on it as he hops by. Bing doesn't jerk his foot back for fear the man might fall.

Limping now, Bing comes to a corner with a traffic light upside down so the green is on top and the red on bottom. He hesitates, not sure if he should cross, and two young women in mid-riff tops, shiny slacks, and knee-high boots laugh at him. They call him a *cabron.* They point at his crotch. He smiles — always the good sport — and they laugh harder. When he crosses a taxicab bears down on him, causing Bing to leap back over the curb. The taxi driver shouts and flings a rude arm signal.

A half block later, Bing's foot kicks a man who is either asleep on the sidewalk or dead. Bing can't tell. At the zoo, he could always tell dead from asleep, but now he's lost the talent. If the man is dead, someone other than Bing should clean him. He glances around for a person to inform of the dead or sleeping man, but others passing by don't look at him or the man. They part like buffalo circling a stump. Bing steps over the man and continues deeper into the city.

He is hot, tired, hungry. Lost. This is becoming unpleasant and Bing can't find a place to go. A boy — 11, maybe — in shorts and a t-shirt with a photo of Bart Simpson on the front falls in next to Bing. The boy looks friendly. Bing nods at him.

The boy says, "*Chick-lay.*"

Bing says, "You will have to pardon me. I do not fathom."

The boy holds out his palm to reveal two dirty squares of white. "You want gum, mister? Chick-lay."

Bing stops walking, grateful for the kindness. "Yes, thank you." He takes the gum and puts it into his mouth. It is sweet and soft and causes salivation.

The boy says, "Fifty cents."

"Why do you say such a thing?"

"Fifty cents for the gum. Pay me."

"You did not inform me it was for sale. You gifted it."

The boy scowls, which changes his whole face. Adds years to his assumed age. Makes him look less waif and more threat. "Everything is for sale. Where do you think you are?"

Bing takes the gum from his mouth and holds it out for the boy. "Here."

Hands splayed on hips, the boy howls. "It's *chewed!*"

"Yes."

"You *chewed* the gum and now you think you can weasel out of paying!"

Bing doesn't know what is expected. His hand is out. He's willing to give up the gum. He doesn't have money. He sees no choices.

"Thief! Bad man! Child molester!" The kid is screaming, tearing at his hair. Shapes materialize from the darkness to form a circle around Bing and the boy. Most are nothing but curious at the noise, but some are enraged that a rich white man would steal gum from a poor boy of the streets.

One incredibly overweight woman in a Mexican blouse steps forward and lets Bing have it in a string of Spanish invective. Bing looks from her to the boy to his hand.

The kid translates. "She says you cheat me."

"Tell the woman I didn't mean to cheat you. You gifted me the gum and then demanded money. I offered it back. It still tastes nice."

The boy translates Bing's offer to return the used gum. This incenses the woman so much she slaps Bing and the gum goes flying.

Amongst the Spanish outcry from the crowd, Bing hears a single voice in English. "Beat the snot from the rich asshole."

There's that word again. He still doesn't understand it. You wouldn't call a person an elbow or a foot. Why call them an *asshole.*

By now, the crowd is large and boisterous and tears stream down the boy's face. Bing searches for the gum. He finds several pieces stuck to the concrete sidewalk, but none are fresh enough to be his wad.

"Let me pass." The crowd parts for a tall brute of a man. Mustache, neck scar, lost tip of the index finger, aluminum baseball bat clutched in both hands — your basic paranoid Anglo nightmare.

He snarls. "Give my brother his money."

The boys sniffs tears. "Fifty cents."

Bing holds his hands out, away from his body. "I have no fifty cents. I have no money."

The man swings the bat into Bing's thigh. Bing goes down like a chain-sawed pine tree.

"Turn out your pockets."

Bing is crying now. The boy isn't and Bing is. He makes it to his knees and looks up at the man with bat cocked over his right shoulder. Behind the man, the fat woman is shouting words that Bing knows mean *Hit him again.*

Bing turns out his pants pockets. They're both clean and empty, not even pocket lint.

The brute man swings the aluminum bat into Bing's ear. Blood spatters the side of his face and onto the sidewalk. He lands with his nose and right cheek against the hard concrete. He can see snake-skin cowboy boots as the brute shifts his weight from leg to leg in preparation for another blow.

"He can give me his pants."

Bing turns his head to look up at the boy who is running the back of his hand across his leaky nose. Something has gone wrong with Bing's ability to hear. Behind the boy's voice flows the sound of running water.

The brute says, "You heard the child. In place of the money you owe, he will take your trousers."

Bing twists about so he is lying on his back where he arches up on his shoulders to pull off the Armani pants. The crowd snickers at Bing's tighty whitey underwear. Bing hands the pants to the kid who measures them against his own legs — six inches too long, three inches too wide.

"Pants aren't worth much without the jacket," the boys says.

The crowd looks at Bing, waiting. The brute raises the bat. Bing's leg hurts. The side of his head hurts. He can't understand why the pain was inflicted. Punishment should be connected to wrongdoing and Bing can't see what he did wrong.

The man with the bat says, "Now."

"That's enough." Rosemary walks into the circle. Due to a combination of back lighting and blood in his eyes, Bing can only see the outline of her hair. He can't see her face, but he knows her voice. Her voice is the sound of wonder.

"How much does he owe?"

"Fifty cents," says the brute.

"A dollar," says the boy. "There's interest."

The brute pops the boy a tap to the head. "Fifty cents. The gringo cheating you doesn't make it okay to cheat the lady."

The kid holds his head with the pants-draped arm and sticks out his other hand.

Rosemary tosses two quarters his way, and, in what Bing sees as amazing, the kid catches them both.

"Everyone can go home now," Rosemary says.

The brute reaches down a hand to help Bing up. It appears to be a bygones-be-bygones situation. By the time Bing is upright, the boy with his pants has disappeared, followed by most of the crowd.

The brute says, "Next time don't accept gum you can't pay for," then he rests the bat on his shoulder, turns, and walks into the darkness.

CHAPTER SEVENTY-SEVEN

Rosemary pulls a Kleenex wad from her bag and blots Bing's ear. Doesn't make him look any less beat up.

"I can't leave you alone for a minute."

"I am happy I can see you." He means it.

Rosemary spits on the Kleenex and rubs his hairline, which only smears blood. There are messes Kleenex can't fix. She gives it up and returns the soaked-through tissue back into her bag. "Come on. Can you walk?"

She takes Bing's hand to lead him away.

He balks. "How did you know where I am?"

She reaches back into her bag for a cigarette. For once, he doesn't give her grief as she lights up and blows smoke away from his face.

"Sarah's phone."

Bing digs into his jacket pocket to feel the Droid he's forgotten.

"She gets lost now and then." Rosemary speaks of Sarah in the present tense. "I track her by the GPS on the phone."

Bing pulls it out. Thin, black, with a daisy pattern back case, a tiny, red light blinking in the upper right hand corner. It's the sole possession he ever lusted after. "Do you want it back?"

"Sarah gave it to you." She takes the phone from Bing's hand and gently returns it to his pocket. She's consciously not looking at him below the waist. "Besides, I may need it to rescue you again."

Bing rubs his thigh. His leg hurts a lot more than his head. The head is mostly gratuitous blood, while the thigh is deep bruised. "That means if I get lost again, you'll look for me?"

"I looked this time. Why wouldn't I look again?"

She starts walking and after a moment's thought, Bing follows. He still doesn't know where they are or where they are going. He has no intention of letting her leave alone.

He calls ahead. "Why did you find me?"

She answers without looking back. "You're too pitiful to abandon."

"Thank you."

They walk a half block down a street Bing didn't see when he came to the place where he ended up. This street is even darker. The buildings have plywood for window coverings. Many of the doors are padlocked.

Rosemary stops so he can catch up. When he comes alongside, she says, "I didn't mean that. About you being pitiful."

"But you said it. Do people say what they do not mean?"

"It's going to take a long time before I'm not angry about what happened. I may say things, now and then, to hurt you. Things I don't really think are true. You'll have to forgive me."

Bing touches her hair. It's what he likes best, even better than copulation. "I don't fathom *forgive.*"

Rosemary stares down into the gutter, which is full of cards advertising a strip club. Photo on one side, address and phone number on the other. They could be in Vegas had the words been English.

She drops her cigarette into the gutter, steps on it, then bends to pick it up and tucks the cold butt into her back pocket. Considering the amount of litter already on the street, the gesture is more symbolic than useful.

"I didn't mean what I said before. At the station."

"About me being a fraud and a swindler?"

"No, I meant that. I didn't mean the part about you being an animal. That was cruel."

They round a corner to a block that seems built for amusement. There is a bumper car place with loud music and a disco ball light, although no one rides the cars. The owner or manager or whoever he is sits on a stool at the front, looking sad, while groups of boys and girls jostle into a video gaming store next door. Rosemary's Jetta is parked in front of the bumper car business. She gives the man three dollars for not letting the kids steal her Jetta.

Neither Bing nor Rosemary moves to open the car doors. They stand together on the driver's side with Bing's hand on the roof. As if watching a campfire for the light and movement, they both look at the video games where there are machine sounds and youthful laughter.

Bing says, "What about the part where you said we are not love?"

Rosemary steps toward Bing. She rests her forehead against his chest, but her hands hang at her sides. Forehead to chest is the only point of contact.

"I didn't mean that either."

"We are love?"

"I was hurt, because of Sarah."

"You miss your sister."

"I miss what we were together. We were so shallow, shooting Jaegermeister, kissing boys in bars. Once we drove to Santa Fe just because we didn't feel like going to sleep. We thought buying clothes was recreation and our opinions on music were vitally important." Rosemary digs her fingers into Bing's arms, deep enough to draw blood. "I'll never be shallow again. It's gone."

Bing knows what to do. He saw it on her TV. He places two fingers under her chin and lifts it gently so her eyes come up to meet his.

"I did what Sarah wants."

Rosemary's eyes go slick. He voice breaks. "I can't for my life see the point in going on without her."

Bing and Rosemary hug. A long hug where Rosemary cries and he pats her hair and thinks about what she means to him. He cares for her hair, and her fingers, and her voice. His happiness depends on hers. The most terrifying thing about being lost in Tijuana was the thought that he might never see Rosemary again.

When Rosemary speaks, her voice is muffled by his chest. "I couldn't save her."

Bing says it. "You did."

Rosemary stops crying, but she doesn't look up. She just holds him tightly.

Bing goes on. "You saved her, but not the way you wanted. Not for you."

CHAPTER SEVENTY-EIGHT

Bringing a barefoot boy with no papers into Mexico is a walk in the park compared to getting him back out, particularly if he's lost his pants and taken a blood bath during the turn-around.

Rosemary wheedles, begs, flirts, fakes tears, and makes vague hints at a bribe, all running up against the stone wall of bureaucracy until she finally talks her way into the office of a supervisor. The supervisor is a woman who knows the difference between safeguarding America and squishing people in the name of policy. She also knows Bing's story. She saw the Balboa Park non-miracle on TV and she knows Bing is no terrorist, drug runner, or illegal alien. To her, he is nothing but another would-be Jesus caught on a stretch of hard luck.

She comes out to the Jetta and tells the rule-obsessives that sending Bing back to Mexico isn't doing either country a favor.

"He's harmless," she says.

Rosemary, who knows better, says, "That's true."

"If you're willing to take him back after what he did, I don't see why the United States government should stop you."

"I appreciate the thought."

"I'm real sorry about your sister."

"Me too."

CHAPTER SEVENTY-NINE

North of Chula Vista Rosemary pulls off the interstate and finds a Greek curb market with a Redbox out front. No gasoline sales. You don't see convenience stores without gas pumps much these days, and, on closer inspection, the Redbox has been broken into and looted. The whole store has that looted look.

"Wait here," Rosemary says.

"I'd prefer to stay near you."

"This dump may be low rent but they'd still call reinforcements if you came through the door in your underwear."

So, Rosemary goes inside and Bing explores under the passenger seat. He finds the jellies he left back at the radio station, an unopened condom packet, and a pair of sunglasses. The sunglasses are purple with yellow lenses and when he puts them on the bug zapper above the market door turns brown.

Rosemary comes out fairly soon, carrying a bag of avocadoes and a six-pack of cut-rate water for Bing, and a pint of Jim Beam for herself.

"This is all they had in the way of fruit." She passes Bing the avocado bag. "Do you know if avocado is a fruit?"

"Dr. Lori says the definition has to do with seeds in the part you eat."

"Tomatoes are a fruit then?" Rosemary cracks open the seal on the Beam bottle. At the smell, Bing retches.

"Give me a break, Bing. I deserve a drink."

Bing twists the top off his water. It's the kind they bottle straight from a tap, then mark up the price. "I deserve a drink too, but mine doesn't smell like week-old emu urine."

"How do you – " Rosemary cuts herself off. She doesn't need the details. She takes a good Beam belt before she starts the car. Bing rips avocado skin with his teeth.

"You know what happened at the station after you left," Rosemary says. "I started talking. I told the others about all the people who ever loved me. Dad left. Mom left. Sarah's gone now. Everyone but you left me, and I'd just driven you away. And you know what Mitchell said?"

"He probably showed you his thumb."

"Mitchell said, 'Are you stupid or what?' And I said, "Right." And walked into the booth and quit my job. I told Turk where he could stick his chi."

Bing pokes a peeled avocado into his mouth, swishes it around, and spits out the seed. "Turk is a pox."

"He's an egomaniacal asshole."

Wisdom hits Bing like the bat did, up against his head. Suddenly, he gets it. "I do not fathom egomaniacal, but *asshole* is an apt word for Turk."

CHAPTER EIGHTY

Rosemary parks in front of her small house, on the same side of the street as the house. Neither she nor Bing makes any effort to get out. Rosemary stares at moths under the streetlight while Bing tears the wrapper off the condom.

"You mind if we sit here a while," Rosemary says. "I can't face going inside and starting the rest of my life."

"Sure." Bing blows up the condom, like a balloon. He pulls the mouth end of the rubber out so it forms a narrow slit and the air flows out in high squeal. Bing thinks this is neat.

It's trash day in Rosemary's neighborhood, when everyone wheels their home dumpsters to the curb so they can be picked up early the next morning. Two houses down from where Rosemary is parked, a raccoon stands on its hind legs to knock over someone's plastic trash dump. The can falls with a *whack* sound and the contents spill out into the street. Rosemary and Bing watch without comment.

Rosemary has had all the suspense she can take. "Dammit," she says. "Tell me."

Bing looks from the raccoon to Rosemary. He concentrates on her throat, with the pulsing vein. "I want to go home."

She slaps the steering wheel. "I knew it." She reaches across and takes the sunglasses off Bing's face. He blinks, as if it's light out even though it isn't.

Rosemary says, "What about me?"

"I do not fit."

Rosemary stares at Bing a long time till he gets self-conscious. He can't decide whether to keep his eyes on the raccoon or play with the condom. He has to do something.

He says, "I try to fit. I enjoy love with you, and riding in cars, and sometimes TV. Restaurants are nice. But I shall never fit."

"I'm sorry."

"Outies are cruel to one another. They make loud sounds and they can see me. They expect me to do what they expect me to do. I don't want to put up with that."

Bing rolls down the window. First, he tosses out the condom, then the sunglasses, then the jellies. He opens the glove compartment and throws out the maps.

He says, "I miss my mother."

Rosemary thinks about her mother. Does she miss her mother? She hardly remembers the woman who played Dungeons and Dragons and had her hair done the first Friday of every month. After Rosemary's dad died, her mother never touched her again, that Rosemary can remember. Her mom stopping loving anybody except some off-kilter always-changing version of God. Loving God and disliking people is a fine way to avoid abandonment.

As she twists the key to start the car, she says, "I don't fit too well in my world either."

Bing turns from the window to smile at Rosemary. "I hoped you might say that thought."

CHAPTER EIGHTY-ONE

Tabla.com plays from a radio site on Dr. Lori's computer. She only listens for the background beat. If hard pressed, Dr. Lori couldn't name a musician or musical piece broadcast by the station she listens to several hours a day.

She's entering the food/weight/waste data in her log. Kano has been losing weight, ever since Bing ran away. He seems to eat, but Dr. Lori suspects some bonobo version of bulimia. She suspects Kano is throwing up and burying the muck before she finds it.

Other than sulking, Betty handled the loss better than Dr. Lori expected, much to Dr. Lori's resentment. Mothers should implode when a child leaves, and Betty gets all the credit for being the mother, at least in Bing's mind, while Dr. Lori is what? The keeper? The provider? The enforcer? Somebody had to make the rules and Betty sure as hell didn't.

Dr. Lori pulls her glasses chain off over her neck. She drains a coffee mug of Drambuie and Cranberry Cocktail, then she pours herself another one, leaving out the cranberry this time. She deserves alcohol. She's had a tougher than average day and average itself has been piss poor lately.

She refused to watch that mockery at Balboa Park, on principle, but she followed it so closely on the internet that she might as well have driven down there. She'd known Bing wouldn't cure the girl. Where did he get the idea he could? He has unique powers when it comes to disappearing, but that's as far as it goes. He can't heal people, not that Dr. Lori knows, and, to her way of thinking, she knows more about Bing than Bing does. Killing the girl had been a surprise.

It's too late to go home and there's no reason to go home any-way. No reason to do anything. She'll sleep in the Airstream tonight. First, however, she has to check on the bonobos. Taeyando's chest has been rattling. Taeyando the queen bonobo is five years older than any bonobo has ever lived, in captivity. There's no precedent for what may be going on in her body.

Dr. Lori shuts off her computer and bends to fasten her rubber boots. Before rising, she shoots the second Drambuie — fire in the belly — then she shuffles down the hallway, wondering how many more years she can do this. It's not fun anymore. Even worse, it doesn't feel important. She's no longer the California Jane Goodall. She feels insignificant.

She opens the enclosure door, locks it behind her, and crosses to the hanging tire nests. As always, the four accepted animals are bunched more or less together, with Ubu over by himself. Tonight, they are more bunched than usual. They seem to be curled around something.

When Dr. Lori passes from the arc of security light to the shad-ows of the nests, she sees Bing. Asleep on his stomach next to Kano. Armani jacket, bloody exposed side of the face, Costco underwear. He chews in his sleep. Betty's arm rests on his back.

Waves of nausea flood Dr. Lori — joy, fury, betrayal, relief, mother's love — the greatest of these is relief. It's as if she has been holding her breath for weeks and now she can inhale.

Lola kicks her feet in her dream. Bing shrugs off Betty's arm and shifts to his side with his hands over his head. Relief, for Dr. Lori, is quickly replaced by fear that she can't keep him. He's seen the outer world. He knows stories of boils and wretched death are just stories, and even though Balboa Park went terribly wrong today — yesterday, now — he'll go back.

Maybe she can settle for Bing part-time. He could travel between the worlds with her taking care of him on this side. Dr. Lori knows better. She knows she couldn't bear not knowing when or if Bing might return.

Betty huffs, blowing air through her lips. Kano moans. Bing stretches and rolls onto his back, and, for a moment, Dr. Lori thinks he may awaken. If he does, how should she play it? Rapture would show weakness. Strict punishment might drive him away again. All she can do is act as if he never left. Keep it casual. No big deal. No deal, at all.

That's when Dr. Lori sees the third hand over Bing's head. Three? One clasped between the other two. All three human. Bing rolls clear onto his back, revealing Rosemary, curled in sleep beneath him.

Dr. Lori's heart pounds. She looks down on the woman she isn't — skinny, lips, hips, thick hair, dressed like she's going to the movies. The nightmare girl's other hand — the fourth human hand — is cupped possessively over Bing's crotch. She's wearing the engineer's cap.

Dr. Lori stares a long time. It seems like most of the night. Finally, she exhales and whispers: *"That little shit."*

We — the observers from above — will never know. Does she mean Rosemary . . . or Bing?

CPSIA information can be obtained
at www.ICGtesting.com
Printed in the USA
LVHW111259050220
645937LV00001B/52

9 780989 395755